"We need to catch whoever is fixated on you," Jack said. "You won't be able to breathe easy until this is resolved for good."

"That's true," Liv agreed.

"So, what if we let your family brush off those anonymous letters, and we can focus on figuring it all out?"

"And how exactly do I explain a bodyguard?" she retorted. "No offense, but even in plain clothes, you don't blend in."

He raised one eyebrow. "So don't explain me."

"They'll assume that you're my boyfriend if you tag along to family events. Unless you're only planning on being here at the store... Or will you keep at a distance?"

Liv met his gaze easily, her expression full of questions. She wasn't about to be passive in any of this, not that he'd expected her to. She was smart, and she wanted to know what she was dealing with.

"How about this," Jack said. "Let them assume I'm a boyfriend. That way, I can stay close enough to make sure you're safe and to keep an eye on the people closest to you."

Dear Reader,

I'm not thin. In fact, I haven't been thin for a very long time, but I also think I'm quite beautiful. I like my body this way—all rounded and soft— and I wanted to write a heroine who was not only a plus-sized woman, but was absolutely perfect in the hero's eyes. That isn't a "romance novel fantasy," either. Beauty is about a whole lot more than size. Thin, plump, round, lithe— whatever your body type, there's a real-life hero out there who thinks you're gorgeous!

This book is a celebration of all of us, in all our natural glory. We have to see the beauty in ourselves before others see it. But when we finally embrace just how stunning we are, it gives us a little twitch to our step that's hard to ignore.

So, here's to you, Gorgeous! Live your day like the natural beauty you are. And if you'd like to connect with me, you can find me at patriciajohnsromance.com.

Patricia Johns

HEARTWARMING

Her Lawman Protector

———

Patricia Johns

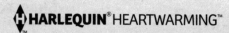
HARLEQUIN® HEARTWARMING™

Recycling programs
for this product may
not exist in your area.

ISBN-13: 978-1-335-63382-8

Her Lawman Protector

Copyright © 2018 by Patricia Johns

Printed in U.S.A.

Patricia Johns writes from Alberta, Canada. She has her Hon. BA in English literature and currently writes for Harlequin's Love Inspired and Heartwarming lines. You can find her at patriciajohnsromance.com.

Books by Patricia Johns

Harlequin Heartwarming

A Baxter's Redemption
The Runaway Bride
A Boy's Christmas Wish

Love Inspired

Comfort Creek Lawmen

Deputy Daddy
The Lawman's Runaway Bride
The Deputy's Unexpected Family

His Unexpected Family
The Rancher's City Girl
A Firefighter's Promise
The Lawman's Surprise Family

Visit the Author Profile page
at Harlequin.com for more titles.

CHAPTER ONE

LIV HYLTON CRACKED open a box of books, uncovering glossy paperback covers. The smell of new books never ceased to hit her brain right in the pleasure center. She was still filling shelves in her brand-new bookshop in Eagle's Rest, Colorado, and she was a stickler for variety. One thing she hated in a bookstore was having access only to the ten top sellers. Sometimes she didn't want a bestseller. Sometimes she wanted a fresh discovery, a delightful distraction…and Hylton Books was going to provide just that to the tourists who came for skiing each winter and for Eagle's Rest Lake in the summer.

With the leaves changing to their brilliant autumn foliage, the tourists were gone—an ideal time to be doing the grunt work of opening a new business. She'd have everything streamlined by ski season.

Liv pulled a hand through her hair and heaved a sigh. Her jeans had shrunk one too many times, and they were getting uncomfortably tight. That's what she was telling herself, at least. She'd gained weight, but she was done with diets. After ten years of marriage, where she constantly struggled to lose weight, she wasn't doing that to herself anymore. At the age of thirty-two, this was her body—no more punishment.

The newly installed shelves were high—a sliding library ladder attached at one side of the store and could be swept along to whichever point along the wall it was needed. That had been hard to come by, but a local contractor had gotten his hands on an old sliding ladder from an archives building in Denver, and it all had come together rather nicely. Like it was meant to be.

Morning light spilled from the display window onto the front counter, and her gaze drifted toward the creased note that lay next to a pile of mystery novels. She'd found the paper on the floor that morning, shoved through the mail slot. It was a simple piece of computer paper with letters cut from magazines—creepy. The last two notes she'd tossed out, thinking they were a prank by some local kids, but this one had settled into her gut and left her nervous.

*Don't say I didn't warn you. Go on back
and leave us alone or you'll regret it.*

This note sounded darker than the others
and less logical. Warn her about what? And
how was she bothering anyone in Eagle's
Rest? She'd been born here, gone to Eagle's
Rest Elementary back when there was only
one elementary school in town. Her grand-
parents, who'd already passed away, had settled here after they got married. Everyone
she'd talked to seemed really excited about a
bookstore coming to town. So, go back? To
Denver, where she'd lived the past ten years
with her ex?

The implied snarl and the confusing logic
behind the note chilled her. She didn't think
she had any enemies here, but maybe she was
wrong about that. Whoever had left this note
didn't seem stable, and who knew what an
unstable person would do for their own con-
voluted reasons? She'd called the police station as soon as she'd read the note, and they'd
promised to send an officer down.

Liv flipped through the stack of mysteries,
putting the books in alphabetical order. But
her mind wasn't fixed on the work at hand,
and she glanced out the front window at the
sun-dappled sidewalk. She was waiting for

the officer to arrive. It wasn't that she thought there was some special magic in a cop's eyes moving over that page. Her ex was a cop, so she knew their limitations, but if they could at least put this into the system, pass around a memo that she was being threatened—something! Maybe she could give local cops a deep discount for shopping at her store and keep a visible police presence on this street. That was an idea.

A small, jagged part of her missed having a cop husband...missed the implied protection. But that was over now, and it was time to face life like everyone else did.

Liv brushed her hands down her hips, wiping the dust from her palms. Behind her, there was a tap on the window. Liv recognized the blue uniform but couldn't make out a face. In her heart, whenever she saw that uniform, it was Evan's smile that popped into her mind, and she was left feeling that mixture of heartbreak and anger all over again. Whatever. An officer had arrived. She wanted someone to look at the note and give her an honest answer—should she be worried or not? She crossed the store and unfastened the dead bolt on the front door. She pulled it open, and as the officer looked up, she stopped short.

She knew this cop—but not from Eagle's

Rest. This was one of Evan's colleagues from Denver. She gave him a quizzical look.

"Hi, Liv." He smiled hesitantly. He was tall and broad, solidly muscled, and "cop" seemed to ooze out of his pores. He had that professionally distant look about him, both comforting and disconcerting at once. But he had a gentleness around the edges, too. Jack always had been a good-looking guy.

"Jack Talbott?" she said. "What are you doing here?"

"I transferred. I'm now stationed in Eagle's Rest."

"Seriously?" That was weird—her hometown wasn't exactly well-known. "And what did you do to deserve the demotion?"

Cops didn't angle for small-town positions. They all wanted more action, like in Denver.

"It's a faster climb to chief in a place this size," he said with an impish smile. "I requested it."

That might be true, but it was still a weird coincidence. He stepped past her over the threshold and ran a hand through his sandy blond hair. She was struck by the sheer size of him. How often did he pump weights to be that beefy?

"The place looks good," Jack said. His

brown gaze swept around the shop, landing once more on her.

She nodded, accepting his compliment. It did look good in here, and she was proud of it, but she had more pressing concerns right now. "Are you here for the note?"

"That was the idea," Jack said. "This it?"

He reached for the paper on the countertop and pulled out an evidence bag.

"I've held it, touched it, smoothed it…" She winced. "I'm sorry. Of all people, I should know better than that."

Jack put the paper into a bag anyway and regarded it for a moment.

"So who's mad at you, Liv?"

"No idea."

He looked over at her, and she could see that he didn't quite believe her. That rankled.

"I don't know," she said more firmly. "I grew up here. I wasn't anyone of consequence. I wasn't beautiful or cruel. I didn't even have a boyfriend until I left Eagle's Rest for college. I have no idea who I managed to tick off."

"Okay…" He nodded. "If you suspect anyone, you need to tell me, though."

"Is this serious?" she asked.

"It's…" He nodded again. "Yeah, it's definitely concerning. When there are personal threats like this one and law enforcement doesn't take it seriously enough, that's when tragedy strikes."

Liv's heart sped up, and she crossed her arms over her chest as if that might protect her somehow.

"There were two others. But those were handwritten, and…" She sighed. "Looking back they were probably more useful to you. But I didn't think they were serious."

"Why not?"

"I don't know. I thought they were kids being dumb, or a prank. The last thing I wanted to do was go to the cops and have some juvenile cousin laughing at me for being so jumpy. They just didn't seem like an actual threat."

"Until now." He lifted up the note.

"Until now," she agreed.

"Where are the other notes?" he asked.

"The garbage. I just…tossed them." She sighed. "So who would do this? What do you think it is?"

"Do you suspect anyone is…abnormally interested in your life?" he asked, not quite answering her question but raising her anxiety yet another notch.

"No." She sighed. "Would I know, though?

I mean, if someone had issues…how obvious would it be?"

"What about Evan?"

Her heart constricted a little at her ex's name, and she frowned, disliking the reminder. "Jack, Evan's in Denver. He married Officer Hot Pants. You should know. You were at the wedding, weren't you?"

Officer Hot Pants was actually Detective Serena Michaels, now Serena Kornekewsky. Evan and Serena had been partners, and the affair had been going on for some time before Liv had clued in… Serena was short, slim and as blond as a Swedish maiden—Liv's polar opposite. That was insult to injury, especially after all the work Liv had put into slimming down.

"But does he hold any grudges?" Jack asked, those dark eyes still fixed on her with uncomfortable directness. "Divorces get ugly."

"Marriages can get ugly, too," she quipped. "And yes, we have some tensions, but this isn't Evan's style. And why should he care that I'm in Eagle's Rest? That doesn't make sense. His life went on."

Jack nodded. "Okay. I'm just checking all avenues here. The thing is, Liv, these kinds of threats can be hoaxes, but most times someone won't go to this much trouble unless they have some personal grievance. The more personal someone's issue with you, the more dangerous it is. I'd feel better if I could keep an eye on you."

Great. So she had some vengeful enemy that she didn't even know about. Liv tried to calm her rising anxiety. But this was Eagle's Rest. She knew this town like the back of her hand. She was surrounded by friends and family here…and Jack had picked Evan's side in their divorce. While it might be understandable considering they were colleagues, it didn't make him her favorite person right now.

"I don't mean to be petty, Jack," she said after a moment. "But I think I'd be more comfortable with another officer."

"Look, I'm just going to say this. I'm a Denver cop. I'm the one with experience in the nastier side of things. The cops here—they just haven't seen what I have."

"You're connected to my ex-husband, and I'm trying to make a fresh start here."

"I worked with him," Jack said. "That's all."

"You were at his second wedding," she replied blandly.

Jack shrugged, then met her gaze. "It's up to you, Liv. But I'm the one with the experience, and they're short-staffed right now. Just ask the police chief. That's why he requested I take this one."

"And you think the local cops can't protect me?" she asked. "Eagle's Rest might be small, but—"

"I think they might be blinded to their own neighbors," Jack interrupted. "And while they are fine officers, I'm a cynical guy, and that's what you need right now. Whoever wrote this meant business—I'm willing to bet on it."

She needed him—that's what he was telling her. But she'd never known Jack terribly well, and something wasn't sitting right with her about this whole situation.

"How come you're acting like this is personal for you?" she asked after a moment.

"Because it is," he replied. "You're one of my own—you were part of the Denver family."

"So what are you saying?" she asked. "Cards on the table. Should I worry?"

"Nah." Jack shot her a grin, the smile softening his chiseled features. "Not while I'm around. You'll be fine."

She felt a smile tickle the corners of her own lips. If he was so dead set on standing guard, she'd be stupid to turn him down. Even if these notes turned out to be an elaborate prank, she'd at least rest easier until that was confirmed.

But worry still nagged at the back of her mind. Was it possible that this was connected to Evan? He *did* owe her something…they just hadn't included that little debt in their divorce agreement… But would he go to these lengths?

"Thanks," she said with a nod. "Just until we figure out what's going on."

JACK HADN'T EXPECTED Liv to suddenly confess her involvement in her ex-husband's scam, but he had noticed her eagerness to get another officer to protect her. She said it was because of his nominal friendship with Evan, but if she *were* involved in a scam, she'd want him as far away from her business as possible. He'd worked in the fraud division, after all, and he was up for a spot in internal investigations if he proved himself on this case. She may need police protection at the moment, but she'd probably prefer someone easier to manipulate.

Jack could see how easy it would be for one of the local guys to fall right into her trap, too. Liv was not only beautiful, but she had wide green eyes that showed old pain and fresh hope. Even her clothes were soft and feminine in a most disarming way. Snug jeans that accentuated those womanly hips, and a loose white blouse that showed just a hint of flesh tone through the gauzy fabric. If he didn't have all the facts in a file on the police chief's desk, he might fall for her charms, too.

Heck, he had before…

"Maybe we should clear the air about Evan's wedding," Jack said.

"I don't think there is much else to say," she retorted.

"He was my colleague, and he invited the whole department to the wedding. It was… basically, it was a schmooze-fest. How did you know I was there?"

"Social media pictures," she said, and then color flushed her cheeks. "And no judging. With all the tags from people I knew, I couldn't avoid it. I saw you in pictures, and I'm sorry, but it sure feels like you chose his side."

"I wasn't choosing sides. I was just…going through the motions. Look, Liv—I never approved of what Evan did to you. But I do aim to stay out of other people's relationships. No good can come of sticking your nose in where it doesn't belong."

Frankly, a small and petty part of him had been thinking that he'd be glad to step in if

Evan was going to walk away. He was still single at thirty-five, but not because he hadn't been looking around at his options. But then they'd started investigating Evan and discovered that Liv had been delivering paperwork to the fraud victims. And he'd been disappointed in a way that stung and made him angry. She wasn't supposed to be like her ex, but it looked like she was in this hip deep.

Liv picked up a book from a box on the counter and then headed for a shelf at the back of the store. She walked her fingers across the spines of the volumes already on the shelf. When she spoke, emotion choked her voice.

"Did you know he was cheating on me?"

She slid the book into place, then turned toward him. Some of the color had drained from her cheeks, and Jack heaved a sigh. Getting into this wasn't going to help his cause here…but then again, if they could get this out of the way, she might trust him a little bit more.

"I did," he confirmed.

She nodded briskly, then came back to the counter, reaching into the box again.

"The messenger gets shot in these sorts of situations," he added. "You know that."

"Everyone knew, didn't they?" She tapped

another book against her hand, and irritation snapped in those green eyes.

"A lot of people knew," he confirmed. "And a lot of people told him he was making a mistake."

"Did you?"

No, he hadn't. He'd never been that close to Evan, and Jack didn't like wasting his breath. Besides, he'd been afraid that his attraction for Liv would be obvious if he started in on Evan for his cheating ways, and he wasn't exactly proud of the fact that he felt that way about someone else's wife. Jack was the kind of guy who believed in right and wrong—it was why he'd become a cop to begin with. And lusting after a married woman fell solidly into the category of wrong. Too bad Liv wasn't as different from her ex as he'd thought back then.

"No, I didn't lecture Evan on his personal failures," Jack replied. "And I know that isn't a whole lot of comfort to you right now, but the thing is, if a man needs his colleagues to reprimand him into monogamy, he's not much of a man."

Liv was silent for a moment, then nodded. "I agree with that."

"And for what it's worth, I have no idea

how he strayed when he had you to come home to."

Besides the fact that they seemed to share a knack for real estate fraud. Jack's department had found more evidence that pointed to her involvement in Evan's schemes—this very bookstore, as a matter of fact. Complaints about some deeply unethical behavior during the purchase of this property five years ago had sparked their suspicions. They'd had enough to start a formal, albeit undercover, investigation six months ago, and their digging had brought them to Liv.

"Too bad Evan didn't feel the same way about monogamy," she said bitterly. "Whatever. It's in the past, and this is a fresh start."

How fresh, though? Was this a part she was playing—stung woman starting over? Or was her fresh start going to involve a nice influx of cash? If she and Evan were parting ways in business now, Evan might owe her an awful lot.

"I'm just curious," he said. "When did you buy this place?"

"Evan and I bought it about five years ago," she replied. "Evan figured it might be a good investment, and I'd been hoping to put it to good use. Never thought that would be after our divorce, of course, but..." She shrugged.

"I asked for this building when we divided our assets."

"Evan was okay with that?"

"This is Eagle's Rest. We bought it for a song from an old woman who needed the money. In exchange for this place, I didn't contest some other stuff. So Evan was happy."

That was strange, considering that Evan had gone out of his way to buy as many surrounding properties as possible. But he'd let this one go? Maybe Liv wasn't planning on parting ways with her ex when it came to their scam, after all. Money might mean more than wedding vows to some people.

"So Evan cheats on you, and you accept a piece of worthless property?" He wasn't supposed to be cross-examining her, but he was curious how she'd defend that.

"It's not worthless," she retorted. "It's chock-full of sentimental value. I was looking at the life I wanted now that I was single, and I wanted to come home. Besides, there's something to be said for low property taxes—especially when you're just starting out."

"Has he shown any interest in this place since?" Jack asked.

She shook her head. "No. Look, Jack, I'm not Evan's biggest fan right now, but he has no reason to try to scare me away from this store. I'm out of his way. He's got the woman he wants, and he's got Denver. Frankly, I think he's glad to be rid of me."

Before Jack could think too deeply about her defense of her ex-husband, Liv glanced at her watch. "I've got to finish up with these shelves before lunch."

That was a dismissal—he could hear it in her tone. Should he push it today? Maybe not...

"Okay," he said. "But I want you to keep your doors locked and your alarm system activated for the time being."

Her cheeks colored. "I don't actually have an alarm system yet."

So the sign in the door's window was a decoy. That was good to know if they got a search warrant and they needed to take a look around later.

"You should look into that," he said. "And be aware of your surroundings. Make a note of anyone who hangs around or shows a little too much interest in your store."

"I need people to show interest, Jack." She shook her head. "I'm opening a new business! I need customers."

"Trust your gut," he replied. He was hoping that her guilt would make her gut a little more touchy than usual, and she'd call him back.

"I will." Liv looked like she wanted to say something more, then gave him a tight smile. "Thanks, Jack. And you guys will be patrolling this street, right?"

You guys. She was still banking on the rest of the police force here.

"You bet," he replied, pulling a card from his pocket. "I'll be in touch. In the meantime, if anything seems weird or uncomfortable— day or night—you call me."

She took the card from his fingers, her gaze lingering on his for a beat longer than necessary. She looked worried, and while he was only doing his job in an undercover fraud investigation, he felt a faint pang of guilt. The testosterone-fueled part of him didn't like tricking a woman into letting him get closer. In fact, while it was perfectly legal to be dishonest in order to get a confession out of a suspect, it never felt morally comfortable to him.

Still, these were the tactics available to the police, and what was worse: some dishonesty to catch a criminal, or letting a criminal go to victimize someone else? When someone was trying to lie and deceive, they didn't tend to come clean with straightforward questioning. Like any undercover operation, there was going to be some deception. A lot of people from his community growing up in a poor section of Denver had been the victims of some illegal police deception in the past, so it was a little harder for him to rationalize it away. Still, for all he knew, he was saving Liv's life before she got in too deep to some criminal ring. There were some seriously scary people who would do anything for a big enough payout. And he was pretty confident that she was in league with them.

"You've got my number there," he said.

"Thank you," she said, then licked her lips. "I appreciate it."

"I mean that." He caught her gaze and held it. "You call me."

Liv nodded and glanced away. He'd done what he could today—planted a few seeds. He'd suggest to the chief that they leave another threatening letter overnight just to complete the process. Undercover operations required some careful setup, and she was still a little resistant to letting him in closer.

Jack headed for the door and pulled it open. "Take care now, Liv."

And when he glanced over his shoulder, he caught those clear green eyes fixed on him, her lips slightly parted and her cheeks pale. She clutched a book in front of her in a white-knuckled grip.

CHAPTER TWO

LIV ARRIVED AT the store the next morning, half afraid she'd find another note, but the floor in front of the mail slot was bare. She sighed in relief, then took a moment to pull herself together. She wouldn't be scared off by a coward who worked in anonymous notes. As the morning passed by, she put away the last of the books, but there were more deliveries expected. She ordered in some lunch—a slice of vegetarian pizza with a salad on the side and an order of potato wedges. She was hungry, but she was also nervous. And when she got nervous, she tended to eat. She'd always been this way, even as a kid. In her elementary school years, she'd been filled with social anxiety and was constantly peckish. She'd get on the school bus every morning with dread in her belly, and she'd have her lunch polished off before she even arrived at school.

Back then, she didn't have a lot to be nervous about. It was just anxiety of the general variety. She'd had friends and several first cousins in the school, so she'd never been alone. A boy had started making fun of her once, and her three older cousins had beaten him up. For better or for worse, those were days when a bloody nose didn't turn into family counseling, and Liv had gone through school both chubby and unharassed. Some called that a miracle, but Liv had a secret— she'd mastered the art of the compliment early. But as a grown woman with a marriage in her wake, Liv was tired of people-pleasing, and she'd started mastering the art of a well-timed comeback.

Liv popped the last of the wedges into her mouth just as someone rattled the front door. She looked up, still chewing, to see her aunt Marie peering through the window. Liv sighed and went to unlock the door.

"Why did you lock it?" Marie asked as Liv opened the door. "This isn't Denver, my dear."

Marie was a petite woman—barely over five feet tall and as trim as she'd been at twenty. She'd aged well, and at sixty, with her hair dyed a respectable brown, she could pass for five years younger.

"Hi, Auntie," Liv said. "Come on in."

Marie looked around, her gaze stopping at

the greasy paper plate on the counter. "Liv, dear, you need to eat better."

Would Marie give that same advice to her stick-thin daughter if she'd just consumed the same meal? Not likely. This was the kind of pressure she lived under, and since her divorce she'd decided to stop apologizing for eating.

"Do you know anyone who hates me?" Liv asked, changing the subject.

Marie blinked. "What?"

"Someone who hates me." Liv slowed it down. "Or hates the idea of this bookstore…"

"No, of course not." Marie eyed Liv speculatively. "What's going on?"

"I got a threatening note. Three, actually. The police think it's serious."

"Threatening what, exactly?" Marie asked.

"Nothing specific. That if I don't leave town, I'll regret it. That sort of thing."

Marie blew out a breath. "You haven't been toying with another woman's husband, have you?"

Liv burst out laughing. "I love how you always see me in the best light, Marie."

"I'm just… It's brainstorming, dear. What would upset someone around here? Homewrecking, I suppose. That's all I can think of."

"I agree that home-wrecking is horrible,

considering Evan's cheating," Liv replied drily, "but I've kept my own home-wrecking to a minimum."

"Well, it's a silly question to begin with!" Marie said with a shake of her head.

"Or it would be, if someone weren't trying to scare me off," Liv replied.

"But this is your hometown. If anyone belongs here, it's you."

Liv was forced to agree. She'd come home to lick her wounds postdivorce. A threatening note—it was weird.

"Is it possibly a joke?" her aunt said after a beat of silence.

"I thought so at first," Liv admitted. "I've never been one to inspire this much drama, but the police think it's something more."

"The police may be wrong."

"True. And if they aren't?"

"You need a man around here," Marie said. "And that isn't me trying to meddle. Maybe put out some big shoes so that people think you have a boyfriend or something. A male presence might help."

Useful. Except she did have an officer making his services available in that department. Maybe she should take Jack's offer more seriously.

"Anyway," Marie went on, "we're having

a family barbecue at our place and wanted to invite you. Unless, of course, you're too full—" She looked toward the paper plates again, and Liv's irritation simmered back up. She was tired of the constant nagging when it came to what she ate. Yes, she was plus-size, but how on earth did that make her lunch anybody else's business? It had been like this since she was young and well-meaning extended family tried to be a "good influence" on her.

"There's something I've been meaning to talk to you about, Auntie. I've been reading some articles on dementia," Liv said, fixing her aunt with her most concerned look. "And there are brain exercises you can do to ward it off."

Marie coughed, the color draining from her face. "I'm *sixty*."

"I *know*." Liv held the eye contact meaningfully. "Should I print off the articles for you?"

Marie turned for the door. "No, you should *not*."

"Because if you change your mind, I've saved them all!" Liv called after her aunt, who hauled open the door. "There are some games that your children can play with you to help keep your mental faculties sharp, as well—there's one with a brightly colored ball."

"Hilarious, Liv. Point made." Marie shot her a scathing look over her shoulder. "I hope you're advising your mother of these mental exercises, too!"

"Only when she criticizes me for eating lunch," Liv quipped.

"Fine. I'm sorry if I offended you, but I do care. Are you coming tonight or not?"

"Wouldn't miss it for the world," Liv said with a sweet smile. "See you."

Marie stomped out of the store, and the newly installed bell tinkled cheerily at her exit. Liv smiled to herself, enjoying this brief victory. She was tired of explaining herself, her food choices, her divorce…all of it. But did she really want to attend this barbecue just to have her aunt mentally tally up her calories? She was tired of being the big girl who nibbled carrot sticks while everyone else gorged on ribs, only to make up the difference when she got home again, ashamed of herself on too many levels. No more faking it. She had to start trusting her own observations and stop worrying about everyone else's. Easier said than done sometimes, but she had a feeling that, like most things, it was a matter of practice.

Liv stood motionless for a few beats as her aunt disappeared down the street, and Liv's irritation slipped away, leaving her feeling mildly guilty. It was stupid—her aunt had been insulting her, and yet she felt bad for having given her a taste of her own medicine. But that's how she'd always felt when she stood up for herself—guilty. That needed to stop, too. The door swung slowly shut but stopped a couple of inches short of closed.

Liv sighed and headed over to see what was blocking the door. It was a small package wrapped in brown paper, *Mrs. Kornekewsky* written in black marker across the front. It seemed to have tipped from the corner into the doorway as her aunt left.

Kornekewsky wasn't her name anymore—she'd been quite happy to shed it. But *someone* was clinging to her marriage...

Liv bent and picked the parcel up. She held it for a moment, wondering whether she should call Jack now or open it herself. Curiosity won out. If someone was going to all this trouble to scare her away, she wanted a clue as to who it was.

She grabbed a pair of scissors and cut the tape, peeling back the paper to reveal a small teal-colored box. The lid came off easily, and she looked down at what seemed to be a collection of photos.

She tipped them onto the counter, careful not to touch them this time—they were a collection of grainy pictures that looked like they were taken on a cell phone, and they showed Liv in various places about town. The grocery store, the library, at a street corner... And nothing else. No note. No explanation. She eased the pictures back into the box, clamped the lid back down and swallowed against the bile rising in her throat.

Mrs. Kornekewsky. Her heart hammered, but under the panic was a certainty—this was connected to Evan. Somehow, maybe even in someone's fevered mind, this was connected to her cheating ex. Was there no getting rid of him, or had their marriage entangled him in her life irrevocably?

Liv pulled open the drawer where she'd put Jack's card and rummaged around until she came up with it. She fumbled as she dialed, and it rang three times before he picked up.

"Detective Jack Talbott."

"Jack. It's me... It's Liv. I got a package. Not last night...sometime today. I didn't see anyone, but when Marie left—" She swallowed, knowing she wasn't making sense.

"Liv. Slow down. What's happened?" Jack said.

"I received a package at some point after I came down at nine this morning," she said, trying to compose herself. "It was addressed to Mrs. Kornekewsky, and it contains pictures of me."

"Okay." Jack's tone turned curt. "Don't touch it again. I'll be right there."

"Thank you." She sucked in a breath, and she suddenly felt better. She wasn't alone in this. And while Aunt Marie might think this was only a joke, Liv was now convinced otherwise. It would take a sick person to joke around like this.

"And lock the door until I get there," Jack said. "See you soon."

Liv ended the call. All of her earlier bravado had evaporated, and she stared at the box on the counter with a shudder. For the life of her, she couldn't figure out who'd hate her this much or what it had to do with Evan. Jack seemed to think it might be Evan, but while he might be a cheater, he still had some respect for her as his ex-wife. Maybe Jack could figure this out faster than she could. Her aunt was right—she needed a male presence around here, and a pair of decoy shoes wasn't going to cut it.

CHIEF SIMPSON EXCHANGED a look with Jack as he hung up his phone. A few officers in the bull pen were typing away on their paperwork; the coffeepot gurgled to one side. Jack tucked his phone into his pocket and rested a hand on his belt.

"It would appear that the pictures worked, sir," Jack said. "Kudos to Buchannan for the drop-off."

This was the most adventure this precinct had seen in decades, or would again, if Jack could guess. Buchannan had gone in plain clothes and, apparently, it had all gone off without a hitch. Now it was up to Jack.

The chief crossed his arms over his ample belly. "Your assignment is clear. You're to tell her it's imperative that you shadow her for her own safety. If she needs further confirmation, bring her by the station and I'll sit her down. But if all goes according to plan, you should be able to begin your investigation."

"Understood, sir. I'll be in touch."

"We're staying in close contact with the team that is watching Kornekewsky, so if he tries to reach her, we'll inform you ASAP."

"Sounds good."

"And, Talbott?" The chief's voice grew firm.

"Sir?"

"Stay close to her, but you don't have permission to cross any lines."

"Lines, such as…" Jack was pretty sure he knew what the chief meant, but some things were safer to spell out in case they had different ideas of where that line started.

"No romantic entanglement. It's easy to bend the rules when you're undercover, and I don't want that happening here. I want this clean. Don't give their defense lawyers any gifts, you hear me?"

Jack was more professional than that, and this wasn't his first undercover operation as a detective, even though it was his first for internal investigations. This was his chance to nab a spot tracking down the dirty cops—something he'd wanted since he was a kid in the projects, watching cops plant evidence.

This felt eerily similar—using planted scare tactics to nab a suspect. Back in the projects, he'd seen the cops who were supposed to protect a community tear it apart—his own cousin had done jail time for a possession conviction based on planted evidence. But that had been different. Berto had been an innocent kid, and the cops who were planting evidence were being paid off by the big drug dealers to divert suspicion away from them. They had to "catch" someone now and again so it looked like they were doing their job. Berto had never been the same again when he got out of prison. When he'd finally pulled himself together, he'd joined a gang, solidifying his life in crime. And Jack had vowed to make it right—get the cretins who'd done this to his cousin.

So while he might find the suspect attractive, he wasn't foolish enough to get emotionally involved with her. This was a search for evidence and a chance to even the scales a little bit. He was firmly on the side of the boys in blue.

"Loud and clear, sir. Strictly professional."

"Good luck."

As Jack headed out of the precinct, he felt a combination of relief and adrenaline. This was a job, and adrenaline always kicked in when he was getting to work, but he was also relieved to be finally heading in there. This wasn't personal, but the sooner they started, the sooner they could suss out the extent of this scam and lay charges. There were a lot of vulnerable people whose investments and livelihoods might rely on it.

It didn't take Jack long to arrive at Hylton Books, and he hopped out of his cruiser and headed around to the front door. Liv must have been watching for him, because she met him at the door and opened it before he had a chance to knock.

"Hi," she said, backing up to let him in. "It's on the counter."

She nodded in the direction of the small box, but she didn't go closer.

"I talked to the chief before I came," Jack said, heading for the box and taking the required look. He knew what he'd find—the chief had shown it to him that morning.

"What did the chief say?" she asked, her voice low.

"He said that you need protection round the clock until we sort this out. I've been assigned to you." He put the box back down on the counter, keeping it within her line of sight. She was silent for a moment.

"Jack, why was it addressed to Mrs. Kornekewsky?" she asked. "Whatever this is, it has to do with Evan. I just don't see how."

"Maybe Evan was up to something," Jack said.

"He's a fellow cop, Jack! That's where you go first thing?" She shook her head. "Evan is a cheating louse, but he's still one of the good guys. As much as I hate to admit that."

Yeah. Jack wasn't so convinced. And "good guy" was a strong description for the husband who'd dumped her.

"It's pretty clear that this has to do with Evan. You might not like that, but it's true. And you used to be married to him, so—"

He wanted to solidify that fact in her mind right now—this had everything to do with her ex-husband. Maybe she'd be more forthcoming with information if they didn't waste time dancing around that one.

"So someone is mad at Evan—" She shook her head. "Everyone in town knows about my divorce. It's the juiciest news Eagle's Rest has had for the last year. Why target me?"

"Is there anything you can think of that might connect him to this town?" he asked.

"Besides this building? I told you we bought it together. His name was on the deed until he signed it over to me."

Now wasn't the time to cross-examine her. He needed her trust, and right now she was spooked, but she wouldn't be dumb enough to incriminate herself.

"Liv, we have time," he said with a shake of his head. He pulled an evidence bag from his pocket and dropped the box into it. "I'll stick with you for the next couple of weeks, so that we don't have to worry about your safety, and we'll figure this out."

"What do you mean, stick with me?"

"What does it sound like?" He shot her a

mildly annoyed look. "You want to face off with a stalker alone?"

"No!" She pulled her auburn hair out of her face. "But I told my aunt about the letters, and she's convinced it must be a joke. I have to admit, I was, too, but she invited me to a family thing tonight. If I show up with a police escort—"

"That might be for the best," he interjected.

"What?" She frowned. "The gossip? The drama?"

"That they assume it's just a practical joke," he replied. "We need to catch whoever is fixated on you, not just chase them off for a few weeks. You won't be able to breathe easy until this is resolved for good."

"That's true," she agreed. "And my family all panicking about it won't help matters."

"Bingo." He smiled ruefully. "So what if we let them minimize this for a while? Let them brush it off, and we can focus on figuring it all out."

"And how exactly do I explain a bodyguard?" she retorted. "No offense, but even in plain clothes, you don't blend in."

He raised one eyebrow. This was why the chief had warned him earlier—his ability to stay close enough to gather evidence relied on a balancing act of his own. "So don't explain me."

"They'll assume that you're my boyfriend if you come tagging along to family events and whatnot. Unless you're only planning on being here at the store...or will you keep at a distance? What's the plan here?"

Liv met his gaze easily, her expression full of questions. She wasn't about to be passive in any of this, not that he'd expected her to. She was smart, and she wanted to know what she was dealing with, too.

"How about this," Jack said. "Let them assume I'm a boyfriend. I'll be a perfect gentleman, so no need to worry about anything. That way, I can stay close enough to make sure you stay safe and to keep an eye on the people closest to you."

"You think my family is involved?" she asked incredulously.

"Frankly, Liv, I don't know what to think. But I'm not taking any chances."

Liv sighed. "So you'll be with me 24/7? You do realize that I other have family events. My cousin Rick is getting married later this month, for example. Are you seriously wanting to tag along for all of that?"

"If I were some nut looking to hurt you, I'd wait until you were alone," he replied quietly.

"My goal is make sure that person never gets the chance."

She looked away from him, and her cheeks pinkened. "And at night?"

"You have a couch, don't you?" he asked.

"I do."

"I know this isn't comfortable," he said. He didn't offer any follow-up on that statement, because he didn't really want to give her a way out. His investigation would be most effective if he had a view into her personal life.

"No, it isn't," she admitted. "But neither is being stalked, or whatever this is. So I suppose we'd better make the best of it."

That's what he'd wanted to hear, and he shot her a smile. "I'll be as unobtrusive as possible. Your safety is my priority." And that wasn't a lie. If she was linked to the kind of people they thought, her safety was definitely a cause for concern. The police department needed her either on the stand as a witness or standing trial—and they needed her in one piece.

"There's that barbecue tonight," she said. "At my aunt's place."

He eyed her, waiting. There was a beat of silence between them.

"If you're coming along, do we make up

our story now?" she went on. "Because they'll be asking a lot of questions."

Jack was actually going to enjoy this part. The chief had warned him against getting emotionally involved with her, but undercover operations involved some acting the part. This was only for appearances, and other than that, he'd keep his professional distance. "All right. So when did we meet?"

"In Denver," she said. "Let's keep this as close to the truth as possible. Less to remember."

Yeah. She knew how to lie effectively, it seemed. "Okay, I worked with Evan and got to know you that way. When did I ask you out?"

"Who says I didn't ask you out?" she countered.

"Because I'm the kind of guy who doesn't waste a lot of time," he replied with a teasing smile. "But it's up to you."

Liv rolled her eyes, but a smile tickled the corners of her lips. "Fine. You asked me out. When?"

Jack thought for a moment. Keeping things as close to the truth as possible *was* the best course… "As soon as your separation was finalized," Jack said. "Because I'm a decent guy."

Heck, he'd been planning on asking her out then, anyway. It was only this investigation into her ex-husband that had put a crimp in his plan.

"Then we've been dating for a year?" she asked.

"Let's call it eleven months," he said. "It sounds more credible if it's not quite a round number. And if they ask why you didn't tell them about me, just say that you weren't sure about me yet, and you're still skittish postdivorce."

"Which I am, so that's believable. I suppose we could play the rest by ear." She paused for a moment. "One more thing. You didn't attend Evan's second wedding."

"Was I invited?" he asked.

"Yes, but you turned it down because you believed in monogamy and Evan's cheating offended you on a very deep level." Her tone was tight—this mattered to her.

"Okay…" He paused. "Liv, I didn't condone his cheating."

"Got it." She shot him a bland look. "But if you're going to be my fake boyfriend, I get to rewrite what I don't like."

"Fair enough. Anything else you'd like to rewrite?" He spread his hands. "It's now or never."

"I'll keep you posted."

Jack shot her a grin. "Do I get to rewrite anything?"

"Like what?" She looked like she might be dreading his answer, and he wondered what she was expecting him to say.

"If I'm going to be your fake boyfriend, I want you to pretend that you're crazy about me," he said. "I rock your world. I curl your toes. I'm the best thing to ever happen to you."

Liv's face cracked into a smile, and for a moment he was stunned by the transformation. He'd always known she was beautiful, but he'd never been smiled at quite like that. He swallowed.

"Fine," she agreed. "But at the end of this, you'd better tell my family how heroic I was and all that, because otherwise I'm not going to live this down."

"Deal." Heroic. Or she'd be proven guilty, and he'd have no explaining to do at all.

CHAPTER THREE

LIV HADN'T BEEN expecting a houseguest when she woke up that morning, so as she led the way up the back staircase toward her apartment, she tried to remember exactly how clean she'd left the place. Did she have bras hanging over the shower rod? Had she left the window cracked open like she normally did to air out the breakfast smells, or had she forgotten? Always nice to introduce your living space smelling like old fried eggs. She was aware that she may have settled back into single life a little too well… Funny how fast that happened. When Evan had first left her, the emptiness had been agonizing.

"One of the officers will swing by my place and pick up a bag of clothes for me," Jack said from behind.

"Where are you staying?" Liv asked as she reached the top of the stairs and fished in her pocket for the key.

"At a hotel, actually. I'm not settled yet."

Not settled was an understatement, but then

men were different. They didn't seem to mind roughing it as much as she did. Liv liked to have a home—comfort, solitude, her personal items surrounding her to make her feel safe. Except safe right now was relative, wasn't it?

Liv unlocked her door and glanced around before opening it all the way. Everything seemed in order—or mostly so. There were a few dishes on the counter, but that was probably forgivable.

"Come in," she said stepping aside to make room for the burly cop. He gave her a nod of thanks, then stepped into the apartment and looked around. She got the feeling that his eyes were picking up more detail than anyone else's would. She knew how cops worked, how they thought.

She'd have a cop staying under her roof for the next little while, and that was a bit uncomfortable. Not only was he very, very male—she glanced over Jack, who was checking window locks—he was muscular and intimidating. But under that shell, she could see hints of a regular guy—the stubble on his chin, the scrape across the knuckles of one hand. Every cop had personal armor they put on when they were at work, but they were human, too. It was the "guy" part of him that made this the most awkward. She'd only just gotten comfortable living alone again, and she didn't need reminders of what she was missing out on.

"I hope you don't mind the couch," Liv said. "It doesn't pull out or anything."

"I'm not exactly a houseguest," Jack replied. "Don't worry about it. I'll be sleeping with one eye open, anyway."

"The water in the bathroom is a bit finicky," she added. "It's either piping hot or freezing. But there is a sweet spot, if you find it."

"I'll survive." He shot her a rueful smile.

"Also, there's a draft that I can't seem to find the source of. We might need to move the couch about a foot if you don't want to freeze at night."

When Evan had shown her the place before they'd signed all the papers, they'd felt that draft and Evan had jokingly suggested a ghost. She hated being spooked, and back then, Evan had loved getting her into his arms... She pushed back the melancholy memory.

"You okay?" he asked. Liv looked up to find Jack's dark gaze fixed on her.

"Fine." She pushed the sadness back. Missing Evan took her by surprise sometimes, even though she knew that he wasn't worth her heartache.

"So when you bought this place, you bought it jointly?" Jack asked.

"Of course." She gave him a speculative look. What exactly did he think of her marriage? Evan *had* loved her once upon a time. "Jack, have you ever been married?"

"Not yet. Lived with a woman once, but we never got to a wedding. Why?"

"Because married people tend to buy things jointly," she replied with a shake of her head. "We were married. We had a life together. I wasn't tucked away in the background somewhere."

"Got it," he replied.

"Although being married to a cop is a whole new kettle of fish," she admitted. "They have too many secrets. I'll never marry another one."

"And all cops are the same?" He pulled away from the window and glanced back at her.

"All cops do the same job," she said. "And it attracts a certain personality type. You pour yourself into your work, teamwork is life-or-death and you stick to your code."

Jack shrugged. "All right. But most of us

have a finer sense of right and wrong than your ex-husband."

Did they? She'd heard of a few affairs in the Denver precinct over the years she was married to Evan. And for all of Jack's declarations of disapproval, he'd been at the wedding where Evan had married his mistress.

"You're done with cops, then?" Jack asked after a moment.

"Completely," she replied with a wry smile. "Call me selfish, but I don't like coming in second place to anything in my husband's heart."

"Fair enough."

She wasn't sure what he was agreeing to—her desire to steer clear of cops or her stance on marital priorities. It didn't matter.

"When was the last time you talked to Evan?" Jack asked.

"A couple of weeks ago," she replied. "He called me, for the record."

The sound of his voice had rattled her. She'd been having a tough morning, and he'd purred into her ear like he had back when they were married. It hadn't been fair.

"What did he want?"

"His grandmother's brooch. He thought I still had it, and he wanted his wife to be able to wear it."

"Did you have it?" Jack asked.

"No, I don't have it," she replied with a sigh. "I'm not petty enough to hijack family heirlooms."

And yet the image of Officer Hot Pants wearing that brooch still rankled her. She remembered how touched she'd been when Evan had given it to her the Christmas after they were married. It had seemed so heavy with meaning… So much for that.

Liv looked around the small apartment, from the open living room and kitchen to the closed bedroom and bathroom doors. It looked like they'd be in some very close quarters together for the next little while, and she didn't like this uneven balance of power in her own home.

"This is going to be awkward," she said suddenly. "We could make it less awkward if we have a few ground rules."

"Lights-out time?" he asked. "Shower schedule?"

"I was thinking more like a tit-for-tat sort of arrangement. I get that I'm the one needing police protection, but that leaves me giving all the information, telling all my personal stuff, and you get to keep your privacy."

Jack grew still, but his eyes didn't leave

her face. "That's the job description, Liv. Is it a problem?"

"For me." She headed to the kitchen, and Jack followed as she talked. "I hated that— the police secrecy all the time—and I don't feel like living with it again."

She started to stack dishes in the sink.

"I'm afraid I can't help much there," he said.

"Oh, but you can." She shot him a smile over her shoulder. "I know you can't reveal police secrets, but you can reveal a bit about yourself. I propose a deal. For every personal thing I tell you, you have to match me."

"With what?" He sounded uncomfortable.

"With information of your own. I didn't choose this! I'm a victim in this whole situation, yet I have a virtual stranger living with me for the next while. That's invasive. I'd feel a lot better if I wasn't the only one having all her personal business laid bare."

Jack laughed softly. "I could see that."

"Well?" Liv grabbed a towel and turned around to face him.

"It's highly irregular," he replied.

"So?" She spread her hands. "You think this isn't irregular for me, too?"

She was tired of trying to shrink herself, take up less space, both physically and emotionally. She'd survived the worst she could imagine when her husband left her, and she'd promised herself never to back into a corner again.

"I'm here to protect you," Jack qualified.

"Which I appreciate," she agreed. "But you're still here, in my home, in my business."

Jack met her gaze for a moment, and she watched him, waiting. He was trying to hide what he was feeling, but a nervous tapping of one finger on his belt gave him away.

"All right," he said at last. "Tit for tat."

"Good." She glanced at her watch. "You might want to call on that officer to collect your clothes. We've got a barbecue to attend."

Liv hated this—officially. She wanted her own space, her privacy. She hated feeling threatened in her own home. She hated that she had to adjust to living with a man again just when she'd been finding some healing in solitude. But there was one tiny part of this that she wasn't dreading, and that was having a good-looking boyfriend—fake as he was—to show off at that barbecue. She was tired of the pity and judgment. Maybe Aunt Marie would have less to say about her food choices if she thought that she'd already hooked another man.

Or maybe Marie would just chastise her for

moving on too quickly. Whatever. It didn't matter. Jack on her arm changed the balance of power around here, and for that small but significant fact, she didn't mind his presence.

Let them talk—she wasn't going to be Poor Liv anymore. She was going to be brave, outgoing, unfettered Liv with a muscular man by her side. And the gossips could choke on it.

JACK PARALLEL PARKED on the street where Liv indicated her aunt and uncle lived. The shadows stretched long and dark between telephone poles. This was an older section of town—small, boxy houses lined up in a 1950's cookie-cutter paradise. Number 11, where Marie and Gerard Hylton lived, had a neat yard without a single leaf on the closely cropped grass, despite the large tree in the yard. It was immaculate.

"Your uncle is retired military, right?" Jack said.

"That's right."

"I can tell."

Jack had changed into a pair of jeans with a leather jacket over a T-shirt. His aim was to at least try to fit in. Liv was wearing a long tartan skirt that skimmed over her hips and swirled around her calves paired with a black sweater that swept over her ample curves and looked so soft that his fingertips tingled with the desire to touch it. She knew how to dress her figure—always had that he could recall.

This was an excellent start to his investigation. When he'd texted the police chief with this opportunity to see the people closest to her, the chief had been optimistic, but he'd included advice—*Watch who she confides in, if anyone. We don't know how far this goes.*

But Jack would have to be careful. He was posing as her romantic partner, and he needed to maintain some perspective. While it was good to keep the family from panicking and bounding into this fake threat, he needed some space to work and didn't want them focusing on him instead. He had to slide under their radar. He was trying to keep a nice clear work space here…if that was possible in a place the size of Eagle's Rest.

"Nervous?" Liv asked.

"Nope." Jack pulled himself out of his thoughts.

"You should be," she quipped, then opened her door and got out of the car.

"Why's that?" he asked as he joined her outside in the evening chill.

"Because you're about to tell the Hyltons that you're dating me," she replied with a low laugh. "And every single one of them is going to have a strong opinion about that."

"For or against?" he asked.

She shrugged. "A bit of both, I imagine. But Hyltons are nothing if not passionate people."

Her choice of words piqued his interest. Passionate, were they? He'd always suspected that under that polished veneer of hers there was some smolder—the kind that might get tugged along into an ill-advised plan for the sake of love. Or money. Or both. He glanced over at her, but she didn't seem to catch the double entendre in her own words.

"They've got a fire going in the backyard," Liv said.

"No time like the present." He held out a hand toward her, and she hesitated.

"Oh, that's right, look the part," she said, and her cheeks tinged pink. She seemed so innocent and sweet like this—and he was going to have to be careful not to fall for his own undercover work.

"That okay?" He dropped his hand. "I'd just assumed. Or we could be a more distanced couple. That's fine, too."

The soft murmur of voices punctuated by laughter floated to them over the breeze, and Liv's expression hardened. "No, you're right."

And she slipped her soft, cool fingers into his palm, shooting him a wary look. "I'm sick of their pity. I want to give them something a little juicier to talk about. But no kissing. And your hand stays at my waist and doesn't wander."

"Wouldn't dream of it." He gave her a quizzical look. "I'm a cop, Liv. I'm not taking advantage."

"Just making sure." She gave his hand a squeeze. "Okay, let's go."

As they crossed the road and headed around the house to the backyard, the voices grew stronger, and he could smell the savory aroma of cooking meat. The backyard was larger than he'd thought. A fire pit in the center crackled and popped. There was a large barbecue next to the rear door of the house, and light from the back windows glowed out onto the lawn. The door stood open, and a woman came out with a platter of burger buns but stopped short when she saw them. People sat around on lawn chairs with cans of pop and beer in their hands, and as Jack and Liv approached, they started looking up and taking notice. The chatter fell silent, and then a child's voice rang out with, "Who's the guy with Aunt Liv?"

That was the beginning of introductions. A

few older men shook his hand very firmly—with enough strength behind their grips that they seemed to be trying to prove something. The older ladies smiled sweetly, murmured things into Liv's ear and cast Jack some sidelong looks. There were a few younger couples who said hello and smiled appropriately, and a small herd of kids who were playing together and stopped to stare. All the while, Jack tried to survey the different groups and sort out who, if anyone, might have a more business-like relationship with Liv than the others. The chief was right—if Liv was connected to her ex-husband's affairs, it might be through other family members. Evan *had* been part of this family for ten years. There might be a few in-law relationships that deserved his attention. Families could be close—his sure had been. So he understood how those dynamics worked.

"The food is set out," a plump older woman said, shooing them toward a folding table covered in Tupperware and casserole dishes. "Go get something now. Paper plates are in the bag on the seat, there…"

As they headed toward the food, Jack leaned in.

"Was Evan close to any of your family?"

Liv shrugged. "He got along with everyone. He used to hang out with my brother, Steve, when we visited."

"Is Steve here?" Jack asked.

"Not today. He's on duty at the fire station."

A brother who was a firefighter, an ex-husband who was a cop… People didn't usually link public servants who risked their lives for their community to fraud, but it happened too often. Firefighters and cops didn't make a whole lot of money, and like anyone, financial pressure sometimes got to them.

"If Evan were harassing me," Liv said, her voice low, "my brother wouldn't be helping him. Trust me. Steve's always been a protective big brother."

And now she was protecting her brother. That piqued his interest, too.

"Is he married?" Jack asked. "Kids?"

"His wife is the pregnant one over there." She jutted her chin in the direction of a blonde woman with a large belly sitting in a lawn chair by the fire with two small kids. They all had plates of food in front of them. She was chatting with some other women close by, interspersing her conversation with admonitions to the kids not to spill, or to sit back down.

"What about you?" she asked. "Siblings?"

Jack eyed her.

"Tit for tat," she said with a small smile.

He smiled grudgingly. "Fine. Yes, I have two brothers. One is married with kids. They're in Denver." He'd been closer with his cousin Berto, though. They'd grown up together and had been closer in age.

"So you're Uncle Jack."

"I'm Uncle Jack. I'm good for cash on birthdays and rides in my cruiser. Those kids take way too much pleasure in the back of a squad car."

Liv laughed, her eyes sparkling as she dished herself up some potato salad. "For you?" He held out his plate, and she gave him a spoonful. "Avoid the jelly salad. I don't know what Bernice does to it, but it's always off."

Jack took her advice, looking up to see a thin woman in her early sixties approaching with a platter of fresh ribs.

"This is my aunt Marie," Liv said. "Marie, this is Jack."

"So you're...a boyfriend, we assume?" Marie asked with a tight smile. This would be one who didn't approve, apparently.

"That's me," Jack said. "Nice to meet you."

"How long have you been together, exactly?" Marie turned her attention to Liv. "You've never *once* mentioned this man."

"Eleven months," Liv replied. She took some ribs onto her plate, and Jack followed suit. The food did look delicious. Marie's gaze followed the food to Liv's plate, then stayed fixed there, her lips pursed. Liv regarded her aunt for a moment, then handed her plate to Jack. "Hold this, would you?"

She licked off her fingers and then pulled her purse off her shoulder and started to rummage through it.

"It's so nice that Liv has met someone," Marie said, shooting Jack a smile. "What do you do?"

"I'm a cop. I just transferred to Eagle's Rest," Jack replied.

"And before this…?"

"I was in Denver."

"Oh…" Marie looked at Liv, her eyes widening. He could see what was happening here, the subtle undermining of Liv's fake good fortune. Every family had an aunt like this, and apparently, Marie was the Hyltons'.

"And yes, I know her ex-husband," Jack said. This was the good part of them having some shared history—if word got back to Evan, it wouldn't be inconceivable.

"Hmm." Marie glanced down at Liv's plate again, then said, "Dear, that potato salad has full-fat mayonnaise. Just thought I'd let you know."

At that moment, Liv pulled a sheaf of papers out of her purse and handed them to the older woman.

"For you, Auntie," she said with a bright smile. "I promised to print off those articles, remember?"

Marie swallowed, licked her lips and then thrust the papers back toward Liv. "I don't need this."

"They're for you, anyway." Liv winked, then took her plate back from Jack.

What was on those papers? Could Marie be involved, too? Jack and Liv walked together away from the table, against the tide of people moving in for fresh ribs.

"Sorry, that was kind of passive-aggressive," Liv said as her aunt marched off. "She's been hounding me about my weight, so I printed off some articles on dementia."

Jack laughed softly. "You don't say."

"It's better than stewing about it for the next month. One of us was going to walk away from this barbecue angry, and I was tired of it being me."

Jack grinned and shook his head. She had spunk under all that sweetness, and some edge, too. Edge enough to be dangerous, he noted. Liv wasn't the kind of woman who went down without a fight, and all the while, she was capable of a stunning, heart-stopping smile.

She was a wicked combination.

CHAPTER FOUR

LIV TOOK A bite of the tangy potato salad and heaved a sigh of contentment. Marie, for all her faults, was a great cook. Her potato salad not only had full-fat mayonnaise, but she added a dab of Dijon mustard and diced pickles for flavor, and a bacon crumble on top. Not bacon bits from a plastic shaker, but actual fried, crumbled strips of bacon. If Marie was so concerned about calories, she only had herself to blame.

Liv watched as Jack took his first bite.

"Man, this is good," he said.

She smiled. "Marie makes this potato salad for every family gathering, but she never eats a bite. Such a waste, in my humble opinion."

"For sure." Jack took another large bite. "Mmm. Wow. So—" He glanced around, swallowing. "Anyone here who might have a bit of a grudge? Or a connection to your ex?"

"A connection?" Liv shrugged. "Every last one of them. He was part of the family."

Jack was eyeing her with an odd directness, and when she met his gaze, he turned his attention to his plate and took another bite.

"You're convinced this is Evan," she clarified after a moment of silence.

"Call it a hunch."

"I don't believe you," she retorted. "What's this based on?"

"I don't like him." A small smile turned up the corners of Jack's mouth, and for just a moment, his eyes glittered with humor.

Liv chuckled. "That's it?"

"He's cocky, and he doesn't seem to have the same guilt mechanism the rest of us have," Jack replied. "Do you have a better guess?"

Liv shook her head slowly, doubt creeping into her mind. "No."

Could it be Evan? It didn't seem right. He had no reason to bother her. He had what he wanted in Officer Hot Pants. Jack knew more than he was letting on—she was willing to bet on it. Still, the memory of those photos in the box gave her an involuntary shiver. Whoever was threatening her—be it Evan or someone else—she wanted to know who and why. The mystery only made it feel more daunting than it probably was.

Or was she only trying to convince herself of that? At the very least, if she had someone in her life with a weird grudge against her, it was probably better to know.

Across the grass, Liv's cousin Tanya was taking a photo of Aunt Beth and Uncle Herb in the low late-afternoon sunlight. The couple leaned in toward each other and smiled brightly. The flash went off, Tanya looked at the screen on the back of the camera and the older couple came in to have a look, too. Then they scooted back to their previous position, smiled again—a little less brightly this time—and lowered their chins. The flash went off, and they came around to look at the screen again.

"So…" A voice hummed at Liv's shoulder, and she turned to see her uncle Gerard. He still looked the part of the drill sergeant, even in shorts and a T-shirt.

"Hi," Liv said with a smile. "How are you?"

"Fine. Care to introduce me?"

"Uncle Gerard, this is my…" Police escort? Bodyguard? The lying didn't come easily to her. "This is Jack."

"Jack." Gerard nodded and extended a hand, and the men shook. "So you're dating our Liv, are you?"

"Looks that way." Jack smiled back cordially. "You're Gerard Hylton?"

"The one and the same."

"Marie's husband," Liv said.

Jack looked down at his plate, newly scraped clean, and back at Gerard. "Lucky man. Your wife is a great cook."

Gerard wasn't easily placated by compliments about his wife. Marie drove her husband crazy.

"I've heard you're police," Gerard said brusquely.

"I am. I'm a detective—I just transferred to town."

"We've done that before—the whole cop-in-the-family routine," Gerard said. "It didn't go well for Liv. We're not keen for a repeat."

Jack's eyebrows went up, and Liv suppressed a moan.

"Uncle Gerard, we're not that serious. You can stand down," Liv interjected.

"Evan seems a little too interested in our land, if you ask me," Gerard went on.

"Honestly, Uncle, you've got to let that one go," she said with a sigh. Evan had offered to buy Gerard and Marie out when they were attempting to retire in Arizona. And Gerard could be touchy.

"And I don't care if your ex is personal friends with Mayor Nelson," Gerard went on. "He could be hobnobbing with the president for all I care. That land isn't for sale."

Gerard's laser glare didn't waver away from Jack. "You cops take care of your own. Well, we Hyltons do the same."

"So you aren't a fan of Evan Kornekewsky," Jack said.

"What do you think?" Gerard barked.

Liv put a hand on her uncle's arm. "Be *nice!*"

"I thought I was," Gerard retorted, then he sighed. "Marie is waving at me frantically. She's afraid I'll say something harsh."

Liv shot Jack a grimace, and Uncle Gerard reached over and gave Liv's arm a squeeze. "You look great, by the way, kiddo. Go get another plate."

She'd always liked Uncle Gerard. He was Marie's complete opposite. In some very good ways the couple complemented each other, and in other ways, they were a lot alike. Big hearts, big mouths and even bigger opinions. Gerard headed back toward his wife, leaving Liv and Jack in momentary peace.

"Sorry," Liv said with a wince.

"Don't be. I like him. He's honest." Jack's squint followed her uncle. "So what's this about Evan and land?"

"A misunderstanding," she replied. One she still hadn't forgiven her ex for, because he'd tossed her into the middle of it.

"Care to elaborate?"

"There's not much to tell," she replied, and she heard the stiffness in her own tone. She was still processing a whole lot of anger, apparently.

"And the mayor?" Evan asked with a frown.

"This is a small town," she said, relaxing a little. "It doesn't mean the same thing it does in Denver. Trust me."

Jack eyed her for a moment, then shrugged.

"I need more of that potato salad," he said after a beat of silence.

"If you were actually dating me, you wouldn't like my uncle half as much," Liv said, following him toward the table. Evan had detested her uncle. They'd sparred at every social event, and her uncle had glowed victorious when Evan finally proved himself the lowlife that Gerard had suspected all along.

"You've had boyfriends who complained?" Jack asked.

"I've had a husband who complained," she retorted.

Jack was silent for a moment, then shrugged. "I like who I like."

Not that it mattered. In a few weeks, she'd have to tell them that Jack was nothing more than security anyway and hope that the drama of all those threats overshadowed the more pathetic truth about her relationship to this hunky cop. Uncle Gerard's bravado was for nothing.

"Liv, how are you?" Tanya said, and Liv looked up to see her cousin approaching, camera in hand.

"Hi, Tanya." Liv tried to smile. She loved her cousin, but the more people she had to lie to about Jack, the worse she was going to feel.

Liv made the introductions, and Tanya and Jack shook hands.

"So…this is new!" Tanya said with a wide smile. "Liv sure can keep a secret. I'm serious. I mean, she's normally pretty close-mouthed about stuff, but this is crazy! How long have you kept him under wraps?"

"Almost a year," Liv said with a wan smile. She'd been thinking about how good it would feel to rub some fake relationship into Marie's face, not Tanya's. This felt like collateral damage—a family relationship that would suffer because of these untruths.

"Almost…" Tanya's smile faltered, and Liv saw the hurt in her cousin's eyes. "What? That long?"

"With her divorce and everything, she

wasn't sure if she'd even like me," Jack supplied.

"Well, it's not my business," Tanya said with a forced smile. "Obviously."

Liv sighed. "Tanya, you and I need a coffee. When are you off work?"

Tanya and her mother ran a local deli together—it was a family affair.

"I have tomorrow morning off," Tanya replied.

"Perfect. How about at ten, at the place on the corner?"

"Okay." Tanya glanced down at the camera in her hand. "I'm putting together a photo album for Grandma for Christmas this year. All the couples and families and all that."

"That's a great idea," Liv said, then suppressed a sigh. She'd have to follow through with appearances on this, too, it would seem. Just great—a photo of Liv beaming adoringly next to some guy she was pretending to date. She was going to have a really hard time living all of this down!

"Look, I'm not upset," Tanya said, lowering her voice. "I'm just surprised. In fact, call me jealous! You're on your second cute cop, and I always did like a uniform. What can I say?"

Liv laughed softly, then Tanya brightened. "Let's get you two over here by this tree,"

Tanya said, nudging Liv over a few feet, then grabbing Jack by the arm and arranging him next to her.

Jack looked down at Liv with a mild expression of alarm. Maybe he was sensing the same thing—a photo gift for Grandma was taking this charade a little far.

"Put your arm around Liv's waist, Jack," Tanya ordered, looking through her camera, then she popped back up above it. "Jack—pull her in, come on! I've had old people look cozier than the two of you."

Liv glanced up at Jack, her cheeks warming with embarrassment. She'd intended to be more pulled together than this... She'd wanted to lose the family's pity, hadn't she? But it was one thing to hold this man's hand and quite another to slide into his arms. Should she call this off? Send Tanya over to some other couple? Before she could decide, Jack's warm, broad palm slid around her waist and he tugged her closer against his muscled side. She fit right under his chin, and he stood behind her slightly, the sandpaper of his jaw resting against her hair.

"Oh..." she breathed. This wasn't...terrible. It was nice, actually. Uncomfortably nice.

"That's better!" Tanya said, lifting her

camera once more. "Liv, loosen up, lean into him a bit."

Liv turned her head toward Jack and smiled for the camera. There was a *click*.

"Perfect." Tanya beamed. "Do you want to see it?"

Liv and Jack leaned over to see the end result, and Liv was stunned. Tanya had a way with photography, but it was more than that—she and Jack looked really good together. He had a darker complexion compared to her creamy paleness. And the way he'd pulled her into his arms accentuated his bulging biceps. She was used to feeling bigger than her dates—even than her husband! But in this picture, she looked nothing but soft and feminine next to Jack's latent strength.

"Nice," Liv said, her voice sounding a little strangled in her own ears.

"Right?" Tanya grinned. "Okay, I'll see you tomorrow morning. I've got to go make Gerard and Marie look loving." She made a face. "Jack, it was a pleasure to meet you."

Tanya headed off with a wave, and Liv looked up at Jack nervously.

"You didn't have to be quite so convincing," Liv said, brushing a tendril away from her face.

"She dared me. What can I say?" He shot her a roguish smile.

"My grandmother has dementia, so I can't even explain this one to her and have her understand the humor behind it," Liv retorted.

Jack winced. "Sorry."

"Whatever. I'll talk to Tanya tomorrow morning and get her to delete the picture."

"You sure you want to do that?" Jack asked. "You looked really good."

"I always look really good," Liv shot back. "Whatever. We knew this would be eggshells, right?"

"We knew it," he agreed. "Besides, if I were a real boyfriend who didn't work out, there wouldn't be any shame, would there?"

"No, but eventually, they'll all hear the truth, and I'd rather they didn't pull up that photo to stare at when they do. I'll look… pathetic."

"You couldn't look pathetic. You're gorgeous."

"Fine, then I'll feel pathetic."

"That's fair," Jack agreed. "So how long are we staying?"

"We're leaving now."

"Is there time for more of that potato salad?" Jack hooked a thumb toward the bowl that was already half empty.

"No." She shot him a baleful glare. "You've caused enough trouble."

Jack scooped her hand up in his and pulled her close again, grinning down at her with a low laugh. "All right, Ms. Hylton. Time for our exit."

Jack was playing a part—smitten boyfriend. That's what she'd asked for, wasn't it? But she hadn't expected to find herself falling into her role, too. The sooner they caught whoever was threatening her, the better. Because any more of this, and she'd find herself enjoying her fake boyfriend a little too much!

After some goodbyes and some lame excuses about a prior engagement, they headed back toward the car. She'd leave her extended family to gossip about her behind her back.

It sure beat Poor Liv.

THAT EVENING, JACK sat at Liv's tiny kitchen table, feeling in the way. Liv's apartment was small, so the kitchen table was on the far side of the living room, and from where he sat, he could see into the kitchen on one side, and then through the living room to the bathroom and bedroom.

Not a lot of privacy, he realized ruefully. He was the one crashing into her personal life, so it wasn't really his place to be looking for some space to himself, but this was a decidedly feminine apartment. Everything smelled faintly of lavender, and for the life of him, he couldn't figure out *how*. But it did.

There were some pillar candles standing on a decorative plate on one side table, and under the window there was a radiator with some women's delicates draped over it—drying, no doubt. It was either a slip or a nightgown—a silken ivory color that shimmered in the soft light of a nearby lamp. He felt out of his element here—an obvious intruder into her personal space. Women were different creatures, and Liv was somehow more feminine than he was used to.

Liv stood in the kitchen making a pot of tea. She bobbed a metal diffuser in a teapot and then hooked the end over one side.

"Do you want sugar?" she asked.

"Sure." What he actually wanted was a strong cup of coffee, but yeah, whatever.

Jack was in a bit of a bad mood this evening already. He'd done his part and acted the doting boyfriend, but this case was going to be harder than he'd thought. Liv's family were a complicated bunch, and they'd take a bit to untangle. Then there was Liv herself. She was too soft, too pretty, and reminded him a little too strongly of the things he was missing in his life. And he didn't want to take the lid off that.

Liv deposited a brimming teacup in front of him—gold-rimmed and floral. It looked so delicate that he was half afraid of crushing it. She sent him a fleeting smile, then sank into the chair opposite him. She buried her nose in her own teacup—similar to his, but with different-colored flowers—and took a lingering sip.

"Hmmm…" She sighed. "This is good."

Jack lifted his own cup and took a sip. It was piping hot and sweet, but other than that, tasteless to his palate. He took another sip, then let his gaze move around the apartment.

"Tell me more about your family," Jack said, pulling his attention back to the woman across from him. "Tanya…she's your cousin, you said?"

"Yes, my father's sister's daughter," Liv replied. "We grew up together, Tanya and I. We've always been close."

"How did she feel about your divorce?" he asked.

"Oh, I don't know. She was shocked—just like everyone else. They didn't see it coming. Evan and I put up a really good united front, so when I said we were splitting up… Well, you can imagine."

"So she was against it?" Jack probed. "On his side? On yours?"

"On mine, of course," she said.

"Where are your parents? I didn't see them—"

"In California." She smiled faintly. "They're retired, living in their RV."

"Hmm." He nodded slowly.

"So my turn, then," Liv said, leaning forward. "Tell me about your brothers. Brotherly dynamics are always interesting."

He sighed. It wasn't wise to share too much personal information, but every case was a unique job, and Liv was making this one harder than it had to be. "Do we really have to do this?"

"Yes." She took another sip of tea, but her gaze didn't leave him.

"Fine. One's an accountant and the other is a plumber."

She nodded. "Are you close?"

"Yeah, we're close. I was closer to my cousin when I was a kid, though. My brothers are both younger than me, so I hung out with my cousin."

"Like me and Tanya," she said.

"Yeah, I guess." He could understand her close relationship to her cousin. Kids were lucky to have family to grow up with.

"So your cousin—what's his name?" she asked.

"Berto. He's, uh—" Jack gave her a pained smile. "We aren't in contact anymore."

"Why not?" Sympathy swam in those green eyes, and she leaned toward him so that her soft perfume tickled his nose.

"He associates with known criminals, so as a cop I have to keep my distance," Jack replied gruffly. Would that be enough to make her back off? Berto had a criminal record of his own, so it went deeper than he was about to admit. But keeping his distance didn't mean that Jack wasn't hell-bent on setting a few wrongs right.

"You must miss him," she said quietly.

"Yeah, I do."

"How did you turn out so differently?" she asked. "You're obviously in a better place."

"We both grew up poor in the projects in Denver," he said. "Berto got caught up with the wrong people, I guess. I can't say I was making better choices than he was. Maybe I was just lucky."

"You chose to join the force," she countered. "That's a positive step."

"Berto might have, too, given the chance," he replied bitterly. "He was arrested the first time when he was barely fourteen. Drug possession. But I'm telling you, Berto never touched heroin in his life. Back then, Berto and I said we wanted to be rich when we grew up. But rich meant something different to us than it meant to anyone else. Our biggest dreams were to move out of those crumbling old apartment buildings, get away from the drug dealers, and get houses with real yards and driveways. We wanted to take care of our parents and siblings. We wanted our mothers to quit those low-paying jobs that ground them down."

"You were sweet kids," she said softly.

"We were poor kids. We had no power, and neither did our parents. Berto ended up like too many of our friends."

"How is your mother now?" Liv asked.

"I take care of her and Dad," he replied. "No worries there."

Jack was stupid to be giving her any information about his family at all. What was it about her? Just talking with this woman made him want to open up. It felt good to let it out, and she listened so easily without judgment. But the more she knew—the more she could pass along to whoever else was working this ring—the more vulnerable he became. She made him feel out of his depth in a whole new way, which meant it was time to shut up.

"Enough about me now. Let's move on to you," he said with a small smile. "Are there any boyfriends, exes, casual love interests that I should be aware of?"

She shook her head. "I'm still licking my wounds."

"Fair enough. How about your store?" He crossed his arms over his chest. "How is it financed, if you don't mind me asking?"

"With a loan, like everyone else." She put her cup down onto the saucer with a soft *clink*. "I'm hoping to be able to make enough profit to pay it off one day. Bookstores have such big competition with online sellers, but there is just something about being able to flip through a book, hold it, look at the other options on the same shelf... I'm hoping to capitalize on the tourist traffic."

"Yeah," he agreed. "I get it."

"Anyway, I've dreamed of owning a bookstore for as long as I can remember. When I was a kid, I used to make books of my own with paper folded in half and a stapler. Then I'd set them up for my own bookstore."

"So why do it now?"

"Because I needed something for me," she said. "I've been cut loose, and I need something that reminds me of...me."

Her connection to the place did seem

genuine. Jack's gaze moved to the kitchen windowsill, where a collection of books sat between two bookends. They didn't look like cookbooks, either.

Liv followed his gaze.

"Just some kitchen reading," she said.

"Kitchen reading." He chuckled. "Like what?"

"A few classics—some Charles Dickens, some Shakespeare, a book on chess strategy."

"Yeah?" He raised his eyebrows.

"I've always liked Dickens. While I wait for pots to boil, I reread some of my favorite parts."

"I was more interested in the chess strategy," he replied.

"Oh, that." She rose and went to the windowsill, plucking out the volume and handing it over to him. "Evan used to play chess, but I stopped playing with him after a couple years of marriage."

"Why?" Jack flipped through the book—it was thick and looked very involved.

"He's a bad loser." She shrugged. "He's also a cocky winner. It wasn't good for our relationship either way."

"So why the interest in chess now?" He clapped the book shut. "If it were me, I'd hate the game, just for bad associations."

"I don't know." A small smile came to her lips. "A girl likes to know she could win, if she were pressed."

Was she being pressed? That was the question. Did her ex-husband have her in a corner, or did she wield more power than he thought? She was a woman who reread the classics while she cooked and used her spare minutes to learn chess moves. She was daunting.

"How good are you at chess?" Jack asked.

"Better than I look." She met his eye with a cool smile. "And better than Evan thinks."

"So you play for spite?" he asked.

"No, I play to win." She shrugged. "There's something about a well-performed strategy that leaves your opponent in the corner. No moves left. Only then realizing what you've done to him."

That was ominous, and it reminded him a little too closely of the people who had been pressured into selling their family homes… they would have realized too late, too.

"It's getting late," Liv said after a moment. "I should really get ready for bed."

"Sure. You don't need to entertain me. I'm here on a job."

Liv rose and glanced around. She seemed to spot the slip on the radiator, because she hurried across the room and snatched it up.

When she looked back at him, she looked embarrassed.

"Sorry about that," she said.

"It's your home," he replied. "Don't apologize for anything. I'm not a guest here, Liv."

She tucked the slip under her arm and headed for a cupboard. She pulled out some sheets, a blanket and a pillowcase.

"I don't have any more bed pillows," she said. "But we could cover a throw pillow with this pillow case, and you should be comfortable. I think." She grimaced. "No one visits me."

"I'll be fine."

Liv licked her lips. "I normally take my shower at night. If you wanted yours first—"

"Liv." His voice came out as more of a bark than he'd intended, and he softened his tone. "I'm *not* a guest. Do what you would normally do, okay? I'm fine."

She pulled a hand through her auburn waves. "Okay. If you insist."

She disappeared into the bathroom, and a few moments later the water came on with a rattle. Jack distracted himself by making up his bed on the sofa. He made his bed at home with military precision, and he did his best to replicate that job here. The sofa was too short, but he'd make do. He noticed that even the sheets had that soft, floral scent about them.

It was all very diverting from the case that he'd rather be thinking over, as was the sound of the shower through the shut bathroom door. He was a man, after all, and Liv was a very beautiful woman. Her divorce hadn't dampened any of her natural spunk, and he wished it had. If she were a little less radiant, maybe he could focus better on the work at hand.

Instead, as he spread the blanket on top of the sheet, he was remembering what it felt like to pull her close for the camera. She felt just as good in his arms as he'd imagined back before he'd realized she was tied up in Evan's mess.

The water in the bathroom turned off, and Jack glanced around the living room, his gaze moving over a bookshelf, an ottoman that had a hinged lid for storage and her closed bedroom door. If she had something to hide, where would it be?

The bathroom door opened, and Liv came out with a billow of steam. Her hair was wrapped up in a towel, and the rest of her ample curves were draped in a white terry cloth robe that she held shut with one hand at her throat.

"Done," she said, shooting him a smile.

She looked different in her robe—her face clean of makeup and her eyes all the more entrancing without the liner and mascara. She looked younger this way, softer. She was barefoot, and he noted that her toenails were painted hot pink. And he liked it.

"The towels are on the rack in the bathroom," she said, heading toward her bedroom and opening the door. "If you're hungry, feel free to raid the fridge. You're guarding my life—it's the least I can offer."

Her lips turned up in a smile and she slipped into her room, then turned back. "Good night, Jack."

His name on her lips sounded sweet, and he gave her a curt nod because it was all he trusted himself to do. He wasn't faking to be her boyfriend here in her apartment. Here, he was a cop, and he needed to remind himself of that. Her big, dewy eyes, her lips, the milky whiteness of her skin—none of that was his business here. And for all he knew, she was working it to keep him distracted.

The bedroom door closed with a decisive *click* and Jack let out a pent-up breath. He was hoping he could sleep at all.

CHAPTER FIVE

MOUNTAIN COFFEE CO. was relatively empty. Liv sat by a window, listening to the hiss of the milk steamer in the background while she waited for her cousin. Outside the window, she watched as a pickup truck stopped at the four-way stop, then eased forward again. She couldn't see the snow-capped peaks in the distance from where she sat. The real view in this town had to be enjoyed from outside, standing on the street and looking up. The Rocky Mountains were awe-inspiring, and even though she had grown up in this town, they hadn't lost their grandeur in her eyes.

The outside door opened, and Liv waved as Tanya came in. Tanya waved back and headed to the counter to give her order, then she came to the table and sank into the chair opposite Liv. Her chestnut hair was pulled back into a ponytail, and it swung forward as she leaned over to give Liv a quick hug.

"Hey," Tanya said with a grin. "It's been too long since we've had a cousin catch-up."

"I know." Liv took a sip of her chai tea. "You look great, by the way."

"*You* look great," Tanya retorted. "Look at you—all glowing. I love your dress."

Liv was on a vintage dress kick lately. This morning she wore a gray woolen dress with an A-line skirt and an asymmetrical neckline that drew the eye toward her curves, and she'd paired it with a sleek red lipstick.

"Thanks. It's new." Liv smiled back. "So what happened after I left the barbecue?"

"What you'd expect," Tanya replied with a shrug. "Wild gossip and conjecture."

Liv chuckled. "I like it."

"You would," Tanya retorted drily.

"Hazelnut latte," the girl at the counter called, and Tanya got up to retrieve her drink.

Liv had left Jack at the apartment that morning. She didn't need protection from a girl talk with Tanya, and she didn't want someone else listening in on them, either. Jack had grudgingly agreed to stay back and take a look around "the perimeter of the store," as he put it. She had to admit, she felt safer with Jack close by, but the timing was terrible.

"Have you talked to Evan recently?" Tanya asked as she slid back into her seat.

"No, why?" Liv took a sip of her tea, leaving a red lip print on the rim of the cup.

"There's trouble in paradise."

Liv considered her cousin for a moment, then put her cup down in front of her. "How do you know?"

"I've kept up with Evan a little bit." She dropped her gaze for a moment.

"And you never told me?" Liv demanded. "You've been chummy with my ex-husband? Seriously?"

"You've kept a few of your own secrets!" her cousin shot back, and Liv bit her tongue. The truth was, until now, she hadn't kept any.

"And he told you that he's having problems with Serena," Liv clarified.

"Yes." Tanya shrugged. "Serena is a whole lot different as wife than she was as girlfriend."

"Aren't we all?" Liv said drily. "So what's she doing?"

"She doesn't understand him. She's getting more demanding. She wants a baby."

Liv tried to tamp down the bitterness rising up inside her. She'd wanted a baby, too, and Evan had never caved. He was all about work—and apparently, all about maintaining an affair with another woman. Serena had won that battle and walked away with

Evan. It was grudgingly satisfying to know that Serena, with her tight little body and a seven-minute mile, wasn't keeping Evan satisfied, either.

"And Evan is telling you all about it?" Liv squinted at her cousin. "Since when?"

"He was part of the family for ten years," Tanya said with a sigh. "But he's not happy, Liv."

"Good." Evan didn't deserve a second chance at relationship happiness. He'd cheated on her, dumped her and then married another woman. It was a step in the right direction if he recognized that new did not equal better. He'd had a gem of a wife in Liv—she was well read, smart and widely considered to be hilarious by her friends. She dressed for her figure, kept her legs shaved and maintained a good relationship with her in-laws. She'd been there for Evan, listening to him, supporting him when his mother passed away and when the IRS came after him for back taxes. And if a loyal wife like Liv wasn't good enough for Evan, then she hoped the home-wrecking Serena henpecked him to death. He had it coming.

"I thought he might be talking to you about it, too." Tanya kept her eyes on her cup.

"I haven't talked to him in a couple of

weeks, and when I did, he was asking for jewelry back."

"Jewelry?" Tanya's eyes widened.

"A brooch. For his new wife." She sighed. "It's not terribly exciting, and I didn't have it. So, no, I'm not chatting with him. I'm free of him, for the most part."

He did owe her something still—but she wasn't even sure she could hold him to his obligations. Maybe she should cut her losses, and he could go off into the sunset with his baby-frenzied bride.

"And you've moved on with Jack," her cousin pointed out.

"Yes, I have." Or that was the way it currently appeared, and Liv was perfectly happy to let her family believe it. Still, looking into her cousin's face, she felt a twinge of guilt.

"How serious is this?" Tanya asked. "Jack seems like a great guy. He's clearly smitten."

"It's not serious. At all. He's a nice guy, but I'm not about to get myself locked into anything."

"Why not?" Tanya asked. "He's cute!"

"He's a cop," she retorted drily. "I have a few hang-ups when it comes to the police force. They do the whole band-of-brothers thing. If you aren't a cop, they don't let you in. And I'm tired of coming second to a job."

"And Jack is the same?"

Liv shrugged. "They're all the same, Tanya."

"Too bad. You looked so happy with him," her cousin replied. "So you're going to dump him?"

"No, I—" Liv winced. "How much do you talk to Evan?"

"I hardly talk to him at all," Tanya protested. "We catch up from time to time. That's all."

Liv sighed. "Because I don't want my personal business getting back to my ex-husband."

"My lips are sealed," Tanya replied. "You know that! Come on. I'm on your side in this."

And who did Liv have in her life, if she couldn't trust her own cousin?

"I'm going to tell you something, and I need you to keep it between us," Liv said. When her cousin nodded, she went on, "Jack isn't my boyfriend."

"What?" Tanya's brow furrowed.

"I hate lying to you, Tanya, and I really need you to keep this a secret."

"Of course."

"I've been getting threatening notes and packages at the store, and when I called the police, they took it seriously. Really seriously."

"So…who is Jack?" her cousin asked.

"He's a police officer. He's posing as my boyfriend to avoid notice, but he's…looking into it."

"Are you in danger?" Tanya lowered her voice and frowned.

"The police are treating it that way," Liv replied. "But Jack is staying with me until he can sort out who's been threatening me and put a stop to it."

Tanya let out a rush of breath. "Wow."

Liv raised her eyebrows and lifted her cup of tea to her lips again. "And the timing is terrible."

"I don't suppose the timing for being stalked is ever great," her cousin replied.

Liv took a sip and smiled. "Maybe not. But I was just settling in, you know? Getting comfortable after the divorce, feeling more like myself. And Jack is…" She cast about for the right word.

"Hot?" Tanya raised an eyebrow.

"Very, very male," Liv qualified with a small smile. "He's such a guy. All muscles and determination. And no, there isn't any romantic possibility between us. He's strictly professional."

"He wasn't professional at all at Aunt Marie's," her cousin countered.

"Apparently, he's also a good actor," she replied. "It's hard sharing a one-bedroom apartment with a man. It's...very close."

"I'll bet," Tanya said with a grin. "You never know what might develop. Protected by a cute cop...woman in distress..."

"I'm hardly in distress."

"You called the cops, didn't you?"

Fine, she was scared, but she wasn't about to cave in and hand her life over to a man she hardly knew, either. Liv leaned her elbows on the table. "I'm finally comfortable on my own. I'm opening my own bookstore... I'm me again, you know? And having Jack around is just...distracting."

"Yeah... I could see that."

Liv glanced out the window, watching the shade flutter across the sidewalk in the sunlight. "He knew Evan."

"Jack did?" Tanya grimaced.

"They worked together in the Denver PD. He was at Evan's wedding to Officer Hot Pants." Liv shook her head. "You know what Evan put me through, and I'm so ready to just put him in the past. I'm glad he never agreed to have a baby with me, because if he had, we'd still be linked as co-parents. But as it is, I'm free! Divorced and done."

"Are he and Evan friends?" Tanya turned her cup in a slow circle on the tabletop.

"No. Acquaintances. Or so Jack claims."

"You think there's more to it—"

"Maybe there isn't," Liv said. "I don't want to be paranoid, but I hate coincidences."

"You should have been a cop, too." Tanya chuckled. "It's all that chess strategizing. You see traps where there aren't any."

"I'll feel better when Evan is well and truly behind me. That's all."

"And when all good-looking officers are out of your home?" Tanya asked with a low laugh.

"Yes! You might think that sounds dumb, but I'm done with dating cops. *So* done. Besides, any man who can lie as convincingly as Jack did at that barbecue—I can't trust that kind of guy."

Tanya smiled ruefully.

"And I need you to lock this all away," Liv said, catching her cousin's eye and holding it. "The truth is, someone *is* threatening me, and the police feel that this is the best route to catch whoever is doing it. But everyone needs to believe that I'm dating Jack and that he's nothing more than a boyfriend."

"Okay." Tanya sobered. "You can trust me, Liv. I've had your back since kindergarten."

Liv pulled her hair away from her face. "Thanks. It didn't feel right to leave you in the dark."

She had to trust someone. Evan had broken her trust, and someone out there was trying to chase her out of town, but Liv wasn't going to allow that to undo her most treasured relationships.

The quicker Jack got to the bottom of all this, the quicker Liv could get back to normal. She had a whole life away from her ex-husband, and she was looking forward to getting back to it.

JACK SAT ON the couch, a photo album open in his lap. He flicked through a few pages, scanning the faces. As it turned out, the ottoman had been filled with photo albums, and he'd already thumbed through most of them. He was getting a feel for Liv—her past, her friendships, her tastes.

He'd also been in contact with the police chief, and so far Evan wasn't doing anything suspicious. He was lying low, which was frustrating. They needed some contact between Evan and Liv, but so far they weren't having any luck.

Jack shut the album and put it aside. There was one last album at the bottom—a pearled white cover. He lifted it out, and as he suspected, it was a wedding album. He opened the cover and browsed through the first pages. Liv had been just as beautiful on her wedding day as she was now—curvy, rounded, glittering. She wore a ball gown that nipped in at her waist, and a diamond tiara glittered in her auburn updo. She looked stunning.

Evan was more subdued in the photos. Always a drink his hand and a lopsided grin on his face. Liv seemed to be the "together" one in that relationship, and Jack had to wonder if Evan ever realized how good he'd had it.

"She kept the wedding album…" he murmured aloud. How many divorced women held on to their wedding albums? He had no idea, and it wasn't like she'd had it on display or something. It was in the bottom of a box. Nevertheless…did Liv still harbor feelings for her ex-husband? People sometimes did stupid things to try to win back an ex.

Jack felt a little twinge of jealousy at that thought, and he quickly tamped it down. She was a suspect—he'd better keep that clear in his head. And for strictly investigative purposes, he had to wonder how much contact the exes still had—how many of their interests were still joined. Liv had delivered documents to one of the victims swindled by

Evan postdivorce. She was still involved—the question was, how deeply?

Was Liv just sitting on this property, faking more personal interest in the store than she really had, until it was time to liquidate? Evan had betrayed her, but perhaps he still owed her something after that betrayal, something that would make keeping her mouth shut worthwhile. Money?

Jack glanced around the apartment. It all looked very…settled. Knickknacks, books, a lot of attention put into home decor. But that didn't mean she couldn't up and move. Maybe she was willing to wait a while for a bigger payoff.

He clapped the album shut and stacked all of the albums back into the ottoman in the same order he'd taken them out.

When Liv had left to have coffee with her cousin this morning, he'd agreed to hang back with the intention of searching her apartment. It was a great opportunity, and he couldn't let it go.

Jack put the lid back onto the ottoman and took one last look around the room. Liv's bedroom door was shut. He'd left her bedroom for last. He checked his watch. She'd been gone for forty minutes. Coffee took longer than that. Besides, he had a cop keeping an eye on the coffee place—Officer McDonald. He'd text Jack as soon as Liv left.

He opened the bedroom door and glanced inside. The curtains were open, spilling late-morning light across an unmade bed.

"Liv, you're messy," he muttered to himself as he gave the room a once-over. But sometimes messes could be useful when doing a quick search. Unless people were neat freaks, they tended to leave things out without realizing it.

Jack went to the window and looked out onto the street below. The bedroom window faced the same direction as the storefront, and he looked across the street at a woman pushing a stroller. The toddler threw a bottle onto the sidewalk, and she stopped to pick it up, then continued on. He turned back to the bedroom.

There was a vanity table with a few bottles of makeup sitting on top next to a box of what looked like more makeup. A laundry hamper sat in one corner next to a full-length oval mirror on a stand. The sleigh bed was wooden and polished to a sheen. Thick mattresses made for a high bed, and it looked… comfortable. After a night on that lumpy sofa, these were the things he noticed.

Jack slid an arm between the mattresses,

feeling toward the center of the bed. He moved quickly around it and did the same on the other side. He lifted blankets and sheets, checked under the pile of pillows, and tried to ignore the fact that the piles of covers smelled sweet and feminine—recently laundered.

The bedside table had a few books stacked up. He glanced down the spines—a couple of mysteries, a book of Wordsworth poetry and *Great Expectations* by Charles Dickens. Apparently, Dickens wasn't only "kitchen reading."

Just behind the stack of reading material, he spotted a journal.

"There we go…" He felt a tickle of guilt. This was private—personal. This was the kind of invasion of privacy that a man didn't pull with a friend, and being undercover could confuse those lines in his emotions. But he had a job to do—he picked up the journal and flipped through the pages. It went back only a few months. As he scanned the entries, he noticed that she talked a lot about her store.

Today, I had to deal with the contractors. I'm a woman, so they figure they can push me around. I need those shelves done by the twelfth. I hate not being taken seriously. But everyone complains about their contractors, don't they? There are days I wish I had a cop husband to throw at them still. Just for ten minutes. Then I'd give him back.

Jack chuckled. Obviously, the contractors had finished because he'd seen the end result downstairs. But whether she'd used honey or vinegar to make that happen, he didn't have the time to find out. He flipped to the center of the book.

I got another letter. It was all theatrical— letters cut out of magazines and glued on paper. Is this Tanya's warped sense of humor?

No, it had been Jack's work, actually. Theatrical…well, she should try putting together a threatening letter that wasn't too upsetting but still did the trick! It was harder than people thought.

He flipped forward to the most recent page, written last night by the date at the top.

Jack is on the couch out there. I don't know about him. He's hiding something. But then, I tend to think that about all cops since Evan. Jack's all official and rocklike. I don't mean as in Dwayne Johnson, either, although Jack is built to about the same proportions. He doesn't open up without some real prying. He's all professional—as he should be—but I hate that. I feel like I need to defend myself for some reason.

I have a man in my apartment. That's a

*first for this place! That's a first since Evan...
And if only he could be a little less attractive.
I need someone nerdy and spindly. Maybe
even married, too, and with a wallet full of
pictures of his bucktoothed kids. But Jack—
he's all testosterone, and I'm responding to
him against my better instincts. He always
was the brooding, über-male type. That much
hasn't changed. And apparently, I'm still the
kind of girl who goes for that. When will I
learn?*

That was where she left off, and he smiled
to himself. All testosterone, was he? He'd
been described in worse ways. And if he was
keeping her off-balance, that could be considered an asset to this investigation.

Except, he wasn't feeling that rush of male
satisfaction because of the investigation—he
was liking the fact that she was attracted to
him. Was he allowed to enjoy that a little bit?

"No," he growled to himself. Of course he
wasn't! He was here to prove her connection
to a case and get as much evidence against
her and her ex-husband as possible. He had a
job to do, and he'd better keep focused.

He heard a voice in the hallway—Liv's—
then a key slid into the lock. Jack's heart hammered hard, and he dropped the journal back
where he found it and took two long strides

to the bedroom door. He was just pulling the door shut behind him as the front door opened.

Liv didn't look up at first, her attention on juggling her keys and a to-go coffee cup. A cell phone was pinched between her cheek and her black woolen wrap. When her gaze flickered up toward him, she stopped short.

"Mom? I've got to get going, okay? Tell Dad I said hi."

She hung up the phone and nudged the door shut behind her.

"Hey," Jack said, forcing what he hoped was an easy smile.

"What are you doing?" she asked, frowning slightly.

"I was taking a look around the perimeter," he said with a shrug. "Just checking out the security of the place."

"Were you in my room?"

He shot her a conciliatory smile. "Very briefly."

She sighed. "That's my personal space. I'd really appreciate it if you stayed out of there."

"And I will."

Liv put her cup and phone down, her keys clattering to the floor. She stooped to pick them up.

"I'm not always that messy," she said, her cheeks growing pink.

"Yes, you are," he said with a short laugh, and she shot him an icy glare. So there it was—he'd finally knocked her off-balance.

"How would you know?" she retorted.

"I'm a cop. I'm trained to look at details. I'm not saying I gave it too much attention, but your bedroom has the look of a room that stays in that state pretty much all the time."

"Just stay out."

"You bet."

Liv heaved a sigh and headed into the kitchen, disappearing from view, and he suppressed a sigh of his own. That was a near miss. Why hadn't McDonald texted him? He looked down at his phone. Nothing. Luckily, Liv was distracted enough by her own embarrassment around the state of her bedroom not to question him further, and he was glad for that. But the words from her journal were still burning through his mind. Was that the way she saw him? He'd been attracted to her for years, and he'd never thought that she'd given him a second look…but one misstep here could land him in some very dangerous territory. This case was his chance to prove himself to the Internal Affairs department— and there was an opening available. He could make a big difference in Denver. He could finally start making the projects a safer place for the kids growing up there by weeding out the dirty cops and pressing charges against those who planted evidence.

"So how was your coffee with your cousin?" Jack said, ambling over to the kitchen.

When he came around the dividing wall, he saw Liv putting together a sandwich on fluffy white bread.

"Fine." She unscrewed a jar of mayo and plunged a butter knife into its depth with a loud *clink* of metal against glass.

"You seem…upset," he volunteered. "Did something happen, or are you still annoyed with me?"

Liv looked up at him. "Tanya deleted the photo of you and me."

"Yeah?"

"I told her."

"What?" he barked. "What did you tell her?"

"Who you are and why you're here. She's my cousin and my oldest friend. I'm not lying to her."

Jack pressed his lips together, trying to control his rising anger. "I thought we agreed—"

"Her lips are sealed. She won't tell anyone. But if I lied to her, it would have affected our relationship, and Tanya is one of the people I value most."

Jack's mind was already spinning toward damage control. The last thing he needed was Evan getting a premature heads-up.

"And your mother on the phone?" he demanded.

"She's in California. What's the harm in her knowing the truth? I can't balance that much lying."

"So your mother's lips are sealed, too," he clarified.

"Yes." Liv lifted her chin in an expression of mild defiance.

"Fine." What else could he say? He'd hoped to keep this contained for a little while longer, but all it meant was that he'd have to work fast and stay focused.

"My mother and my cousin are nothing to worry about," Liv said. "Trust me."

Trust her. That was the very last thing he could do!

CHAPTER SIX

JACK LOOKED TIRED the next morning—more so than he had been recently. Liv eyed him across the breakfast table sympathetically.

"The couch is agony, isn't it?" she asked.

"It's fine. I keep telling you I'm not a guest."

He kept saying it, but it was hard to wrap her emotions around. When someone was staying in her personal space, she couldn't help but feel somewhat responsible for his comfort.

"Did you sleep last night?" she asked, taking a gulp of her tea and one last piece of toast.

"Uh…not a lot," he admitted. He looked at her for a moment, as if deciding if he'd say more, then he added, "I was thinking about your relationship with Tanya…and about Berto."

She swallowed her bite of toast. "Where is Berto now?"

"Prison—he broke parole."

"For a good reason, at least?" she asked hesitantly.

Jack shook his head. "Nope. The thing is, once he was arrested that first time, something in him changed. There are some guys who can reform. There are others who were broken too early."

"How old was he when he was arrested again?" she asked quietly.

"Fourteen. That's a formative age. He just…gave up." Jack cleared his throat. "I don't want to talk about him, though."

"I think you need to," she countered. "Obviously, you still care about him. You were close once, and losing someone in any way— you have to grieve it."

"I've had plenty of time for that," he replied with a small smile that didn't reach his eyes. "It's been twenty years."

"Time means nothing if you haven't dealt with it," she replied. "Talking is *healthy*, Jack."

Jack met her gaze for a moment, and she could see all those conflicting emotions in his dark eyes, but then he pushed back his chair and stood up.

"You're opening the store today," he said. "Let's focus on that."

And while Liv was excited for today, she

could feel that rock-solid cop side of the man battling with his very real emotions. He was another cop trying to hold it all in, and she'd been married to that before. A woman had no hope of beating through those walls, even if the man needed it.

Liv finished breakfast, and they headed downstairs, where Liv took a final look around her shop—at the neatly organized shelves packed with books, the clean corkboard waiting for local announcements and advertisements, the cash register primed and ready to go.

Jack found a stool and arranged it by the window, where he got a view of the street, but his gaze was locked on her. It felt strange to be sharing this moment with a relative stranger.

"Well, here goes…" Liv had a flutter in her stomach as she unlocked the front door and flipped the sign around to Open. The sidewalk was empty, so no one came dashing inside to part with their money, but she was open all the same.

"Congratulations," Jack said.

"Thank you." She shot him a smile, and for a split second, that stony expression of his cracked and he smiled back.

"This is a dream realized for me," she said.

"How about you—are you where you wanted to be when you were a kid?"

"Me?" Jack laughed softly. "Yeah, almost."

"What's missing?" she asked.

Jack shot her a rueful smile but didn't answer, and it was just as well because Liv's cell phone began to ring. She dug it out of her purse and glanced down at the number. Her stomach sank and she rubbed a hand over her eyes, considering.

"Who is it?" Jack asked.

"Evan," she muttered.

She didn't want to pick up. Whatever Evan wanted, it could wait. But before she could stop him, Jack reached over and picked up the call, hitting the speakerphone button. Then he shot her an expectant look. Apparently, Jack wanted to listen in on this conversation.

"Hi, Evan," Liv said, trying to force her voice to sound natural.

"Good morning." Evan sounded jovial, to say the least. "How are you doing?"

"Fine, but busy. What can I do for you?"

"Is your store swamped with customers?" he asked, suddenly hesitant. How did he know about her opening day? Liv looked up at Jack, eyes wide.

"Um—" She swallowed. "What do you need, Evan?"

"I'll take that as a no," her ex-husband replied drily. "Well, congratulations, anyway."

"How did you know I was opening today?"

"I marked it on my calendar when we talked last. I care."

"Great." But it did soften her a little bit.

"We still help each other out even if we didn't work out romantically, don't we?" he asked.

This was suddenly getting more personal than she cared to share with Jack—bodyguard or not. Liv took the phone off Speaker and turned away from Jack slightly so that she could at least feel like she had a little privacy. "Didn't work out romantically? You sound like we had a few dates! Good grief, Evan— we were married for a decade!"

"I know, I know…" Evan's tone softened further. "I'm just saying, I think we could be on better terms than we are."

"And what use is that?" she retorted. "We don't have any kids, and there is no reason to stay in touch. You have your life and I have mine. Period."

"I care," Evan repeated softly, and he sounded so much like the old Evan that her heart gave a squeeze. "Besides, I still owe you those first-edition books my grandmother left to you, don't I?"

Liv's heart skipped a beat. They were worth a lot of money, those books. Technically, they were hers, but they were connected to Evan's family history, not hers. "And you'll part with them now?"

"It's only fair."

"A lot of things were fair, and yet you trampled those boundaries," she quipped.

"Oh, stop it," Evan said with a sigh. "Grandma left them to you, and granted, she'd thought they were staying in the family. But still…considering your love of books, I think it's only right that you should still have them. Besides, if you took me to court, you'd win."

"And how does *your wife* feel about that?" she asked primly.

"About court?" Evan asked innocently. "She's not keen on it."

"I'm not suing you!" she retorted. "So quit playing games. How does Serena feel about you handing over those first editions?"

"She's not the hateful woman you think she is," Evan said quietly. "She's fine with it."

Liv glanced back toward Jack and found his gaze still locked on her, his granite expression unchanged. She smiled weakly.

"You could ship them," Liv said at last.

"I'll figure it out," Evan replied. "Just so you know, I'll make sure you get them."

"Thank you. I appreciate it." She didn't like being in this position with Evan—it wasn't comfortable. He always managed to make her feel like he was the one pulling strings.

"And I was wondering if you might be willing to pick up some papers from someone. He's an older guy and can't figure out how to send documents securely," he added.

"Evan, I'm not your wife."

"I know, but you're there, and I'm here, and…I was hoping for old time's sake you might not mind."

His voice was still so soft, so tempting, and she had to admit that she was leaning toward agreeing. He was giving her those first editions, after all. But when she looked up, she saw Jack watching her, and it jolted her back into the present.

"No," she said more firmly. "Drive out and pick them up yourself if you're so concerned, but we're not married anymore, and I'm not your assistant."

Evan sighed. "Think about it."

She licked her lips. "Final answer, Evan. Goodbye."

Liv hung up, looking down at her cell phone. Why was she always so eager to please that man, even after their divorce? He'd been able to get her to do just about anything over the years with that one line—*Think about it*. Never accepting her *no* and always patiently waiting for her to come around. She was tired of playing these games.

"What was that?" Jack asked, pulling her out of her thoughts.

"I don't think you have to worry about Evan," she said quietly. "Whatever hard feelings he had toward me seem to be in the past."

"How do you know?"

Liv tucked her phone into her pocket. "His grandmother left some valuable first-edition books to me in her will. She passed away about the same time Evan left me for Officer Hot Pants, and considering they were from his side of the family, I really didn't think he'd part with them."

"He thought you'd sue him?" Jack asked with a slight frown.

"I guess." She shook her head. "I'm just moving on with my life. I wasn't going to pick new fights with my ex. Anyway, he's going to send them to me. I'm…shocked."

"Yeah…" Jack chewed the side of his cheek.

"What?" she asked.

"He asked you to do something," he said.

"A personal favor," she said with a shake of her head. "And I'm not doing it."

"What kind of favor?" he pressed.

"Picking up some documents and FedExing them out to him," she said. "I used to do that sort of thing for him all the time when we were married. It looks like Serena isn't up to speed on how he likes things. But I'm not doing it. I'm sick of this."

"What documents, exactly?" Jack's gaze had turned laser-focused.

"I don't know." She shrugged. "It doesn't matter, does it? Sometimes he buys some pieces of property and sells them again when property values rise."

"Is this one of those sales?" he asked.

"I don't know!" She was getting irritated now.

"So why would he suddenly part with these valuable books now?" Jack asked.

"You know as much as I do," she replied, then pulled her hand through her hair. "I have to admit, he was remarkably…sweet."

"Softening you up," Jack confirmed.

"There are rumors that his marriage has a few cracks already," Liv admitted ruefully. "Maybe he's appreciating what he had."

"Maybe."

Liv sucked in a breath. She'd imagined the

day Evan realized all he'd lost when he left her—imagined it over and over again. What woman didn't want her cheating ex to feel the sting of everything he'd missed out on when he'd tossed her aside? And now that day had come—or so it seemed—and it was a whole lot less satisfying than she'd thought. In her fantasies, Liv would come back at him with a great insult, crushing him in his vulnerable state, just as he deserved. But hearing Evan sound so much like he used to back when he'd loved her...that had slipped underneath her defenses.

"He got to you," Jack said, and he looked mildly surprised. Liv realized that her eyes had misted, and she blinked it back. This was one of those times she wished she was alone to deal with her grief.

"It's complicated in the usual divorce kinds of ways," she admitted. "I'm used to hating him, and then he turns around and does something downright decent. It reminds me of the way he used to be, back when things were good between us."

A whole lot had happened in the last few days, and Evan's call had been poorly timed. Liv straightened a pile of coupons she'd set aside to give away with purchases, and she felt a lump closing off her throat. Her eyes welled with unshed tears in spite of her best efforts to blink them back. Of all the days for Evan to call, it had to be this one…

"Hey." Jack got to his feet and crossed the store. He put a warm hand over hers. It was a comforting gesture, and when she glanced up at him, she saw worry in his eyes. "He really did get to you…"

"I didn't ever feel ugly," she said, her voice tight. "Growing up, I had some self-esteem issues, but by the time I got married, I felt beautiful. I figured I had a lot to offer a man. I mean, I tried to lose some weight, but that wasn't about feeling unattractive. It was just…habit, I guess. I liked my shape, I just wanted to bring it down a dress size. I don't expect you to understand that." She pulled her hand out from under Jack's. "I really liked who I was and how I looked until Evan left me. That was the first day I looked in the mirror and wondered if I'd been delusional all that time."

"Not delusional at all," Jack said gruffly. "You're gorgeous."

"I'm sniffly. You have to say that," she said, snatching up a tissue and dabbing it under her eyes lest her makeup run.

"I don't say anything I don't want to," he replied, his voice soft and low. "I always did think you were beautiful. You can draw every eye in a room. There's just something about you… And Evan was the lucky one. You are better than him. You always were."

Liv looked up at Jack again, her breath caught in her throat. He looked utterly truthful, his dark eyes locked on her, and for once, that granite expression had softened. She was inclined to believe him…

The bell above the door tinkled, and Liv looked over to see three local women coming inside.

"You're finally open!" one of them chirped. "At long last."

"I am," Liv said, forcing a smile to her lips and straightening her shoulders. "Come on in. Have a look around."

The women's conversation turned toward one another as they headed for the bookshelves, and Liv shot Jack a grateful look.

"I have a meeting at the station," Jack said with an apologetic smile. "But don't worry—there will be officers patrolling this street."

"Okay."

He lifted his cell phone. "Call me if you need me, okay? Meeting or not, you're the priority."

"Will do. But I'm sure I'll be fine." Optimism seemed prudent right now. Her life had to keep moving forward, and whoever was trying to scare her couldn't stop that from happening.

Jack turned and headed for the door, and she watched him go. He was built like a tank, but he moved with lithe confidence. She was reluctantly disappointed to see him go, and it wasn't only because he was the one standing between her and an unstable threat. She was getting used to him being around…and starting to like it.

What could she say—she was still a woman, and Jack Talbott was a ruggedly handsome man who'd been sleeping on her couch…

"Excuse me, do you have the newest Julia London series?" one of the women asked, drawing her attention away from the door as Jack disappeared.

"I do," Liv said with a smile. "I have her older series, too. She's great, isn't she?"

Back to work.

JACK GLANCED AT his watch as he walked into the Eagle's Rest Police Department. He was on time, and the chief would be waiting for him. He nodded to the receptionist, flashing his badge, as he headed past her desk and into the bull pen. He was relieved to have gotten out of Liv's store. Spending so much time with her lately, he was getting blinded to the case, and he hated that. He'd started opening up to her, too…and just now in the store, her emotional reaction to her ex-husband's call had sparked that natural protective instinct inside him. He was slipping in too close—he knew it. Jack was also seeing her at her most vulnerable, and that was doing a number on him. Whatever feelings he'd developed from afar before her divorce were back. Liv wasn't the kind of woman a guy could wipe out of his mind that easily.

"Morning, Jack," Chief Simpson said as Jack tapped on the open office door.

"Good morning," Jack replied. The chief nodded him in, and he closed the door behind him.

"Have a seat. Do you want coffee?"

"No, I'm fine," Jack said, easing into the too-tight chair. "Thanks, though."

"How is the investigation going?" the chief asked, fixing those glittering blue eyes on Jack. "Any progress?"

"Look, if I'm going be undercover with this woman, I need better support from the PD," Jack replied. "McDonald was in position at the coffee shop yesterday when I was doing a sweep of Liv's apartment, and I got a text from him saying she was gone a full ten minutes after she'd come back to her apartment. I was counting on him. I'm not going to be effective if—"

"McDonald feels terrible," the chief interrupted. "And yes, he dropped the ball. But he also discovered something useful to our investigation. The cousin that your suspect was having coffee with has been in frequent contact with Evan Kornekewsky."

"What?" Jack snapped. "The cousin—Tanya. Big brown eyes and a camera."

"That's the one. She's the one who's been receiving phone calls from Evan twice a week for the last eight months. They seem downright chummy. If not something even more intimate."

"Kornekewsky doesn't exactly shy away from infidelity," Jack muttered.

"Exactly. He may have something going on with Tanya. He seems to like that family... We might be able to use this. If you're supposed to be dating Liv, then maybe you could position yourself to be...useful to their circle."

"One hitch there," Jack replied. "Liv told her cousin our secondary cover—that I'm only posing as her boyfriend in order to protect her."

"So soon?" Chief Simpson asked with a

shake of his head. "How did you find that out?"

"She told me," Jack replied. "She also told her mother."

"So much for keeping secrets," the chief replied.

"Or she's more calculating than we're giving her credit for," Jack replied. "The cousin could be her decoy to keep suspicion away from her…" Not that he actually believed that right now. Or was she playing him? "I wanted to go with her to the coffee shop—she insisted that it would be weird. She wanted some personal space. Considering my cover, I couldn't exactly declare the cousin wildly dangerous, now could I? So I used the opportunity to sweep the apartment."

"Did you find anything?"

"Nothing incriminating. She keeps a diary, so she likely has others stored away somewhere. They might hold the evidence we're looking for."

"Hmm." Chief Simpson made a note on a piece of paper.

"She got a call from Evan this morning," Jack added. "She seemed surprised to hear from him, a little shaken by it. He asked her to do him a favor and pick up some documents from an old guy."

"Nice!" The chief cheered up. "And?"

"She turned him down, but since her cousin knows who I am, I think we can assume that Evan does now, too," Jack went on. "So that was either a ploy to make her look guilty to draw us away from him, or it was a message of some kind."

"But so far, she still thinks you're here because someone is threatening her," the chief added. "But you're right—our time is limited."

Liv could raise all of his suspicions when she talked about her love of chess strategy, and her guilt suddenly wasn't so unbelievable. If Liv was as guilty as they thought, and if her cousin with whom she wanted privacy to meet was in contact with Evan, well, then it was possible that the welling tears and spontaneous personal revelations were simple manipulation. And he'd fallen for it.

"Since we have to assume that our cover story has gone all the way back to Denver, we'll have to make sure that everyone in the Denver PD believes you've been transferred out here," the chief added.

Jack grimaced. "No offense, sir, but that's going to be seen as a demotion."

"Agreed." The chief chuckled sardonically. "So the Denver chief is already passing along the rumor that you're being quietly disciplined for an attitude problem."

"Great." Jack rubbed a hand over his short-cropped hair. There was nothing quite so reassuring as a blow to his personal reputation. "Taking one for the team, am I?"

"When we catch him, we can set the record straight," the chief replied.

"A little added incentive," Jack replied drily.

"We need proof about what's actually going on here," the chief said.

"Any idea on how I'd secure that proof?" Jack asked.

"Don't leave Liv Hylton's side," the chief replied with a small smile. "A couple of days ago, we went to a judge to get a court order for audio surveillance in her apartment."

"Audio surveillance?" Jack shook his head. "I don't think that's necessary. I can get the evidence—"

"Talbott—" the chief interrupted. "Can I offer a word of advice?"

"Yes, sir."

"When you're working in Internal Affairs, you're investigating friends, colleagues, buddies. This is part of the job. When you know a suspect personally, it makes everything harder. But regardless, we need evidence that will stand up in court."

"I stand by what I said, sir," Jack replied. "I'll work more comfortably if I'm not being constantly recorded, too. I want to dig up all the evidence possible. I'm fully committed to this case, but I don't want recordings in her home."

He knew he was being testy about this, but it felt wrong. What if he discovered that she was innocent? What if her words were twisted and used against her? She'd have no warning! If dirty cops could twist evidence, who was to say there weren't any working in Internal Affairs?

But this might be his own issues from his youth coming into his emotions, too. He'd seen a lot of dirty policing, from bribery to bullying, and Liv was either guilty or very vulnerable right now. His emotions were kicking into protective mode.

"This isn't your call, Talbott," the chief replied.

Jack clenched his teeth. "Understood, sir."

The chief sighed, then shook his head. "Internal Affairs is going to ask me for a reference before you're offered any position. And I realize that getting your head around this stuff can be hard. That's why IA needs the best of the best. It takes mental fortitude. I worked in IA for fifteen years before taking this position as chief of police, and it helps to remember that bad cops ruin lives. You're the check and the balance. No single person can wield that much power without answering for it."

As if Jack needed any reminders of that. He'd seen the catastrophic consequences of a pack of dirty cops firsthand. Not everyone wanted to testify against some drug dealer, but they were threatened into it by the local cops. It was cooperate or get set up for something they didn't do. He could still remember his cousin's anguished pleading: *It wasn't me! I didn't do it! I'm not selling drugs! It wasn't me!* He'd sounded more like a kid than a teenager. And why target him? Jack still didn't know—but some cop had benefited from it. Maybe it had been as simple as getting another arrest so the cop looked like he was doing his job.

There were a lot of vulnerable people in this town, and if the police were right, Eagle's Rest was ripe for the picking. Evan Kornekewsky had plans for Eagle's Rest—although what he was going to do with all that land he pressured the vulnerable into selling at rock-bottom prices, Jack didn't know.

But one thing was certain, he couldn't pull it off alone. Everything on paper, from joint accounts during their marriage to Liv's direct involvement in getting signatures for sales, pointed to her guilt. But there was still a chance that she'd been duped, too. A very slim chance. Was she being set up like Berto had been? Was she part of the illusion? Or was she just as guilty as she looked?

CHAPTER SEVEN

LIV GRABBED A can of tomato soup out of the cupboard and pulled open the utensil drawer, rummaging around for the can opener. Outside the kitchen window, lightning lit up the evening sky in a blinding flash. Rain hammered against the glass in wild, whistling gusts. The day had been sunny enough, but by nightfall, clouds had started moving in, sailing over the moon, and a brisk wind had picked up. At least the storm had waited until closing time—Liv would take whatever luck she could get.

But the inky clouds and the moaning wind felt ominous, especially with the prospect of a stalker out there. She shivered.

"Just let me order us Chinese," Jack said, and Liv glanced back at him.

"In that downpour? Besides, I don't feel like Chinese. I want tomato soup and grilled cheese." She shot him a grin. "You're welcome to order your own takeout and drag some poor delivery guy into the deluge, if you prefer that to good old-fashioned comfort food."

She found the can opener and a whisk and thumped the drawer shut again.

"I don't like making you cook for me," he countered.

"I'm not cooking for you," she said with a low laugh. "I'm cooking for myself, and you're invited to join me."

"Semantics." He chuckled.

"Whatever gets me the perfect grilled cheese."

And her grilled cheese sandwiches were fantastic. She used sharp cheddar, softened butter and thick slices of crusty white bread. No takeout place could come close.

"So how were sales for your first day?" Jack asked.

"Not bad." She turned toward him again. "People seemed pretty supportive, overall."

"That's good."

"I hope it lasts." She licked her lips. "I was looking for whoever sent those notes—and no one seemed…disgruntled or unusually interested in me. What did you think?"

"I agree," he replied. "I've told you all along who I suspect."

"This isn't Evan." She shook her head. "Come on, Jack. He just called to offer me those first-edition books. Why would he try to scare me off?"

"So Evan, who lied, cheated and maintained an affair without you noticing, is suddenly trustworthy?" Jack retorted.

Liv felt her own irritation rise. Just because she'd been cheated on didn't make her suddenly blind or stupid. "Who said I never noticed?"

Jack's expression softened. "I thought—"

"Hindsight is twenty-twenty. Yes, I noticed. He was more distanced. He worked late a lot. He pulled a lot of overtime that he never seemed to get paid for. I wasn't completely stupid, I just hadn't come to the most obvious conclusion yet. I was giving him the benefit of the doubt."

"You're doing that still—giving him the benefit of the doubt," he countered.

Was she? It was possible. But none of this made perfect sense, and that confusing tilt was driving her crazy. She was missing some vital detail here that would help her understand. Why would Evan want to bother her? Why would anyone want to chase her out of town?

"What about you?" she said. "Did you ever get cheated on?"

"Changing the subject?"

"Keeping it fair!" she retorted. "Come on. Fess up."

Jack shrugged weakly. "Once. In college. There was a girl I was dating, and I guess I thought it was more serious than it was."

"Meaning she was dating more than just you," Liv clarified.

"Yeah. And I'm not that kind of guy. If I'm with someone, I'm loyal. If it doesn't work, then fine. But I don't play around."

"Very noble." She held his gaze for a moment, then turned back to the can of soup. "So what happened?"

"I saw her out with another guy. There was no room for misunderstanding. When she next called me, I said maybe it was better to see other people, and that was that."

"Not very dramatic." Liv shook the soup concentrate into the pot, then reached for the milk in the fridge.

"Sorry. You wanted more?" he asked with a low laugh.

"Maybe I do!" Liv filled the can with milk and poured it into the pot. As she whisked, she turned back toward Jack, holding the pot in front of her. "I think great love deserves some great emotion."

"In my case, it wasn't great love," he replied with a shrug. "In yours... I can't comment."

"So no one managed to break your heart?" she asked.

"I don't know. Maybe." He heaved an irritated sigh and looked away.

"Who? Come on. Tit for tat," she said.

"It wasn't a woman I even dated. And she didn't break my heart. She just...turned out to be someone different than I thought, and it really disappointed me."

"I don't think that even compares," she said with a short laugh.

"This isn't a competition," he retorted.

"I'm not making it one."

"You are, with your demand that I open up just as much as you do. It's not like we're friends."

His words stung, and Liv froze. She was forcing this...but why? Did she want a friend so badly right now that she was trying to strong-arm him into complying?

"Liv, I'm sorry if that came out more harshly than I intended—"

"No—" She held up a hand. "You're right. You're here professionally, and I hate that. I don't want some cop overrunning my life, and I don't want to be an open book to anyone anymore. So I hate it, but…that's not your problem."

There was another crack, a flash of lightning, and this time the lights went out, too, leaving them in darkness. The rain still pattered against the glass, and there was a low moan as the wind whistled around the building. Liv blinked against the pitch-blackness as her eyes started to slowly adjust.

"You okay?" His voice was low and close. She reached out, her hand connecting with the hard rope of his muscled arm, and her stomach gave a flip.

"Fine." Liv closed her eyes for a moment, willing herself to ignore how that bass rumble made her feel. Was it loneliness that was making her react like this? Because Evan had made her feel weak in the knees, too, and she wasn't making the same mistake again. "I've got candles, and I know there's a lighter or two around here somewhere."

"I didn't mean that we're not friends, Liv. I shouldn't have said that."

"Yes, you did." Her throat thickened with emotion, and she tried to swallow it back. "Let's not pretend you meant anything else. And that's fine. You don't owe me anything but your professional expertise—which I appreciate, by the way."

Silence stretched between them, and his hand brushed against her shoulder. She could just make him out the darkness—his broad, dark shape looming comfortingly. Too comfortingly. He wasn't here for her—not strictly.

"We all have hang-ups, Liv. Mine are just… less interesting."

"And Evan is my hang-up," she admitted. "I don't mean to take him out on you, either. I wanted to wipe myself clean of him, but it's easier said than done."

"If Evan were blackmailing you, or strong-arming you into something—" Jack's tone became hesitant "—would you tell me?"

"He isn't," she said. "What are you talking about?"

"Nothing." He sighed audibly in the dimness. "I'm going to head out and inspect the perimeter. I need to check in with the station, too."

"Sure."

What she'd really wanted to say was, "No, stay here," but she wouldn't do that. If it weren't for this stalker, or whoever he was, she'd be on her own in this storm, anyway. She'd rummage around, find candles and sort it out herself. Now was not the time to start leaning on another rugged cop.

Liv watched his form retreat to the front

door. Then there was the metallic scraping sound of a gun cocking.

"Jack?" she called.

"Yeah?" His voice was quiet.

"Be careful out there."

She didn't know what she was scared of. This was a power outage—and there were plenty in this town when mountain storms roared through. But there was something about this night—the pounding rain, the flicker of lightning and that sense that she was more alone than she'd previously realized.

"I always am," Jack said. He disappeared out the door, and his voice filtered back in to her. "Lock up, would you?" Then he pulled the door shut behind him with a soft *click*.

Liv crossed the room and locked the door, adding the dead bolt for safe measure. Another crack of lightning lit up the apartment, the flash coming in from the living room window this time, making the room feel darker in its aftermath. But the window shone gray, the one source of light until she found candles. She paused for a moment, torn between searching the blackened kitchen for the candles and heading for the big window over the radiator to look outside.

The window won, and she stepped around

the familiar furniture until she got to the rain-spattered glass. The rain was coming down in sheets, so she couldn't see far, but in the shadows, she thought she saw a figure...with a cart or something. Could that be right? Not in a storm like this—and not in a place the size of Eagle's Rest. Big cities might have homeless people stuck outside in the weather, but not here.

She squinted, trying to make out the details, and as the wind suddenly changed direction, there was a momentary clearing, and Liv's heart thudded to a stop in her chest. It wasn't a man—it was a woman. With a baby stroller that appeared to be empty. And she was looking straight at Liv in the window. She looked like Serena... but that couldn't be.

Another crack of lightning; a sheet of rain slammed into the window. Liv waited, barely daring to blink, and when it cleared enough to see again, the woman was gone. A shiver crept up Liv's spine.

"I saw that..." Liv murmured aloud. "That wasn't my imagination. I saw that!"

JACK SAT IN his car for a few minutes as he checked in with the station. They were getting closer to being able to lock down a case against Evan—a forensic accountant was combing through his finances right now, unbeknownst to him, and they'd have the evidence for court when the rest of the case was strong enough. Which was great, but he still felt irritable and out of sorts. This time with Liv was difficult for him because she was nosing into his deeper feelings, which were dangerous territory.

He'd been halfway in love with that woman from afar. Stupid, yes, but when he'd discovered that she was a part of this property fraud scheme, it had hit him hard. He'd thought better of her, and the fact that he was so disappointed in her wasn't to his credit. But he had been wanting to ask her out, and hoping for a whole lot more than one date. She was his ideal woman. Minus the criminal bent, of course.

Jack felt obliged to do one round of the building for the sake of appearances, and rain plastered his clothes against his skin. Autumn nights in the mountains were cold, and the rain only made it worse. It must be close to freezing out here. He hunched his shoulders against the chill. He was frustrated—mostly because Liv was still able to knock him off-balance. He was supposed to be the one in control, and with one comment from her he could be sent sprawling. Emotionally speaking, at least. And he didn't like losing the upper hand when it came to his emotions.

Had that been on purpose? He'd been asking about Evan, and she'd brought up his own history. She didn't know he'd been talking about her, obviously, but was she trying to distract him from something he was getting too close to unearthing? Standing in the rain, that seemed like a possibility.

He headed back into the building and up the stairs that led to Liv's apartment. His shoes squeaked with rainwater, and rivulets of moisture trickled down his back. When he got to her door, he knocked.

"It's me, Liv," he called. He heard the dead bolt scrape, and she pulled open the door.

The apartment was aglow in candlelight. Two pillar candles were lit on a side table next to the couch, and she'd brought out a candelabra fitted with another five candlesticks. The ambiance was soft and inviting, but Liv's expression was anything but. Her face was white, and she glanced toward the window quickly, then grabbed Jack's arm and pulled him inside.

"Did you see anyone out there?" she demanded.

"No. I went all the way around and everything looked fine. What's the matter?"

"The woman—with the stroller. Did you see her across the street?" Liv demanded.

"No. There was no one there."

"I saw her." Liv looked at him pleadingly. "I know this sounds nuts, but she was staring at me…in my window. She wasn't just looking around—she was watching me."

Jack turned the lock in the door behind him, his mind spinning to catch up. Liv didn't strike him as the paranoid sort.

"Where was she?" he asked.

"Across the street." She pointed to the living room window, and Jack went over and stared out into the storm. He couldn't see anyone. The street was empty, as was the store across the street. Empty and quiet, as anyone would expect.

"She was just standing there!" Liv said. "With a stroller, the rain pouring down on her, and she was staring right into my window!"

"Where did she go?" he asked, his skin prickling at the eerie description.

"She disappeared."

There was no stalker. There was no emotionally unstable enemy. That was all made up to ensure that Liv let him into her life, and it looked like it was working. Maybe even a little too well.

Liv licked her lips, arms crossed under her bust. She looked over Jack's shoulder and out into the street. Goose bumps rose on her arms, and she gave a shiver. Before he could think better of it, Jack ran a hand down her arm, her skin feeling warm against his chilled fingers.

"No one there," he said. "But I'll keep an eye out. You can count on that."

If she had seen someone, maybe the mystery woman was connected to Evan's group. And maybe it was nothing more than her imagination working overtime. But standing this close to her, looking down on that silken auburn hair, inhaling the warm fragrance of her skin, his mind kept moving away from the job at hand and into much more dangerous territory.

He realized his hand was still on her arm, and he removed it.

"Okay…" Liv nodded a couple of times. "It just…spooked me. Do you think that's the person trying to scare me?"

"Could be." Jack felt guilty for perpetuating her fear. He was supposed to make use of weird coincidences for the case. If it weren't her own imagination doing the work for him, he'd request another threatening letter to be dropped off. But try as he might, he couldn't mentally argue that sense of guilt away. "But whoever it is, they're long gone now. Do you think you could describe her?"

Color finally flushed Liv's pallor, and she shook her head. "I wish I could. There was a lot of rain coming down, and... She was average in pretty much every way. Her build, her height. And she was wearing a jacket of some sort. Her hair was wet. Blond hair? A pale-skinned woman. And she was pushing a running stroller—you know, the kind with the big wheels."

"Was there a baby inside?" Jack asked, his voice low.

"No, it was empty—" She met Jack's gaze.

"Okay. I'll include it in my report." This was all pretty specific. Oddly specific.

"One more thing." She looked away for a moment, then licked her lips. "I know this sounds like I was imagining things, but she looked like...Serena."

"Evan's wife?" he asked in surprise. Yeah, that did make it seem a little more made up.

"That part may very well have been my imagination," she added quickly. "What with Evan's phone call, Serena has been on my mind. And with that amount of rain, I couldn't really see much detail."

"Okay. I'll make a note of it."

"I almost wish you wouldn't." She grimaced. "A woman was there. I just can't swear that it was her. For the record."

"Understood. But tonight, you're in good hands. No one gets to you unless they get through me, and I'm a great deterrent."

A small smile turned up her lips. "I know. Thank you, Jack."

Jack glanced down at his sodden shirt, then undid the buttons. He peeled the fabric from his body, goose bumps standing up on his own flesh at the chill. He caught Liv's eyes traveling over his torso, then she quickly dropped her gaze. It had been a while since he'd been appreciated by a woman.

"I'll get you a towel," Liv said, turning away. While she was gone, Jack grabbed a fresh pair of jeans and stripped off his wet pants, too. He was just buttoning them up when Liv returned with a white towel.

"Thanks," he said, using the towel over his dripping hair, then rubbing it over his chest and arms, drying off the rest of the way. He grabbed another T-shirt from his duffel bag and pulled it over his head.

"Are you still hungry?" Liv asked.

"Actually, yeah," he said with a low laugh. "You still think takeout is such a bad idea?"

"I whipped up a cold supper," she said,

picking up a candle and heading into the kitchen. She returned a moment later, the candle in one hand and a platter in the other. She had sliced pepperoni, crackers, cheese, some fruit—and his stomach growled in response.

"Let's sit where there's light," Liv said, and led the way to the couch in the center of the candles. She put the platter on the ottoman, and Jack joined her on the couch, sinking into the soft depth, close enough to feel the warmth of her skin emanating against his side.

"I'm sorry if I overstepped earlier," Liv said, her voice low. "I do that sometimes. I don't mean to. I just… I think people are interesting and I assume they think the same of me."

"You are interesting," he replied quietly. "Maybe too much so."

"Why's that?" She reached for a cracker and a slice of cheese.

He'd been holding this back for a long time, and seeing her that scared had snapped a thread inside him. All of his reserves seemed to be unraveling.

"I'm supposed to be a professional here," Jack said quietly. "I'm…starting fresh in this precinct, and I can't take any chances with my reputation."

"And I'm a problem?" She shot him a wry look.

"Liv, you're—" The words caught in his throat, and he leaned forward, his elbows on his knees. "God, Liv, you don't get what you do to men, do you?"

He glanced back at her, and her shining eyes moved over him in stunned silence.

"You're gorgeous. You're bright. You're funny. I've got a type of woman I tend to be attracted to, and I don't find her too often..."

He should stop. He knew that. This was crossing lines. If there were audio surveillance, he'd be in deep trouble.

"I know. Evan has a type, too." Liv rolled her eyes. "He likes his woman from magazines—"

"Shut up, Liv," Jack growled, and Liv's eyes widened in surprise. He laughed softly. "It's you. You're womanly and soft in all the right places. I've been noticing you for years, but you were married to my colleague, and I'm not the kind of guy who crosses those lines. But you're—" his voice deepened "—most definitely my type."

"I am?" Her voice sounded breathy.

"Look at you..." He couldn't help himself now. He'd opened that floodgate, and he wasn't about to slam it shut again. He reached over and ran a finger down her cheek, then rested the pad of his thumb on her chin. His gaze moved down to her lips and stopped there.

Liv didn't say anything; he was desperately tempted to cover those soft lips with his— He swallowed, trying to pull his mind away from all the things he wanted to do with her right now. None of it was professional.

"Jack…"

Jack cleared his throat and dropped his hand. "Sorry." He pushed himself to his feet, embarrassment flooding over him. He knew why he was here—so why did he let himself go there with her? She was the suspect!

"I'll chalk it up to candlelight," Liv said.

Jack turned back toward her, and even standing a few feet away from her didn't change how his body responded to her. She was more than his type—she was the woman he'd been yearning after for years. Stupidly, of course. He'd never expected anything to come of it…

"Let's eat, okay?" she said, nudging the platter toward him.

Just then the lights flickered and came back on. The smoke detector chirped, as did the microwave in the kitchen. The soft, confidence-inspiring ambiance evaporated, and Jack felt suddenly exposed.

"Let's eat," Liv repeated, leaning over and blowing out the candles. "I don't know about you, but I'm still starving."

Jack sank back into the couch next to her and reached for a piece of pepperoni and a cracker.

"Yeah, me, too," he said, and she leaned toward him, nudging him with her shoulder.

"Jack?" she said. "I dare say we're getting to be friends."

"Yeah." He popped the food into his mouth so that he wouldn't have to say anything else, but she was right. They were connecting on a more human level now, and if he weren't the one responsible for proving her guilty, he would call her a friend.

Heck, he'd probably career right past friend and pull her into his arms.

CHAPTER EIGHT

THE WOMAN WITH the stroller was hard to forget, and Liv found her gaze moving toward the store window repeatedly the next day. She'd convinced herself that the part where the woman looked like Serena was concocted in her own imagination. Maybe she was more jealous of her ex's new wife than she wanted to admit. Whatever. And outside the store window she did see women with strollers—but they weren't the one from last night. There was a pregnant woman pushing a twin stroller with two toddlers strapped in. There was a mom with a newborn in a rather expensive-looking stroller—but this woman was dark-haired... Not the same woman. Liv knew that, but she couldn't help being a little jumpy all the same.

It wasn't just the memory of the strange woman out in the storm that clung to Liv, though. The whole evening had been... intense. Electricity must be the great civilizing influence, because without it everyone seemed to go a little feral. Jack included.

He was more than good-looking—he was intoxicating. Jack was strong, rugged and the type of man who made a woman feel safe and protected. He was certainly a bad-guy deterrent, and he made her feel all sorts of things she didn't want to be feeling at all, let alone for another cop.

If it had stopped there, and he'd simply treated her like a civilian in need of protection, she might have been able to brush it all aside as a natural reaction to a stressful situation. But he'd said something that had been playing over in her mind all night long: *It's you. You're womanly and soft in all the right places. I've been noticing you for years, but you were married to my colleague, and I'm not the kind of guy who crosses those lines. But you're most definitely my type.*

She shivered again at the memory. *For years*, he'd said. He'd been noticing her across rooms, at precinct Christmas parties— When else would Jack have seen her? She'd spoken to him a few times at various parties and functions. She'd always found him polite and decent, like all of the cops her husband worked with. But she wasn't the kind of person who looked outside of her marriage, either. It was strange to think that she was so physically desirable to him. She was used to the world catering to the size twos, not to the plus sizes. But in that man's eyes, she was... definitely his type.

The bell over the door tinkled, and Liv glanced up as Jack came back into the store. The workday was nearly over, and the light was growing dusky. He'd been out checking on something for another case, he'd said. But she'd missed him. Seeing him again, she felt her cheeks heat. She hated this—the awkwardness from last night still standing between them. She'd wanted him to open up, and had he ever!

They hadn't mentioned it again come morning. He'd silently eaten a bowl of cereal, and she'd whipped herself up an omelet. They'd simply gone about their morning routine, and then she'd come down to open the store for her official second day. Then Jack had become conveniently busy. So had she, for that matter.

"Hi," Jack said.

There was a young mom in the kids' section, sorting through some picture books. Her baby was in a wrap, strapped to her body. So they weren't exactly alone.

"Hi," she said with a smile.

"Closing up soon?" Jack asked.

"No—well, I would ordinarily, but the Eagle's Rest Chess Club is meeting here tonight."

"So soon?" Jack frowned.

"Why not? They've been meeting in Nate's basement all this time, and when I offered the store, they were kind of excited."

"Who's Nate?" Jack perked up. "Old friend?"

"Oh, he's one of our local legends. He's won some pretty big chess championships. He's impossible to beat. I wouldn't call him a friend. I don't know him that well. But you know how life is in a place this size. Everyone at least knows *of* one another."

"Was he a friend of Evan's?" Jack opened a small notebook and jotted down a note, then closed it.

She frowned. "Jack—"

"I'm being thorough," he replied, cutting her off.

She sighed. "Fine."

The woman approached the register to pay. She'd selected a few picture books and a couple of parenting tomes. Liv rang up her order.

"You have a great selection," the woman said with a smile. "And you're walking distance from my place. It's perfect, really."

"I'm glad," Liv said. "Pass the word along—I need all the business I can get."

The woman smiled and accepted her bag. "I sure will. See you later."

The woman turned to leave, and Liv's heart sped up a little bit. "Wait!" she called, and the customer turned back, looking mildly surprised.

"Were you out in the storm last night?" Liv asked, the words coming out of her in a rush. "With a stroller?"

"What?" The woman shook her head and took an instinctive step back. "No. I wasn't."

"Sorry." Liv forced a smile. "You looked a little familiar, is all. Have a great day."

The woman left the store, and Jack shot Liv a quizzical look.

"Apparently I'm paranoid now," Liv said with a sigh. She flicked the sign in the window to Closed and glanced outside. A streetlight popped on, then another one.

"Are you sure you didn't imagine that woman with the stroller?" Jack asked.

"I know the difference between a rampant imagination and a real person standing in the rain," she said. "I know it wasn't Serena. It couldn't have been. But someone was there."

"Okay." He nodded, and Liv pressed the button to open the money drawer.

"You don't believe me, do you?" she asked, pulling out the bills and beginning to count.

"No, I do. But I have to ask these things. Do things look different in the light of day? If they do, that's not a problem. These things happen to the best of us. I just need you to think back on what you saw and tell me if you still think it was a real person out there."

Liv turned her attention to counting for a moment, jotted down a number, then looked over at Jack irritably.

"I'm not prone to hysterics," she said, turning to the coins next, but she was irritated. She was being stalked by someone who wanted her out of town, and if she'd just gotten a good look at this person, the least she could ask was for the police to believe her.

"Okay, good." Jack nodded.

Liv did the math, took out her bank deposit and finished up the last of the closing-out procedure. Just as she was sealing the plastic deposit envelope, the door opened and the first few chess players came inside.

"Come on in," Liv called cheerily. "I've cleared out the center space. And if you wouldn't mind pulling out the folding tables yourselves, it would help a lot."

Those tables and folding chairs were actually being stored for a cousin who'd bought them for her father's seventieth birthday party and then had nowhere to keep them. They'd come in handier than Liv had ever imagined.

Liv headed for the storage space where they were located, but she felt a hand on her arm, tugging her back. She looked at Jack, her eyebrows raised.

"I got it," Jack said, and moved past her to pull out the tables. Granted, he did it far more easily than she would have, but she was still annoyed with the man. He might find her beautiful, alluring, attractive—her words, not his—but he also thought she was imagining things from last night. And if she had to choose, she'd rather have him see her as intelligent, quick-witted, insightful. And levelheaded.

Jack and the chess players set up the tables. The club had a few different chessboards, and they arranged them on the various tables. Liv went to lock the door and stood back, watching as they got settled and picked their opponents.

"I don't think you're prone to hysterics," Jack said as he ambled back to where she stood. He leaned against the counter next to her. "For the record."

"I'm not sure I believe you," she retorted.

Jack laughed softly. "I'm doing my job, Liv."

"Fine." She could grudgingly give him that one.

"Are you going to play tonight?" Jack asked, nudging her with the side of his muscled arm.

"No, no…" She shook her head. "I'm the business owner here. I'm not part of the club. Besides, they've got an even number."

"And an extra board," he pointed out.

There was one extra table and chess set ready to go, and Liv looked over at it longingly. She was already thinking ahead to moves, countermoves, traps and checkmates. It had been a while since she'd had a decent opponent to play against.

Liv glanced up at Jack. "Care to play?"

"Sure." He grinned back, and the confidence in that look made her stomach flip. What was with this man and his easy ability to make her swoon like a schoolgirl?

"I have something to prove," Liv said, leading the way to the table and pulling out one of the folding chairs. She picked up two pawns, rolled them in her hands, then held them out in her closed fists. "Pick one."

Jack tapped a hand, and she opened it to reveal a black pawn.

"You're black," she said. "I'll be white."

They both sat down, and for a moment, they were caught up in arranging their pieces.

"What do you have to prove?" Jack asked, his voice a low rumble, that dark gaze flickering up toward her.

"That if anyone is prone to hysterics, it'll be you," she replied with a small smile.

"Trash talk?" He raised an eyebrow, and a slow grin spread over his face. "Liv Hylton, this is a whole new side to you. I think I like it."

JACK WATCHED LIV as she set up her pieces. She moved methodically, almost reverently, and he had that slight sinking feeling he got when he was pitted against a stronger, heavier, faster officer in hand-to-hand combat training. Normally, Jack was the biggest guy in the room—he was used to that—but not always.

Except this time, his opponent was stunningly beautiful, and he'd much rather take her on physically than strategically, at the moment. But he wasn't going to let his attraction to her get in the way of putting a dirty cop behind bars where he belonged. And he wasn't going to let her off, either, if she was involved.

He'd opened up more than he'd planned to

last night. And that was the part of this assignment he hated—walking that line to gain her trust. He felt like he was betraying her every step of the way.

Jack glanced around at the other players. All of them were focused on their own boards—hovering over the pieces—except for Nate. Nate was watching them with a quizzical look on his face. Nate Lipton was one of the old-timers who'd been pressured to sell his property and had come to the police.

"You say you don't know Nate too well," Jack said, keeping his voice quiet. "He's sure interested in you."

"I'm pretty," she said softly. "That happens a lot."

"You're standing by that? Nothing more?"

"Are you saying I'm not attractive enough to draw an eye?" She looked up at him, holding his gaze.

"Not saying that at all… I think I proved that last night."

She looked back down at the board. If she did know what her ex-husband had done to Nate Lipton, blithely sitting in the same room with him would say a lot about her capabilities.

"I also played chess with him a few times," she said after a moment.

"Who won?" Jack asked.

"Him." She smiled sweetly. "And I lose very graciously. I'm a pleasure to compete against."

Jack chuckled. Somehow, he doubted that. She liked to win to the point that she read chess strategy while she waited for pots to boil. But then, he shouldn't underestimate the power of a beautiful woman over a lonely man. Wasn't he in a similar situation right now?

"I move first." Liv moved a pawn with a decisive *click* as the piece hit the board.

Jack moved his pawn, and she moved her knight, hopping over the row of pawns to put it front and center. He paused before making his next move.

"But pretty or not, the old guy is the only one watching us," he said.

Liv made a move, then glanced in the direction of Nate thoughtfully. "Do you think he's lonely?"

"I thought you'd know that." Jack lifted his rook, then realized if he moved, she would be lined up to take it. He put it back down.

"He's brilliant," Liv said. "Absolutely brilliant. And I think he was married years ago, if I recall properly. I think there was a divorce, and now he's on his own—that brilliant mind, and on his own…"

"He's got a chess club," Jack pointed out, and chose a move that was safe from any of her ploys.

"I suppose…" She looked the board over, then moved her own rook into a position that seemed random enough to him, but he had no doubt it was the first step in something victorious. She'd recognized that old Nate Lipton was vulnerable, at the very least. But he wasn't quite so unprotected as she thought.

"Are you worried about ending up brilliant and alone?" Jack asked, casting her a teasing smile.

"Sometimes."

He sobered, because she wasn't joking, and she met his gaze easily. She wouldn't be alone in life unless she wanted it that way.

"I thought you wanted to settle in here by yourself."

"I do. I'm getting over a nasty divorce. I need to be me again." She moved another piece, then glanced toward old Nate, whose attention was back on his own game. "But some people can stand as warnings about your future, can't they?"

She might want to look to people who were in prison for her personal cautionary tales, Jack thought ruefully.

"I'm more worried about bad guys," he

replied. He turned his attention back to the board. "And catching them."

"You're evading," she said.

"Yup." He shot her a grin, then made his move. "A little bit."

"Winning on a board makes me feel in control," Liv said, moving her bishop. "But it's not real life. It's contained. The rules are simple. Winning is easy—it's just a matter of outthinking your opponent."

Jack looked around the board. He'd have to sacrifice a piece, because he couldn't move without putting himself in harm's way. Outthinking her opponent... She took that for granted. Maybe her uncontested confidence would be her downfall yet. He chose a piece and made the move with more confidence than he felt.

Liv didn't take the pawn he expected her to. Instead she zipped across the board with her queen and captured his rook. He hadn't seen that one coming.

She raised those green eyes to meet his. "In the end, it's only a game."

He considered the board again, looking for his options. He didn't have too many. He made a move.

"You can't do that," Liv said. "You'll put yourself in check."

"Okay, then." He chose another move. Liv moved her queen again, and this time, he saw his path. Two moves later, he had her king cornered. "Checkmate."

"My goodness, you just took over the board, didn't you? Well…I learned something today. You are very good," she said with a brilliant smile, her glittering green gaze locking onto his. "Good game, Jack."

His name sounded sweet on her lips, and she reached across the board to shake hands. As Jack took her fingers in his, he saw a sparkle of mischief in her eyes.

"You let me win," he said.

She shrugged faintly. "And didn't you like it? I told you I lose with grace."

"I'd rather be beaten fair and square," he retorted.

"Then line up your pieces," she said, the smile evaporating. "And your wish is my command."

Jack laughed softly. "You're scary."

"And that's why I know how to smile and let men win," she retorted. "They prefer it that way."

"But what about you? That can't be fun," he said.

"It isn't. I told myself I'd stop dumbing

down," she said quietly. "And for the most part, I do."

"Does that mean you let Nate win, too?" Jack asked as he lined up his pieces once more.

She smiled a slow, warm smile but didn't answer his question. "I start."

This game went much quicker, and no matter how Jack tried to keep ahead of her, she quickly closed in on his king and had him subdued in a matter of minutes.

"Checkmate." She raised an eyebrow.

"Good game." His voice was low and he met her gaze with a wink. "You're very good, Liv. And you know it. So stop pretending to be some coy little minx with me."

"Are you sure you prefer it this way?" she asked.

Jack met her gaze with a slow smile of his own. "Definitely. I like a woman who takes what's hers."

Liv began to clean up the pieces, dropping them back into the velveteen bag.

"What did you learn?" Jack asked after a moment.

"Pardon me?" She glanced up.

"You said you learned something when playing with me. Was that a line, or were you telling the truth?"

"I always learn something," Liv said, dropping the last pawns into the bag and drawing the string. "This time I learned your weaknesses."

"Which are?" He leaned his elbows on the table.

"You start too aggressively. You don't have patience for a good trap." She rose to her feet, standing over him so that his gaze could slide up her voluptuous figure to those deep green eyes. She was very wrong in her assumption, of course. He had plenty of patience for a good trap, but it was just as well she didn't know it.

"And my strengths?" he prodded.

"You distract me with your chitchat."

"So that's how to beat you—get your mind off the game?" he asked with a roguish smile. He wouldn't mind taking up that challenge… if only it wouldn't jeopardize the case and his life's mission to get into Internal Affairs and finally do some good.

"It would seem," she said.

How much was Liv hiding from him? He wished he knew. Maybe there was nothing and she was innocent. He was starting to hope that she wasn't in too deep, at the very least.

She was likable. Maybe even more than

likable if he let himself go…and that was the problem. He was a professional to the bone, but he was starting to feel more for her than professional curiosity. If he had to arrest her at the end of all this, it was going to hurt. There was no way around it.

CHAPTER NINE

L IV ROLLED OVER in her bed, the soft scent of distant cooking enveloping her slumber. Her eyes fluttered open and she lay on her side, staring at the clock on her bedside table. It was almost eight—which wasn't a problem because today was Sunday and the store would be closed. Even small business owners deserved a day off once a week.

She inhaled deeply and realized that she did indeed smell frying potatoes…and she could hear a soft *clink* coming from the direction of the kitchen. She sat up, pulling her hair away from her face. Was Jack cooking?

She must have been tired to sleep so soundly. That was the best rest she'd had since the letters had started. But she had to admit that having Jack around did make her feel safer. She didn't feel like she had to sleep with one eye open with Jack in the apartment. If anyone broke in, they'd stumble across that muscular cop first. And she had a feeling that even asleep, Jack was perfectly prepared to handle anything.

Liv got out of bed and quickly got dressed in a pair of jeans and a loose, beaded peasant-style top. She padded barefoot to the bathroom, and ten minutes later her hair was combed, her face was washed and she was wearing a light layer of makeup.

Ordinarily, she'd sit in her kitchen in a bathrobe, but with Jack here she couldn't be quite so free and easy. He wasn't a guest, but he was still *there*.

As Liv headed into the kitchen, Jack looked up from the stove.

"Morning," he said.

"Good morning." She glanced around and spotted a plate of crispy bacon and a dish of scrambled eggs. "You planning on sharing any of that?"

"Of course." He turned back to the stove. "I felt like it was time I pitched in, and you keep turning down my offers of takeout."

"That's nice. I appreciate it."

He could cook. It shouldn't surprise her. Any man had better be able to fend for himself, but it was still nice. Evan had been a good cook, and it was one of the things she'd appreciated about him. He used to cook on weekend mornings—

Her heart clenched at the memory, and she tried to push it back. Evan had stopped that thoughtful gesture a couple of years before he left her. And here was another man in her kitchen, whipping up a delicious-looking breakfast, and she didn't want to soften to him.

"So how well does Evan know the mayor?" Jack asked, and it felt like he'd somehow read her mind.

"Uh—" She sighed. "They met through my father. My dad went to school with Mayor Nelson, and Evan hits it off with pretty much everyone. I think they golfed a few times. But in a place this size, a lot of people have connections to the mayor."

Jack turned off the stove and slid the potatoes from the pan into a bowl. He came to the table and deposited the dish next to the others.

"Let's eat," he said.

Liv grabbed some plates from the cupboard and some cutlery, and then they settled around her little table. The potatoes had been fried up with some onions and a little dill—

"I don't have dill," she said, looking up.

"One of the other officers picked up some groceries for me and dropped them by."

How much had happened before she woke up? "That was…nice of him."

"I'm not here to eat your groceries," he said. "And since I'm on official duties while I'm with you, the department picks up the tab."

That was the reminder she needed—official duties. She didn't have to connect this to Evan, or to any of the other guys she'd dated in the past. They were two people who needed to eat. That was it.

"Tell me about Nate," Jack said.

"Did Evan know him?" Liv asked, picking up the thread of the conversation.

"Yeah. Were they…buddies or anything?"

"Not really. They used to play chess together. Nate taught Evan everything he knew. Evan used to think he might be able to play in some competitions. Nate sold us his house after his wife died. If that's the kind of thing you mean."

Jack nudged the eggs toward Liv, and he dished himself some potatoes. It smelled amazing, and Liv didn't need any more encouragement.

"When was that?"

She did the mental math. "Five years ago? No…six or seven years. I don't know."

"Was it an average sale?" he asked.

"I guess. He was thinking of selling, anyway, and Evan really wanted that land. I guess it was just good timing for everyone. Why this interest in Nate?" Liv asked, reaching for a strip of bacon.

"I'm being thorough."

"I saw a woman with a stroller, not Evan. Or Nate." She lifted her gaze to meet his. He was hiding something—there had to be more of a connection for Jack to keep coming back to her ex-husband. Cops didn't follow loose ends for nothing.

Jack eyed her thoughtfully for a moment, then he said, "I believe you saw a woman with a stroller. I'm just not convinced that she's the root of the problem."

"But why?" Liv insisted. "And don't pretend that you're just following a gut instinct here. I know how cops think, and your fixation on Evan doesn't make sense unless there's more to this. So what's really going on?"

"There is a connection between the letters and your ex-husband, but I'm not at liberty to reveal the details." He was every inch a cop in that moment—the reticence, the stony expression... Liv shook her head.

"Not at liberty," she said drily. "I'm the one being harassed and threatened, and you can't tell me why you think my ex-husband is connected to this?"

"I can't."

Liv heaved a sigh. "He's shown no ill will toward me in the last year. He's remarried to another woman. He's offering to give me the books his grandmother left for me in her will…but that's all some ruse?"

"What do you think?" Jack asked.

"I think my ex-husband is a cheating louse who won't stay faithful to Officer Hot Pants, either! That's what I *think*," she retorted. "But an inability to be a faithful spouse doesn't make him into a stalker. If anything, he cared about me too little! I don't see a connection. At all."

Jack nodded slowly. "Okay. Noted."

But Jack did see a connection, and he wasn't about to share it with her.

"I hate this—" she said. "This, right here. You cops are all the same. It's all about protecting your information and never betraying any personal feeling."

"This isn't about personal feelings," Jack replied. "This is about your safety."

"And I'll be a whole lot safer if I have all the information," she shot back. "Why is Evan a threat? What points to him?"

A tingle edged the back of her neck. Her ex-husband had always been good at hiding things with his charm, and she needed to know what she was missing. Because she couldn't see it!

"You'll just have to trust me," he said.

Liv stared at him, her irritation rising. She wasn't a child to be protected. She was a grown woman who needed to know the risks.

"I'm one of the good guys, Liv," Jack said quietly. "You know that, right?"

"You're a cop, Jack," Liv said tightly. "You're part of a tight-knit group who figures you're a step above us common civilians."

"Not true."

"Really?"

She glared him, and he met her gaze but didn't share her anger. That might be even more frustrating—the fact that she was the only one feeling off-balance here. He knew more than she did, and that wasn't right.

Liv's cell phone rang, and she sighed and shook her head.

"I'm going to answer that," she muttered, heading into the living room to fetch it. She saw Aunt Marie's number and picked up the call.

"Hi, Auntie. How are you?" she asked.

"I'm good," Marie replied. "I'm downstairs."

"What?" Liv went to the living room and looked down into the street. Sure enough,

Marie was standing on the sidewalk, her head tipped back so she could look up at Liv's window.

"Hi," Marie said, and she smiled and waved from below.

Liv felt warmth at her side at the same moment that Marie's eyes widened in surprise. She looked over to find Jack just behind her. Great—Marie was a little old-fashioned about these things, and her assumptions were going to be a lot more scandalous than reality.

"Oh...you're entertaining," Marie said, her voice lowering.

Liv couldn't help but laugh. "You met Jack. He's just visiting. Come on up."

"No, really, I should probably—" Marie looked around as if seeking an escape, then she looked back up at the window, her expression strained. "I was just coming by to say I was sorry, Liv."

Liv's heart melted. She and Marie might butt heads, but her aunt loved her. They were just from different generations. "Come up, Auntie. Please."

"Okay. I'll see you in a minute." Marie ended their call and disappeared from view as she headed toward the outside door.

Liv turned around to see Jack eyeing her uncertainly.

"Marie's coming up," she said.

"Yeah, I caught that."

"She just wants to make up, but I can't sort things out with my aunt with you around," she said. "You understand that, right?"

"Of course." He nodded toward the kitchen. "Feel free to feed her the breakfast I made. I'll head out for a few minutes. Just do me a favor and let me know if you've got any other plans."

Because he would come along, obviously. And he'd protect her. But the problem was that he was seeming less like a cop and more like a part of her life lately, and that had to be stopped. Even bickering with him in the kitchen had been oddly comforting. She needed protection from whomever was threatening her, but her emotional safety mattered, too.

There was a knock at the door, and Liv went to open it. Her aunt stood in the hallway, her phone still clutched in her hand. She glanced over Liv's shoulder with a slightly forced smile.

"Come in," Liv said with a low laugh. "Jack is just on his way out. You hungry?"

"Yes." Marie smiled. "I am."

This was the thing about family—time might pass, issues might come up and people might even argue, but they were still family. They outlasted husbands, and they were there at the end of the day.

Jack grabbed his coat and slipped past Marie into the hallway.

"Nice seeing you again, Marie," he said with a warm smile. "I wish I could stay, but I've got some stuff to take care of, so—"

Jack's gaze moved beyond the older woman and he shot Liv an apologetic look.

"We'll talk later," he said quietly.

She nodded, and Jack disappeared. She could hear his footsteps descending the stairs, and her heart gave a little flutter. She was ticked off at him right now—annoyed that he was such a cop, even though that was exactly why he was here. But her emotions were getting jumbled where this man was concerned, and she needed to find her balance again, stat.

"Come in and eat," Liv said. "I haven't had breakfast yet."

It was time to get her feet back on the ground.

"THE JUDGE GAVE us the warrant for auditory surveillance two days ago," Chief Simpson said as Jack came into the precinct.

"Two days ago?" Jack retorted. "How come no one told me?"

"I just did," the chief replied. "Nothing is hooked up yet."

Jack nodded numbly. It still felt wrong. "How did you do it?"

"We managed to link some of the money that was used on these sales through joint accounts that included both Evan's and Liv's names. The judge found the evidence sufficient. So we're good to go. We sent in an officer and installed the bugs while the apartment was empty, and we're just getting ready to start the surveillance now. Officer McDonald is in the meeting room setting up the equipment already."

Jack stared at the chief in shock, rage bubbling low beneath the surface. They'd done this behind his back—without his knowledge. They'd left him out of the loop!

"When were you planning on telling me?" Jack snapped.

"When you needed to know."

McDonald—the officer who couldn't even do his own surveillance outside the coffee shop properly—was going to be listening in on Liv's intimate world. And it wasn't McDonald's ineptitude that was goading Jack, either. Liv was expecting a private conversation with her aunt, and this was invasive. Which was the point—they needed evidence, but apparently, he was playing the role of protector for Liv Hylton, and his emotions seemed stuck there.

"You cut me out of this on purpose," Jack growled.

"I did you a favor," the chief retorted. "You're in too deep."

"I'm in control!" Jack shot back, then turned away and bit his tongue. If he wanted that position in IA, he'd better not antagonize the chief. He needed some time to get his brain around this. Obviously, the chief was right—he was in too deep. But he couldn't admit to that.

"Officer Talbott," the chief said curtly, and Jack faced him again.

"Yes, sir." His words were clipped, but he kept careful control of his tone.

"You recognize that from here on in, anything said inside the apartment will be recorded."

"Yes, sir. I'm clear on that."

"Good." The chief gave a nod. "A straight confession might be too much to hope for, but try to get her to tell you as much as possible so we can get some new investigative leads. Maybe the cousin is involved. We want as much evidence as possible. McDonald won't wait for you to get started recording."

Jack wouldn't get any time to adjust. And he wasn't about to leave McDonald alone with those recordings. He felt like his beefy, intimidating presence might help, somehow. Illogical as that was. He headed for the meeting room, and when he opened the door, Officer McDonald was already set up and was adjusting some dials.

"You're just in time," McDonald said cheerily. "I've almost found the right frequency."

Liv's voice could be heard amid some hissing and crackling, then it came in clear. She was laughing about something, her voice lilting and relaxed. He felt a pang of guilt and tried to push it down.

"Let me put the kettle on," Liv said.

"Pull up a chair," McDonald said, opening a notebook. "We might get lucky today. You never know."

He should have told the Internal Affairs team that he had some personal feelings for Liv. That would have been smarter than simply accepting the case. He'd been angry at Kornekewsky's gall—taking advantage of innocent people—and if Liv was involved, he'd figured it was better that he learned that before he got himself entangled with her. It might have been dumb of him, but Jack had honestly thought that his sense of justice would overrule his attraction to her. Besides, it was his chance to prove himself and start pressing charges against dirty cops. That was why he'd joined the force to begin with, wasn't it? He was close enough that he could taste it. He just hadn't counted on justice feeling like such a betrayal.

Apparently, he'd been wrong about his dedication to pure justice, because while his head told him to keep his distance, every other part of him was drawn to the woman…including his heart.

The door opened, and Jack glanced back to see Chief Simpson come inside. Jack stood back while his boss took a seat. He didn't want to sit down. He was coiled as tight as a spring, and he crossed his arms over his chest, scowling at the receiver and recording equipment.

"…the baby shower is the day after tomorrow," Marie was saying. "I know it's short notice, but you can't organize a shower for a woman who hasn't confirmed her pregnancy, and Viola held out on us!"

"And no one asked?" Liv again.

"Well, after what happened with you…"

What *had* happened with Liv? The women fell quiet and there was the soft *clink* of silverware against glass. Eating? Cleaning up?

Tea? It was hard to tell, and McDonald stayed posed over his notebook, waiting. The chief looked at Jack.

"Have you spoken with any of these people?" the chief asked.

"Marie Hylton," Jack confirmed. "This is the first I've heard of a Viola. I could look into her if you want."

"The more we know, the better," the chief said, turning his attention back to the speaker as the conversation resumed again.

Liv's voice sounded restrained. "Not celebrating someone else's baby doesn't make my grief any easier, you know. You don't ever get over the loss of a child."

"I know," Marie replied. "I'm sorry, Liv. In our defense, we didn't know how to address it when you lost your baby, and you didn't really talk about it. We thought that when Viola was ready to tell us about this pregnancy she would. But she didn't. Pregnancy isn't always simple, is it? And maybe avoiding the subject wasn't the right move... Liv, dear, is this going to be too difficult for you?"

"What am I supposed to do?" Liv's voice trembled. "Stop celebrating when my friends and family have children because I couldn't? No, I'll be there. And I'll put a smile on my face."

It seemed clear that Liv had lost a baby… and Jack hadn't known that. There was a lot that happened in a marriage that no one on the outside was privy to. And maybe that was a good thing to remind himself of. Just because Liv had been done wrong, that didn't mean that she was innocent. McDonald kept writing in his notebook, and the chief's face maintained its expression of concentration.

"In your last report you mentioned that Ms. Hylton saw a woman with a baby stroller outside her window," the chief said suddenly. "Could it be related to her state of mind?"

Jack cleared his throat. "I was going to ask if that was a police plant."

"No. Not us." The chief shot him a shielded look.

"She thought the woman looked similar to Kornekewsky's new wife. So… I don't know."

Had Liv imagined it? Was she carrying around so much grief that she was starting to see ghosts of the life she'd longed for? That was a heartbreaking thought. Or perhaps it was connected to the case somehow.

Liv was talking again: "Seeing that Evan was cheating on me, maybe I should be glad he didn't want to try again for a baby. But I still want to be a mom, Auntie. Is that self-ish?"

"Well, it isn't like you're exactly shriveling up with age just yet," Marie replied. "And you have Jack, who seems downright smitten with you. How serious is it between you?"

Jack felt heat creep up his neck, and he wasn't sure why. This was part of the job—he'd played the role well if Marie was convinced.

"Oh…" Liv sounded embarrassed. "We aren't."

"He was here this morning—"

"Yes, but… I just mean, you never know where a relationship will go."

There was an awkward silence. Would she cave in and tell her aunt the truth—or at least the truth as she knew it? The silence stretched for a moment or two, and then Marie broke it.

"He's handsome, though," Marie prodded. "You two look good together."

"Oh, he's very good-looking," Liv said, and Jack breathed a sigh of relief. "Very, very good-looking. But I've been married to a cop before, and I'm not going down that path again."

McDonald looked back at Jack with a grin, and Jack scowled back at him. Yeah, yeah. The guys would rib him about this—the handsome cop, ever so good-looking. And that chafed, because in another life, he'd have given his left leg to hear Liv say that about him.

"So why are you dating him?" Marie asked.

There was a pause. "Like you said, he's gorgeous. All that muscle and those eyes that lock you down… I'm divorced, not dead."

His eyes could lock her down? He hadn't realized that. And now that he did, he wasn't going to be able to forget it too easily. There was something in her voice—something almost like a growl—that told him she felt the chemistry between them, too. He shouldn't be enjoying that.

"You might able to use her attraction toward you to get her to open up," the chief said thoughtfully. "You'd have to walk the line, obviously. Nothing that could jeopardize the case. But if she trusts you and starts talking—"

"No." Jack hadn't meant his tone to sound so harsh, and he winced.

"No?" The chief rose from his chair and nodded toward the other side of the room. "Is there a problem, Talbott?"

Jack followed the chief into relative privacy and glanced over at McDonald, who was taking notes of the women's conversation as it continued. Jack could hear Liv's soft tones filtering toward him, even though he couldn't make out her words.

"It's not a problem, exactly," Jack replied, turning back to his boss. "I can't manipulate her romantic hopes for the case, though, sir. That's crossing a line."

"I didn't ask you to cross any lines," the chief replied with a frown. "I never would. That would jeopardize the case."

"I'm attracted to her, sir," Jack admitted.

"She's a beautiful woman. It takes a certain mental fortitude to do this job," the chief replied. "Do you have it?"

"I have the fortitude, sir," Jack replied. "But I'm asking for you to trust my instinct on how close to get to Ms. Hylton in order to get the information we need."

"Fair enough," the chief replied. "You're the one in the field, and IA wanted you for a reason."

"Thank you, sir." Jack nodded curtly.

"Talbott," the chief said, his tone softening. "Do you need to step back?"

Jack paused, considering for a moment. This was his chance, if he needed to take it. He could simply say that he was more personally involved than was good for the investigation and back out. It would cause some friction. The investigation would be set back by weeks. They might not ever regain that ground. Jack shook his head. "No, sir. I've got it under control. If you swap me out for another officer at this point, you won't get her trust."

"I agree, and I'm glad to hear it," the chief said, slapping him on the shoulder. "You have our support, in whatever form you require. Get yourself centered, and then get back in there."

The case had to come first. He'd deal with his emotions later when he could safely take the lid off that bubbling pot inside him. But right now, he knew what his job required of him, and he knew why it was important.

That would have to be enough.

CHAPTER TEN

WHEN AUNT MARIE left that morning, Liv stood in the center of her living room for a few beats, her thoughts swimming. Marie had made a big effort to make up beyond just saying she was sorry.

They'd talked about a lot of things— Evan's cheating, the children Liv had yearned for but never had, this ruggedly male cop in her life… Marie wasn't the kind of woman who sided with a cheating ex, and for that Liv was grateful. Marie believed in right and wrong, and Evan had proven himself an unredeemable scoundrel in her aunt's eyes. If only Tanya felt the same—Liv suspected her single cousin was slightly in awe of Liv's sophisticated ex.

But Liv had realized something as she'd chatted with her aunt over breakfast: she was starting to fall for Jack. It was stupid—he might be acting the part of her boyfriend, but he most certainly wasn't. And if she were faced with the choice of whether to legitimately date him or not, she'd say no thanks.

She was tired of being a cop's wife, always coming in second to the job, and then second to the mistress! Forget it. When she was ready to date, she was going to find a nice stable guy with an ordinary job who could tell her about his day without using phrases like "classified information" and, when he'd open up about something, "civilian-level clearance."

Marie had had one last piece of advice before she'd left that morning: *Then don't toy with him, dear. It isn't nice.*

Liv had almost told her aunt the truth then, but something had stopped her. Jack was doing his best to protect her, and she needed to cooperate. He'd asked her to play along. Liv wasn't a heartless woman toying with a besotted boyfriend—she was a woman being threatened by some unknown stalker. She had no choice but to have Jack around…even if it tarnished her reputation somewhat in the meantime and even if it was starting to affect her own emotional equilibrium, too.

"I need space…" she told herself.

All she wanted was some time to think… some time away from her frustratingly masculine bodyguard who made her feel feminine and beautiful just by looking at her. That wasn't what she needed. She was supposed to be acclimatizing to the single life!

Liv grabbed a piece of paper and a pen and scratched out a note:

Jack,
I'm going out for a drive around the lake. I'm sure I'll survive it. I'll be back in a couple of hours.
Liv.

She dropped it in the middle of the kitchen table and reached for her purse. She felt lighter already. She locked the door and trotted down the stairs and outside into the cool fall air.

After her divorce, her dreams of opening the bookstore had given her hope, given her something to work for. The store was not only a dream fulfilled, but a chance at a different kind of life. She looked up and down the street, and in the bright, cheerful sunlight, all her worries about threatening letters seemed far away. Nothing terrible could happen on such a beautiful day, could it? Besides, she'd have her bodyguard back by the time the sun set.

Liv's car was parked behind the building. She tossed her purse onto the passenger seat, then got in the driver's side. This was her one day off, and she wanted to make the most of it, get her mood back in order. Whoever was threatening her could not win this—they wouldn't take away her ability to enjoy the new life she'd worked so hard to put together for herself.

Liv pulled out of her parking space and onto the main street. She headed south, past the old laundromat, a local history museum run by volunteers and a few hotels that catered to the tourists who came to ski. The hotels were virtually empty this time of year, when school was in session and the weather wasn't cold enough to make a trip to the mountains appealing to most people.

Back when Liv had been a teen working at Eagle's Rest's one and only McDonald's, she'd hated this tiny town with its limited options. But now, it just felt like home, and after her time in the city, her marriage, her heartbreak and her subsequent divorce, these familiar streets felt less suffocating and more soothing. They were her safe haven...or so she'd thought until those letters started to arrive.

The town quickly melted away into winding mountain roads. She took a fork to the left that curved around the crystal blue mountain lake. Eagle's Rest Lake was aptly named, since the towering spruce trees that carpeted the mountainside housed a large number of the majestic birds, and if people knew what to look for, they could spot the twiggy nests high up in the branches.

Liv's cell phone rang, and she touched the button on the dash to pick up the call via Bluetooth.

"Hi, Mom," Liv said.

"Hi, Liv, honey. How are things going over there? I've been worried."

"Oh, it's fine," Liv replied, checking her rearview mirror. The road was empty behind her. "I've had Jack with me nonstop, so I'm perfectly safe."

"Is he there now?" her mother asked.

"No," she admitted. "I'm taking a drive. I just needed some space."

"I wish you wouldn't evade the police protection," her mother said.

"I know, I know. I'll head back soon. I'm driving. What can happen? So how are you?"

"I was calling to talk to you about something, actually," her mother said. "You know that old cottage by the lake—the one your Uncle Ned left to your dad?"

"Sure." Liv instinctively glanced toward

the lake that shone like dazzling crystal through the trees.

"You know we've been trying to sell it—"

"Did you find a buyer?" Liv asked, her interest perking up.

"We did…" Her mother sounded wary. "Evan."

"Evan!" Liv pressed her lips together in irritation. "Evan? Where on earth is he getting all this money from?"

"What do you mean?"

"He's been buying up all sorts of properties around here. I mean, I know he inherited some money when his uncle died, but all those down payments… You've got to do the math!"

"I'm supposed to know?" her mother asked. "That man always was secretive."

"Why does he want some run-down cabin, for that matter? That place doesn't even have electricity!"

"I didn't ask," her mother replied. "He called us and asked if it was still for sale and offered to take it off our hands."

"For how much?" Liv demanded.

"For less than we were asking, but I don't think we can be choosy right now," her mother replied.

"And you never stopped to think that I might

not want my ex-husband around?" Liv said, then suppressed a sigh. "Look, I'm sorry, Mom. I know you guys need the money, but—"

"I was wondering if you and Evan were reconnecting," her mother said sheepishly. "I thought maybe he was trying to get close to you again."

"He's remarried, Mom," Liv replied curtly. "I'm not exactly the 'other woman' type."

"I know. But if he realized that Officer Hot Pants was nothing compared to you, broke up with her and asked for you back—"

"I'd tell him to get lost," Liv retorted.

"Good. Good. I wasn't saying it's a good idea," her mother replied. "I had to check. So…should I tell your father to find another buyer?"

Liv sighed. Her parents were retired now and living in California. The money from the sale would help their retirement a great deal, and she hated the thought of them waiting for even longer to find a buyer for that old plot of land. It was lakeside, granted, but it wasn't zoned for anything more than a cabin. Still, her gut tingled with suspicion.

"Mom, why do you think Evan is buying up so much land in Eagle's Rest?" she asked.

"I don't know… I know you two bought some properties together for when you retire—"

"He's bought at least two more properties since we split," she replied.

"So he's still buying up land around there," her mother said, then sighed. "I don't know, dear. I wish I could explain it. That man has never made sense to me."

"I'd gladly stop caring what he does, if he'd just get his hands off my town," Liv said irritably. "But, no, I don't want Evan and Hot Pants sunning themselves in Eagle's Rest every summer. That would be misery."

"If he's bought other properties out there, you might not have a choice," her mother said. "But I'll tell your dad to forget it. He can sun himself somewhere else. I'm sorry to even have brought it up, honey."

"It's okay, Mom. It isn't your fault. But thanks for that. I'll talk to you later, okay?"

They said their goodbyes and hung up.

Would Evan never go away? He wasn't dangerous like Jack seemed to think, he was just…nagging, annoying, always seeming to have his finger in the pie next to hers. And the very last thing she wanted was to share her hometown with the home-wrecking Hot Pants. Or Evan, for that matter. A divorce was supposed to end things, especially when there were no children in the mix. She *should* be able to be free of him.

Was that what the offer of those first editions was about? Was he trying to soften her up so she wouldn't encourage her parents to find another buyer for that land? But why would he want it, anyway?

It didn't add up!

A flapping sound alerted Liv to a problem with the front right wheel. The steering wheel tugged to the side, and Liv slowed, put on her hazard lights and pulled to the side of the road in the chilly shade of mountain evergreens. A flat. Great!

Liv sat for a moment, both hands on the wheel. A pickup truck rumbled past, not even slowing down. These roads were narrow, and when drivers drove at high speeds, the side of the road was far from safe. But she was only about ten minutes outside town.

When the road was clear again, she got out of the car and headed around to the trunk. Liv knew how to change a tire, and she busied herself with pulling out the spare and the jack. A squirrel chattered at her from above, and when Liv peered up at it, she saw an eagle take off from the upper branches of the trees. She stopped to watch as it rose into the sky, and then vanished from view. She'd seen many eagles in her years here, but they never ceased to take her breath away.

An engine rumbled, and Jack's car pulled up behind her. He parked, checked his mirrors, then hopped out. He looked mad, his dark eyes glittering and every movement under careful control.

"Hi," she said, casting him a wan smile, then turning back to the job at hand. So he was angry—she didn't really care right now. "How did you find me?"

"There's only one scenic route around the lake, so I'm told," he retorted. "What are you doing out here?"

"Taking a drive. Why are you following me?" she shot back.

"It's my job!" Jack walked around to the flat tire, then squatted down and ran his hand along the rubber.

"Forgive me for wanting a few minutes to myself," she said. "I like you, Jack, but I'm not used to the constant company anymore."

Jack looked up at her. "You want a hand?"

"Not really!" she snapped back. "I'm perfectly capable. Contrary to popular belief around here."

"You sure?" He raised one eyebrow. "Because this flat was no accident."

"What are you talking about?" The air seemed to chill around her, and Liv leaned in closer—close enough that the soft scent of his aftershave tickled her nose—as Jack pointed to a short cut in the rubber beside the rim.

"It's a slow leak, but this was on purpose."

FOR ALL OF Jack's calm reserve, he was just as surprised as Liv looked. She stared at him, the blood draining from her face, and then her gaze whipped up and down the road. He hadn't done this, and while it was possible it was just some random act of vandalism, it did leave him unsettled. The other cops were convinced that the eerie woman in the rain had been a figment of Liv's tortured imagination, but he wasn't. He'd gotten to know her over the last while, and she wasn't the type to follow ghosts and fancy.

This tire was obviously real, too, and he was starting to get a tickle of warning. Except vandalism happened, right? Probably just some bored, ill-supervised kids fooling around with a knife. He couldn't read too much into this—although if *she* did, it would help their cause. He recognized that.

"My tire was…intentionally stabbed?" she breathed.

"Looks like." He held out his hand. "Pass me the jack, would you?"

This time, she didn't argue and handed it over. The sun disappeared behind a cloud, and the air chilled noticeably. The sparkle from the lake fifty yards off dimmed, and Jack set to work raising the car. When the car was elevated the few inches he needed to change the tire, he nodded toward the trunk.

"Grab me the lug wrench," he said.

Liv went to the trunk and started rummaging around. She didn't seem to be finding what she needed, so he rose and ambled over to where she stood. When he got to her side, she brushed the back of her hand against her cheek, and he could see tears misting her eyes.

"Liv…" He hated this—frightening her. This was all part of the greater plan. She needed to be ill at ease. If she was scared, she'd turn to him for protection and hopefully tell him what she was involved in. But still, he didn't like being the cause of her fear. It felt needlessly cruel, and he hated seeing her fighting back tears like this. Except in his defense, this one wasn't on them!

"Liv," he repeated, and she looked over at him, blinking back the emotion. "Hey…"

He was going to reach for her hand, but instead, he slipped his hand along her waist and tugged her toward him. It was instinctual—and a terrible idea. He knew it the minute his hand touched her waist, because it felt too good, and he was quickly sliding past all those professional boundaries. But he couldn't quite stop himself, either.

"You okay?" he asked.

"What do they want?" she whispered, her eyes searching his. "Why me?"

That's what he wanted her to tell him—why would someone like her ex-husband want to give her trouble? What were they involved in that might get dangerous? It could be argued that he was saving her from future violence by getting her to open up now. And maybe, if they were lucky, she'd testify against Evan in exchange for a lesser sentence for herself.

"You tell me," he said quietly.

"I have no idea." She shook her head. "I'm nobody. I opened a bookstore. This can't be about that. I don't get it. What did I do to deserve this?"

She licked her lips, looking furtively toward the road again. Jack followed her gaze, but there was no one on the road just now—all was quiet except for the rustle of wind in the trees. Quiet. Private... And her apartment was no longer private at all. There was something about this moment—the luxury of being stuck with her on a mountain road with no one recording their words, demanding explanations later...

Liv felt soft and warm under his touch, and looking down at those plump lips, all the logic seemed to be draining from his head. He'd looked at those lips for years—longing to taste them—and never once been this close.

Still, he was on a job. He had to stop this!

"If you know anything..." he said, and a chilly breeze picked up and curved around them. Jack hadn't meant to tug her closer still, but they'd both moved at the same time. When she looked up, his mouth was hovering over hers. She was so close, her soft body pressing against him, and when a wisp of hair blew against her lipstick, he lifted his hand and brushed it aside. Her skin felt hot and silky against his calloused fingers. As he looked down into her face, her lips parted ever so slightly.

Oh, hell...

That was about all he could resist. He slid his hand behind her neck and pulled her into him, his lips covering hers in a desperate kiss. His eyes fell shut as he held her close, and he felt her sigh against him.

Finally was all he could think. She was finally in his arms. He was finally tasting those plump lips with his own. His pulse sped up, and he had a deep, searing longing to take this much further.

He wouldn't. Even this was too far. He pulled back, the cool air flooding between them once more. He pressed his lips together and attempted to steel his resolve. Liv blinked up at him, looking rather surprised and ruffled, too. Her lipstick was smeared, and he used the pad of his thumb to wipe it.

"What was that?" she asked.

"A mistake." He let one side of his mouth turn up in a not-terribly-apologetic smile.

"Definitely a mistake," she said, but then her gaze met his again, and he caught himself leaning in once more. He stopped before his lips met hers, letting out a soft moan.

"This is my fault," he murmured.

"Oh, I agree," she murmured back. "All yours."

He laughed softly, then took a reluctant step back. "I'm sorry. I find you incredibly beautiful, and—" Where was his excuse? He was a cop, supposedly here to protect her. He had no business making a move on her—especially given the fact that he was secretly investigating her!

"It's okay." She shook her head. "We're two healthy, attractive adults, and we've been spending a whole lot of time together."

"So you've been feeling this, too," he clarified. He knew it—he'd heard her admit to it in surveillance, but that wasn't the same as having her tell him straight. And he wanted to hear it intended for his ears.

"I'm...trying to get used to living alone," she said, and he heard the catch in her voice. Shoot. This wasn't the honesty he was looking for. "I'm lonely. I'll admit that. And I have a type, too. You, Evan... I like big, strong, stubborn louts."

"So I'm just one of a type, am I?" he asked with a small smile.

"Let's just call this...an understandable mistake. I need to focus on me right now—on breaking my pattern. No more cops."

"Okay. That's probably wise." Wiser than she realized. "I won't do that again."

"Thanks." She turned back to the trunk and pushed aside a plastic bag, revealing the lug wrench. She pulled it out and handed it over.

He accepted the tool. "And just to prove how professional I'm capable of being, you were about to tell me why someone might be interested in tormenting you."

Liv rolled her eyes, but she didn't look scared like before, and that made him feel a little bit better—a little less like the manipulative heel that he was.

"I told you," she said. "I got the letters and then the pictures. And then I saw that creepy woman out there in the rain…and now this." She paused, something new sparkling in her eyes. Then she looked up at him, her eyebrows raised. She'd just made a connection.

"What?" he prodded.

"You're so convinced my ex-husband is connected to this," she said.

"Yeah, I am."

"Well, Evan offered to buy an old cabin from my parents a day or so ago. My mother just told me about it. And it makes no sense. He left me. He's remarried! What does he want with a cabin by Eagle's Rest Lake?"

"You don't know?" he asked.

"I have no idea. He's suddenly giving me his grandmother's first-edition books, he's trying to buy my late great-uncle's cabin… What's with Evan and my family lately?"

Jack crossed his arms over his chest, meeting her gaze. "You tell me."

"I wish I knew!" She shook her head and turned away. "None of this adds up."

"Well, until it does, you need to stick close to me," Jack said. "No more leaving notes and taking off."

"You're going to regret that," Liv said with

a small smile. "Because there's a baby shower coming up…and it's a Jack and Jill."

"Meaning?" Jack frowned.

"It's for both men and women. And since you're my fake but adoring boyfriend…"

Jack smiled ruefully. "All right. I'll be there. But I'm serious, Liv. No more giving me the slip."

"Okay."

"And, Liv?"

She looked up at him, worry swimming in her eyes.

"I'll behave myself. I'll be professional. That's a promise." He held her gaze. "Okay?"

"Okay." She nodded.

Now to fix the tire. All logic pointed to simple vandalism, but something in his gut wouldn't settle. Liv was right—not everything was adding up here. Either Liv was duping him and he was blind to it, or there was more to this than the police knew.

Was it possible that they were targeting an innocent woman?

CHAPTER ELEVEN

JACK'S KISS WASN'T as easy to forget as Liv had pretended. That had been to save face. She didn't want him knowing how he made her feel! It didn't matter.

Over the next couple of days, Jack kept his distance, too, and she wasn't sure if she was relieved or not. While she knew he wasn't what she needed in her life right now, that kiss had seared itself into her mind, and she'd been reliving it in her quiet moments…

His strong arms pulling her close, that almost inaudible hum he'd made in the back of his throat before his lips had covered hers… His kiss had been gentle but urgent. He was a man who knew what he wanted and knew how to kiss a woman. She'd been left slightly weak in the knees, and when he'd leaned toward her that second time, she had to confess, she wouldn't have stopped him.

Liv told herself that she wanted him to back off a little bit, give her some space to breathe, to think. And he had been quieter, more observant and less interactive since that day. He hadn't once touched her—not even in passing.

That's what I asked him for, isn't it? she reminded herself. And Jack was doing what so many men failed to do—he was respecting her wishes. No need to speak twice. She'd told him she needed space, and he was respecting that boundary.

So as they were getting ready to leave for the baby shower, Liv wondered if their public image was going to change, too. This baby shower would be hard enough for her without having to navigate all the family concern over the state of her fake romance. There was only so much she could handle at one time, but then again, maybe she was about to test that theory.

Liv got dressed in a pair of gray slacks and a pink cashmere sweater that flattered her figure, made the most of her ample hips and made her creamy skin glow. She used more muted makeup this afternoon—a plum lipstick and shimmery eyeshadow. She pulled her hair into a messy bun at the back of her head, and when she was satisfied with the end result, she opened her bedroom door and stepped into the living room, where Jack was waiting.

"Wow," he said, his gaze doing a quick up and down. "You look great."

"Thanks. You, too." Jack was dressed in a pair of khaki pants and a button-up shirt that tugged slightly around his biceps. She sucked in a breath, trying to sound less uncomfortable than she felt. "I need to know what to expect today."

"How so?" He looked at her uncertainly, and she wondered how awkward this was for him, too.

"The last time my family saw us together, we were acting the part of happy couple," Liv replied. "Are we doing that again?"

"I don't see any reason to change it," Jack replied. "Do you?"

She felt a well of relief. She hadn't realized how much she'd been enjoying having a guy to trot around to these family things until she was facing the prospect of losing him...if that could even be the right way to think about it.

"No, I think that would be for the best," she said with a nod, then she met his gaze apologetically. "How much do you hate this, Jack?"

"What?" Jack narrowed his eyes.

"This—playing this role. I realized I've been thinking about how it affects me, when it affects you, too."

"I'm not hating it half as much as you think," he said with a small smile.

"No?" she asked uncertainly.

"I get to make an entire town believe that I've scored the prettiest woman in Eagle's Rest. It's not exactly agony on my part."

Liv felt some heat rise in her cheeks and broke eye contact. "Just making sure. There's nothing more humiliating than having a man feel trapped."

"I'm not trapped. I'm just trying to be the professional I am." He shot her a warm smile. "Am I allowed to hold your hand again? You know, just to make sure we're in the role when we arrive at…whose place again?"

"Aunt Jean's."

"Aunt Jean's." He held out his hand, and she slid her fingers into his warm grasp. He gave her hand a squeeze. It felt so good—warm, protective, strong. She resisted the urge to lean into that muscular arm. Whatever she was feeling right now wasn't logical, and if she gave in to it, she'd only feel foolish later.

"Sure," she said, and couldn't help the smile that came to her lips. "It's for a good cause."

Liv drove to Aunt Jean's house on the west side of town. Jean owned a large '80s style house on two acres of land. They had three bounding German shepherds that were nearly full grown but still acted like pups.

Liv parked on the grass like everyone else, and when they got out of the car, she looked up at the mountain scene that rose up behind the house. The jagged peaks were perpetually dusted with snow, even during the summer, but at this point in the autumn, the snow had moved down the mountain to the halfway mark.

"What a view," Jack said.

"It never gets old," she agreed.

She wasn't looking forward to this baby shower. She loved having a big, united extended family, except for times like these. She couldn't just bow out of a baby shower without deeply offending someone. Her family knew too much—even the deeper reasons she might have for wanting to avoid an afternoon like this one.

But now wasn't the time to lose her resolve. She could make it through this, too. Besides, having Jack with her changed the dynamic a little bit.

He scooped up her hand as they headed toward a walkway that led around to the side door of the house. No one used Aunt Jean's front door—it was the kitchen entrance for everyone.

Liv pasted a smile onto her face as she

opened the side door. The dogs woofed in delight and ran toward them with a clatter of toenails against linoleum, and a few of Liv's aunts and cousins who stood chatting in the kitchen looked up to see who'd arrived.

Liv said hello, gave some hugs and led the way through to the living room, where Viola was seated in a place of honor—a large wicker chair that was decorated with pink and blue balloons. Her belly domed out in front of her, and her husband sat next to her, a big smile on his face.

This was the scene that Liv had wanted for herself—the pregnancy, the proud husband. When she'd lost her baby, she'd been four and half months along. It was supposed to be the safe zone… But Viola didn't look scared. She was about five months pregnant, and looked adorable.

Liv's breath caught in her throat, and she swallowed hard. She ruffled the heads of the dogs, then went over to give her cousin a hug and congratulate her.

"I'm so happy for you both!" Liv said, squeezing her cousin. "Really, truly."

"I'm happy for you, too—" Viola looked around her toward Jack. "He's cute. Where'd you find him?"

"At a police station, where else?" Liv joked.

"You know my track record. I'm going to get myself some punch. Do you want some, Viola?"

"No, no, I don't dare," her cousin said, chuckling. "This baby is sitting on my bladder right now, so…"

Liv grinned and met Jack's gaze. She angled her steps in his direction. Jack met her halfway and nudged her toward the refreshments that were on a sideboard across the room.

"You okay?" he murmured.

"Yeah. Fine." She glanced up and found him looking down at her with concern in those dark eyes.

"You don't look fine," he whispered back, handing her a plastic cup of punch.

"I'm—" She met his gaze. She had been going to tell him that she was perfectly fine, but she wasn't. And somehow he'd picked up on that. "I hate these, but I'll survive."

"Okay." He nodded slowly. "But if you need an excuse to get out of here…"

"Don't tempt me," she said, shooting him a smile. "I have to stay a polite amount of time."

The party went on with games and nonalcoholic toasts. More family arrived, and Liv milled through the groups of people, Jack sticking close. The Hyltons supported one another, if nothing else. Babies weren't brought into the family without getting a royal welcome.

After Viola opened the presents, music suddenly started to play, and a ball made out of wrapping paper and bound up with ribbons from the gift opening was handed from person to person as fast as they could pass it along. No one needed the rules to this game explained—it was a Hylton tradition. The person left holding the ball when the music stopped would be the next one to have a baby, or father a baby, whichever the case may be.

Liv's heart sank. She hated this part...now, at least. There had been a time when her superstitious nature used to thrill at the thought of being left with the ball in her hands, but not anymore.

There was laugher and squeals as people pushed the ball from one set of hands to the next.

"No, no, no!" a middle-aged aunt yelped, laughing. "Here you go—I'm done with babies!"

One of Liv's older uncles playfully held on to the ball for a couple of beats while his wife wagged a finger at him. "Not with me, you don't!"

Liv looked toward the food table again, wondering when the cake could be cut so she could leave already. Then the ball of wrapping paper was thrust in her hands just as the music stopped. The silence was absolute and as heavy as lead.

Her heart thudded to a stop at the same time, and she looked down at the ragged ball in dread. She shut her eyes for a moment, wishing it away. They knew—everyone knew—and she could feel all the eyes turning toward her. She felt tears well up in her vision. What was she supposed to do now?

"Hey, I thought love and marriage was supposed to come before the babies," Jack's good-natured voice boomed out. "Give us some time, would you?"

He plucked the ball from her hands and tossed it toward another young couple, then he slid a strong arm around her waist, tugged her against his muscled torso and his lips came down on hers. The kiss was warm and firm, just longer than a peck.

Everyone started to laugh, and some of them whooped in encouragement.

"Go, Liv!" one of her cousins called out, and Liv's eyes blinked open as Jack pulled back.

"Let's go," Jack whispered.

She nodded, and Jack kept his arm around

her waist and led the way through the kitchen and toward the side door they'd come in by. He was taking control of the moment, she realized, and she was deeply grateful. Even though she had no idea how he'd realized how hard this was for her... Was she that transparent?

All she wanted was to get away. Jack pulled open the door, nodded and smiled at her cousins, and then they were outside in the biting chill of an October afternoon, and the tears she'd been fighting spilled onto her cheeks.

JACK TUGGED LIV after him, kicking the screen door shut behind them. He knew exactly why this baby shower was hard on Liv...he just wasn't supposed to know yet. So how was he going to explain himself for taking over in there?

He'd seen her face when that ball of wrapping paper had hit her hands—the pain in her eyes. He couldn't just let her flounder, everyone staring at her...

"You okay?" he asked tentatively.

Liv's chin trembled, and more tears slipped down her cheeks. He pulled her against his chest, smoothing a hand over her hair, and she let out a shuddering sigh into his neck. He closed his arms around her, resting his cheek against her silken hair. He wanted to fix this—make it better somehow—but he knew he couldn't. This was well out of his control.

And he wasn't supposed to be trying to fix her problems. He was supposed to be taking advantage of moments like this. He just couldn't bring himself to do it.

"Hey…" he murmured against her hair. "Hey."

Jack wasn't sure what to say. But holding her seemed to be helping, so he tightened his arms around her. After a few more sniffles, she pulled back and wiped her cheeks with the palms of her hands.

"Sorry about that kiss," he said, his voice low.

"At least it gave them something better to think than Poor Liv," she said, forcing a wobbly smile.

"Let's get in the car," he said. "I can drive."

Liv handed him the keys, and they headed to where her car was parked. It would be better to get away from prying eyes, anyway. He knew she needed to talk about the baby she had lost. He didn't want this private moment recorded by the police department, though. She deserved her privacy when it came to such a personal matter, and they'd already invaded it once. So after they got into the car, Jack turned toward her.

"What happened out there?" he asked.

"Baby showers are hard for me," she said with a sigh. "I lost a baby three years ago. I'd wanted to be a mom so badly, and when I got pregnant, I was over the moon. I told everyone. I didn't wait—you're supposed to wait, you know. Not that it would have mattered. I was four and a half months when I lost the baby, so…" She glanced toward him.

"I'm really sorry," he said quietly.

"Evan wasn't as excited. He was…awful, really. He said stuff like, 'Don't get your hopes up. You never know what will happen'…that kind of thing. Anyway, it turned out he was right."

Jack felt a wave of anger rolling up inside of him. Evan Kornekewsky was a real piece of work.

"He's an ass," Jack muttered.

"Yes." Liv shrugged. "And he was cheating on me at the time, so maybe he already knew he was going to walk out on me and didn't want the complication of a child in the mix."

"I don't care what his reasons were," Jack replied. "You needed support, and that baby was his."

"It was an awful time," Liv said, pulling a

tissue from her purse and dabbing at her eyes. "I was heartbroken. We hadn't found out the gender of the baby yet, but I was already in love with the little thing. When I miscarried, we found out it was a girl."

Jack reached over and moved her hair away from her face, letting his fingers linger on her damp cheek for a moment.

"I'd already bought some maternity clothes, and I'd started to show—" She dabbed her nose with the tissue. "But I have to get over it. Life goes on."

"I don't know about that," Jack replied. "Life might go on, but you'll never forget her."

"No, I never will." She looked up at him and gave him a teary smile. "It helps to talk about her. Thank you."

"Whatever you need." And he was serious about that, he realized. In this moment, he wasn't the cop investigating her, he was…a friend? That couldn't be right. Maybe he was just a decent man supporting a woman who needed a little comfort right now, who'd been done wrong one too many times by her idiot of an ex.

"What I need is to be able to celebrate other people's babies," she said with a shake of her head. "I thought I could today."

Liv tucked the tissue away and then slowly looked toward him.

"Why did you kiss me?" she asked suddenly.

"I—" How was he supposed to explain himself. "You looked like you needed an escape, and it seemed like the most expedient way out of there."

"Oh…"

"Was I right?" he asked uncertainly.

"Probably." She smiled wanly. "Can we just go home now?"

"Yeah." He adjusted the mirrors, then turned the key. "At the very least, everyone is now talking about you and that handsy boyfriend."

Liv laughed softly. "Yes, they are. That's a guarantee. When all this is over, I might not tell them the truth at all. I might just say that you and I broke up."

"What reason will you give?" he asked, shooting her a rueful smile as he put the car into Reverse and backed out. He got turned around and signaled a turn onto the road.

"Oh, I don't know…maybe you'll have turned out to be a mama's boy."

Oh, really? So that's what she thought was under the surface? He had an undeniable urge to set her straight. "I'm not a mama's boy."

"No?" She eyed him teasingly. "Then maybe you'll have been a career-focused cop, and I realized I was doing the same thing I always do—going for the wrong kind of guy."

"I could even give you a grand public gesture, trying to get you back," he said with a laugh. "They might like that."

"Would you?" She sounded so sincere that he looked over at her to check, but there was laughter in her eyes. "Don't worry, I wouldn't put you through that. I'm imagining you outside my window with a boom box held over your head."

Jack groaned. None of this mattered. He was joking around with her, forgetting that when all of this was over the criminal charges would be laid, and that protective family network would be stunned at what had been going on right under their noses.

But a nagging uncertainty had taken up residence at the back of his mind. He wasn't quite as convinced of her guilt as he'd been before. There was a threat out there, and it wasn't coming from them. It was possible that Liv was a better actress than he was giving her credit for, but he'd seen the fear in her eyes by the road. When people were scared, they got honest. And she'd been scared by the things the cops had set up, and by these new threats, as well. But she hadn't cracked, or even shown signs of strain. While it was hard to believe that a husband could be involved in this level of fraud without his wife knowing, it was possible. Normally, the wife was in on it—they benefited, too, after all. And while Evan had divorced Liv, she had moved back to the very town where Evan had been pressuring the elderly to sell.

Her joint accounts with her husband had been involved with the sales. And there were an awful lot of coincidences. But it was possible that they were only that—coincidences. They needed proof, not suspicion.

The drive wasn't long, and within a few minutes they'd parked behind the store in Liv's regular spot.

"Thank you for the rescue today," Liv said. "I don't know what I would have done if you weren't there."

"It's all part of the job," he said, but he knew that was wrong. That hadn't been the job—that had been something more personal.

They got out of the car and headed around to the front of the building, but as they approached the door, Jack saw something taped to the store window—an envelope.

"What's that?" Liv asked, and she stepped past him and pulled it off the glass.

"Let me—" Jack pulled a pair of latex gloves from his pocket and put them on before taking the envelope from her fingers. He shook it, then tore a strip off the side so he could slide a folded piece of paper out and into his palm. This wasn't familiar. If there was going to be another plant, he would have been advised.

Jack unfolded the paper and looked down at scratchy handwriting across the page.

Liv, Liv, pretty, pretty Liv—you know you don't belong here. Don't you? You know that. Don't make me prove anything. I don't like to be forced. I don't like myself then, Pretty Liv.

Jack's blood ran cold. This wasn't the police department's work—he was willing to bet on it. To be sure, he'd contact the chief right away, but the wording… Whoever had written this sounded stark raving mad.

"Oh, my God…" Liv breathed, and she put a hand on his arm, her fingers digging into his shirt. Jack slid an arm around her waist to stabilize her.

"I'll have an officer pick this up," Jack said, forcing himself to sound more self-assured than he felt. "But yeah…this is serious."

"I don't get it!" she exclaimed, her voice trembling. "Who would do something like this? It's sick!"

Jack looked up and down the street twice, searching for anything out of the ordinary. There was nothing. Then he picked up his phone and dialed the chief's direct number. He didn't use this number unless it was an emergency, and this counted.

"Let's go upstairs—" He pulled open the door and gestured her inside as the phone rang against his ear. He scanned the stairwell as Liv bent to pick up some mail that had landed in a pile on the floor.

"Talbott?" the chief said as he picked up.

"That's right, sir," Jack said. "We've got another letter—this one taped to the window."

"Wait—" the chief's voice lowered "—we didn't drop one."

"I know." Jack put a hand on Liv's elbow and they started up the stairs together. "And this one is…worrisome."

"Is Ms. Hylton with you right now?" the chief asked.

"Yes, sir."

"Any suspicions of who might have dropped this one?" the chief asked.

"No, sir."

"I'll send an officer down to pick it up. You're at Ms. Hylton's home, I take it?"

"Yes, sir."

There was the muffled sound of voices, then the chief came back on the line. "McDonald will be there soon. Obviously, protect the evidence. We'll scan for prints and anything else we can get off the paper."

"You bet, sir. Thanks."

As Jack hung up the phone, they reached the top of the staircase. The game had officially changed. Before this, they were the ones trying to scare Liv, but someone else had joined in—someone much better at writing threatening notes. Up until this point, Jack had simply been managing her experience, but it looked like he wasn't the one in control anymore.

A new player had joined the game, and Jack had no idea who.

CHAPTER TWELVE

LIV WATCHED JACK lock the door—the dead bolt as well as the regular lock. There was something different about Jack now. He'd gained an edge she'd never seen before. He scanned the room twice—steely gaze moving over every surface, delving into every corner—and then he went to the window, his eyes slicing up and down the street.

"Jack?" she said tentatively.

Jack continued his surveillance out the window for another few beats before he turned back toward her.

"Hmm?"

"Why is this letter freaking you out more than the others did?" she asked.

"It isn't," he replied with a frown. "I'm just doing my job."

That was a lie—she could read it all over him. After being married to a cop, she knew their lines. Everything hard was "just the job," and whenever they got scared or angry, they hid behind that badge. They used it like a shield to cover their human frailties.

"I told you about the woman in the rain— *that* was creepy," she said, "and you didn't react like this. You've seen both a threatening letter and a pile of pictures left gift-wrapped on my doorstep, and you didn't act like this."

"Like what?" he said irritably.

"This whole surveillance thing you just started. Door-locking, scanning the room, watching for intruders. You suspect something more this time, don't you?"

Jack sighed. "This letter has a different feel to it. It's…creepier."

It had all been pretty creepy in Liv's opinion, but somehow this letter had hit Jack differently. He was seeing something she couldn't—something that should probably scare her more deeply than it already had. What was she missing?

"So in your professional opinion, what is this?" she asked, trying to keep her voice level.

"I wish I knew."

"Then you aren't blaming this on Evan anymore?"

"I haven't decided," he said.

"Don't you have an idea, at least?" she pressed.

Jack scrubbed a hand through his hair but didn't answer.

"What, you can't tell me? This is *my* life at risk, Jack! This is my shop being threatened! And you won't tell me what we're looking at here?"

"Whoever is threatening you will have to get through me to get to you!" he retorted. "I've got it under control."

"No, you don't!" she shot back. "You're freaked out!"

Whoever this was had just frightened the muscle-bound cop assigned to protect her. That was not a good sign.

"I'm not freaked out." His took a deep breath. "I'm fine. You're fine. I'm very good at my job, and you have nothing to worry about as long as you stick close to me."

Like she'd even consider taking off on her own now. Whatever was happening, she needed protection. And as uncomfortable as it might be, Jack was the best option.

"I'll cooperate," she said seriously. "No more giving you the slip."

"Good." His expression softened. "Now, what's that?" Jack gestured to the pile of mail in her hands. She'd forgotten about it in the panic of the moment.

"Just mail... I picked it up," she said feebly,

glancing down at the envelopes in her hand. The first few were junk mail, but the last envelope looked like it was from the town of Eagle's Rest.

"Nothing out of the ordinary?" Jack asked.

She shook her head, then glanced at that last envelope from the city. She used to leave all the business mail for Evan to take care of. Though they'd had joint accounts, she'd never seen the statements, or even thought to check up on accounts that weren't her basic checking and savings. She was all about the retirement savings—the money she wouldn't let him play with when it came to property buying and house flipping. She wanted that safety net, and he wanted the risk.

Liv turned the letter over, then sighed. She might as well open it—she needed to do something to get rid of this jittery feeling. She tore it open and scanned the contents. She frowned, then read it again.

"What?" Jack asked. "What is it?"

"My property taxes have been reassessed," she said, her breath catching in throat. "I owe five times what I did before."

How was that for pulling her out of the moment? How on earth was she going to pay this? One of the perks of opening her store in a small town was that the property taxes were affordable. But with this kind of jump in what she owed... Her mind was zipping through the arithmetic. She'd had a very slim margin before, but now—

"Do you mind?" he asked, holding out his hand. Liv numbly passed the letter over, watching him read it. Then he looked up at her, his expression confused. "What changed?"

"Nothing that I know of!" she retorted.

"Something changed." Jack tapped the paper against his palm. "The town wouldn't raise property taxes for no reason. These are directly related to the land's worth."

"It has to be a mistake," she said, shaking her head. "There is no way my store is worth that. We have a few tourists but not enough to drive up the values that much. Trust me—if it were worth what that letter says, I'd have sold and taken the money."

"Yeah?" Jack raised an eyebrow, and she could feel the questioning in his look again— like he was suspicious of her or something. But that was crazy. She was the victim here. "It might not be a mistake at all."

"It has to be," she retorted. "Jack, what do I do? I can't pay this!"

"First things first," he said, pulling out his phone. He took a few moments, scrolling through his browser, then he tapped in a phone number. "I know a guy who is a tax assessor in our county—"

"You do?" She looked skeptical.

"I have all sorts of useful contacts," he replied. "Give me a minute, would you? I'll check into this."

Liv sank into the couch, listening to the low rumble of Jack's voice as he talked on the phone. She was tired all of a sudden. So very tired. Coming home to Eagle's Rest was supposed to be her chance to breathe, her chance to get back to her roots, to *herself*. She was tired of being the ex-Mrs. Kornekewsky. It was time to embrace being Liv Hylton again and to chase a few of her own dreams. Evan had taken away too much, and he owed her a fresh start, at the very least.

But ever since she'd arrived back in her hometown, she'd been dealing with a stalker, and now a financial crisis threatened her store. She didn't have extra money—it had all gone into her business. Living in Denver had been easier, ironically enough. She might have had her ex-husband in town and all the reminders of the marriage she'd lost, of the baby she'd lost…of her hopes trampled. But in the midst of the clutter of her old life, at least no one had been threatening her safety! Had she come this close to living her dream as a bookstore owner only to have it torn away at the last minute? Liv leaned forward, resting her face in her hands.

Maybe she should just do what the letter-writer wanted and get out of town. It would be easier…if that really would satisfy the person. But what if he followed her and tried to chase her out of her next home. Not knowing what this was about was the hardest part of all. What could she possibly have done to make anyone hate her this much? It made no sense!

She heard Jack say goodbye, then he came back into the living room. He crossed his arms over his chest and chewed the inside of one cheek.

"I have a few answers," he said.

"Oh?" Liv looked up hopefully.

"The tax assessment is legitimate," Jack said. "All the properties in this area have had their values reassessed because of some minable resources under our feet."

"Minable resources…" Liv frowned. "What kind?"

"Gold. Apparently, there's all sorts of it. It's hitting the news now."

"Gold! That doesn't seem possible." She felt suddenly breathless. "Well…there was this journalist years ago who made a wild claim that there might be something here, but he was disgraced, and… This really doesn't seem possible," she repeated.

"Why not?" he asked. "Eagle's Rest used to be a gold miner's town, didn't it?"

"Yes, that's true," she said, "but besides the little bit they found panning the river that runs out of the lake, there wasn't much gold here. The town collapsed and only revived as a tourist attraction for skiers."

"Well, they missed something, because this land is now incredibly valuable."

This little shop was worth some actual cash? It was hard to believe, and Liv took a moment for that to sink in. Jack was looking at her—his direct gaze pinning her to the spot. He was waiting for her reaction, she realized.

"I don't know what to say," she said feebly.

"This doesn't…explain anything for you?" he asked.

"Explain what?" she demanded, shoving herself off the couch and rising to her feet. "What, Jack? What am I supposed to suddenly understand? I'm sick of this—the constant demand that I pull the answers out of my head, out of my past, out of thin air! Figuring out the criminal element is supposed to be your job, not mine!"

"Liv, someone wants you out of town.

Maybe even dead." He raised the most recent threatening letter, flapping it in front of her. "Someone wants you out of here…and so far, you've been holding out on me."

"I'm not!" she snapped. "Why don't you believe me?"

"Because this is personal. This is no random attack. And I think you're protecting someone."

"Evan?" She laughed bitterly. "You honestly think I'm protecting *Evan*?"

"He tried to buy your parents' land below value," he said.

"I can't explain that," she replied tiredly.

"So you're willing to toy with your life?" he shot back.

"I'm not toying with anything! I still have no idea what's going on, but apparently, you do know something." Anger rose up inside her, effectively capping the fear that was threatening to boil over. "Yes, he's been buying up land around here, and maybe this does explain that. But how was I supposed to know about it? I left him all those little plots of land in the divorce! It was all mortgaged, anyway. What did I want with all that debt? And he was happy to keep it! It looks like it's worth a whole lot now, though…"

"Looks like."

"You know far more than you're admitting to, but you won't tell me! So which one of us is holding out?"

Jack stared at her and she met his eye, glaring right back. He pressed his lips together in a flat line, and she could see the anger in the set of his jaw. But he was controlling it.

"Would you tell me if you were involved with something that got out of hand?" he asked after a moment.

He suspected her of something. That was what this was. He was here to protect her, but somehow he'd gotten the wrong idea.

"What do you think I've done?" she asked breathily. "I thought you were here to protect me!"

"I am."

"Jack, I'm telling you the truth." He *had* to believe her. "I have no idea what's going on, and if this is connected to my ex-husband in any way, I have no interest in protecting him. But I also have no interest in blaming him for something he didn't do. I'm just trying to start over here! But it seems like you know something about him that I don't, so—has Evan done something? Is this land he's been buying up a legal issue or something?"

It wasn't inconceivable, she realized. Evan had always been the kind of man who had secrets, and she hadn't kept tabs on the banking like she should have.

Jack sucked in a long breath, then slowly shook his head. "If there was something that went wrong…something you might have gotten involved with, not knowing how bad it would get—" he sighed "—it would be better for you if you told me now. I could help you."

"Jack, there is nothing to tell you." She searched his face pleadingly.

"Okay." He nodded briskly.

"Do you believe me?" she asked.

"I didn't mean to spook you. I'm sorry."

That wasn't exactly an answer.

"But did Evan do something?" she repeated.

"You'd know better than me," he said with a faint shrug. "And you say he hasn't."

"I say he hasn't done anything *to my knowledge*," she corrected him. "There's a whole lot I probably don't know."

"Fair enough."

So that was it? Jack was letting it go just like that? He'd been solid and logical. He'd been her protector…and now he was being shifty, too.

Was she going crazy? Or was there something much bigger going on that she hadn't seen?

"I'm going to go make another call," Jack

said, hooking a thumb behind him. "I've got an officer coming by to pick up the letter, too, so I'll meet him out there."

"Okay," she said.

Jack tucked the letter into a plastic bag and pulled open the front door. "Lock it behind me," he said gruffly. But when his eyes met hers, they softened. "Okay, Liv?"

Liv nodded, and when he pulled the door shut behind him, she flicked the dead lock into place.

Nothing made sense anymore, including Jack. And that scared her most of all, she realized, because Jack had been the last person she could fully count on. He'd been the sane one in the middle of all this craziness. She'd been leaning on him, looking to him, trusting his instincts...

What on earth was happening?

JACK'S BOOTS THUNKED against the stairs as he trotted down to the main floor. He felt antsy, itchy, like there were crosshairs working over his back.

There were bugs in Liv's apartment recording that conversation, and Jack knew he should be mentally going through exactly what he'd said. Had he said too much? That was the problem with Liv—he couldn't keep his professional distance from her, and he forgot himself a little too easily. She wasn't a friend, or a buddy, or a woman he could date. She was a *suspect*.

He'd gone too far—pushed her to confess. But he'd had his own reasons for that, too. If she came forward now, told them everything she knew, it would go better for her. It would show that she was willing to cooperate before being nailed with whatever charges that would stick.

And yet even as that occurred to him, he had an image in his mind of Berto pleading for his own innocence. *I didn't do it! I don't know what's happening!* He wanted a career chasing down dirty cops so he could set a few wrongs right, but he wasn't willing to lambaste an innocent woman in order to get his chance!

Jack reached the bottom of the stairs and pushed open the door, stepping out onto the street. The cold, fresh air swept around him in a welcome embrace. He'd been sweating, he realized.

A woman was walking by with a preschooler in tow. She gave him a cordial nod, and Jack's gaze slid past her to the cars parked along the street. There were only three, and they were all empty.

Whoever had dropped off this most recent

note had come and gone. But he had to wonder…did they know about the notes the police had been planting? Or was this a weird coincidence? Because Liv's cousin Tanya was in communication with her ex-husband. She could have passed that information along, and Evan might have decided to contribute to the fun.

But why now? Like Liv said, her ex had been friendly lately. She and Evan seemed on rather good terms considering the fact that they were divorced, so why would Kornekewsky suddenly decide to scare her to pieces with a seriously creepy note?

Jack's mind was spinning. Or—and this was a possibility—she *was* innocent, and she really was getting jerked around from all sides. He was wary about believing that one because he *wanted* it to be true. And that was the problem from the start—Jack was emotionally involved with this woman. And he was supposed to be keeping that under control.

When Jack looked at Liv, he didn't just see an accumulation of evidence or lack thereof. He saw Liv—a beautiful woman, a sharp mind, a sweet soul. He'd thought he could separate his attraction to her from the case, but this wasn't just attraction. Yes, she was beautiful—alluring, voluptuous, ever so kissable. But he wanted more than simply getting her into his arms. He wanted to protect her, to soothe her fears, to make her smile. He wanted to hear her ideas, enjoy her company. None of that pointed to a purely physical attraction.

And he'd started to worry about what jail would do to her. All signs had suggested she was involved in her ex-husband's schemes, but Jack had gotten to know her over the last couple of weeks. He'd dealt with a lot of shady characters in his time. They all claimed innocence and lied through their teeth, but Liv wasn't like them. The kind of fear he saw in her eyes couldn't be faked. Even though she'd had her name on those accounts, and even though she'd delivered some documents, it was possible that she'd been manipulated.

It was also possible that he was being manipulated.

A police cruiser drew up to the curb, and Jack opened the front door.

"Here's the evidence," Jack said. "It was handled as briefly as possible."

McDonald accepted the bagged note, turning it over a couple of times as he looked at it. "Pretty, pretty Liv…" McDonald grimaced. "This is a departure from the ordinary."

"Yes, it is," Jack agreed. "I don't like it. Something's up."

"I'll bring it in," his colleague said. "Do you need any more assistance?"

"No, I'm good. I'm just doing a perimeter check, then I'll go back up and see if some time has made Liv more inclined to talk."

"Sounds good," McDonald replied. "I'll let the chief know."

Jack slammed the door and gave McDonald a nod. He didn't want anyone else nosing into this, he realized, because he wanted to be sure first. He needed to know what was going on.

The cruiser disappeared around the corner, and Jack pulled out his cell phone. He dialed the chief's number. It rang once, then the chief picked up.

"That you, Talbott?"

"Yes, sir, it's me," Jack replied. "I'm curious to know if Tanya has been in contact with Evan Kornekewsky in the last few days."

"We've checked her phone records, and there have been several phone calls from suspicious numbers," the chief confirmed. "If Evan is making the calls, he's using burner phones, though, because we can't seem to catch him."

"He'd know how to evade surveillance," Jack said.

"As well as the rest of us," the chief said with a bitter laugh. "What's your sense here, Talbott?" the chief asked.

"I don't know," Jack replied. "But Liv just received a letter from the town informing her that her property value has skyrocketed, and she owes a large chunk of change in property taxes."

"There have been some news stories this morning," the chief said. "The value of the land around here just jumped due to minable gold."

"And Liv looks genuinely upset. She can't afford to pay the new taxes."

"It's genius," the chief said ruefully. "If she can't afford her taxes, the only solution is for her to sell."

"It would seem, except there's been no offer to buy her out, as far as I know. She's simply sitting on this property, unable to pay her taxes."

"Hmm." The chief sucked in an audible breath. "Okay, let's review what we've got here. Liv Hylton moved from Denver back to Eagle's Rest, where her ex-husband, Evan, has been applying pressure to elderly landowners in the area. Her name was on all the accounts used for buying and selling. She has been reported to be the one to hand-deliver documents for signing to at least two of the complainants. She's hosted a chess night in her store for a group of older people including Nate Lipton, who was the first resident to report being pressured to sell his house at a deep loss. And now, suddenly, she's receiving notes we haven't planted... Any chance that one of the homeowners who lost their investment is getting some revenge?"

"It's always a possibility," Jack admitted. "She's scared, and I'm willing to bet she's as confused as she claims. I've pushed her really hard, and she's not cracking."

"Jack, I'm going to point something out here—" the chief began.

"I've gotten too personally involved," Jack concluded.

"Yes."

"I know." Jack sighed. "And I see all the evidence against her. It's circumstantial, though, except for delivering those documents. It's possible that she didn't know the pressure her husband was putting on these people. At least that's what her lawyer will surely argue."

It might even be what Jack would argue at this point.

"Unless you can get a confession," the chief pointed out.

Jack was silent, considering. "I put on some pretty big pressure in there to get her to talk, so I'd better back off for a bit. I don't want to spook her."

"I'll trust your instinct there," the chief replied. "She's going to need to sell—and if she turns to her ex-husband and suggests that others do the same, we'll have collusion."

It was genius…and it would have spun right past him.

There was a shuffle behind him, and Jack's heart thudded to a stop. He slowly turned. Liv stood in the open doorway, her clear green gaze fixed on him, her expression stunned. He hadn't heard that outside door open, and by the look on her face, he wasn't going to be able to save this. He pulled his phone away from his ear, and the chief said something he didn't make out.

"I'll give you a call back, sir," Jack said, hanging up the call.

Liv didn't move. The biting breeze ruffled her hair around her face, and she swallowed hard. She opened her mouth as if to speak, but nothing came out. Her cheeks were pale, and for a moment he was afraid she might collapse. But then the glitter in her eyes transformed from shock to blistering rage.

"Liv—" Jack took a step toward her, but she put a trembling hand out to stop him.

"You're *investigating* me?"

CHAPTER THIRTEEN

LIV'S MIND SPUN. More lies, more confusion. Jack was here to protect her from whomever was leaving these threatening notes…wasn't he? But from what she just overheard of that one-sided conversation, *she* was the suspect! She'd been around cops long enough to know how this worked, and the realization was like a slap in the face.

Her stomach dropped. Jack had been lying…and she'd trusted him. She'd truly thought she'd spot a liar if ever faced with one again after her divorce from the best liar she'd ever known, but she hadn't spotted him. She'd been swept right along with the lie. But it wasn't just that she'd been lied to. It was that Jack had lied to her—Jack, the one man she'd thought she could trust.

"Liv—" Jack repeated, and she could see the agony swimming in his eyes. There was no doubt about it—she'd caught him.

"No!" She pulled her shaking hand against her body. Realizing that she was in full public view, she looked around. A man eyed them curiously from across the street.

"Let's talk inside," Jack said, lowering his voice.

It was a good idea. She turned on her heel and stomped up the stairs, his heavy footfalls echoing hers as they headed back up to her apartment. She pushed open the front door and spun to face him as he followed her inside. She felt a familiar emotion welling up—betrayal.

"So what's going on?" she demanded. "I'm the suspect now? I thought you were here to protect me!"

"I am here to protect you." He met her gaze, and she realized in that moment how much stock she'd been putting in his ability to look her in the eye.

"Who were you talking to? You called him sir, whoever it was. Your boss? You said you'd been pressuring me to talk, so you'd better back off for a bit."

He was silent, his lips pressed together.

"What does that *mean*?" She wanted to shout, but she didn't. She'd caught him—why wouldn't he just tell her what was going on? It was infuriating!

"Liv, it's complicated," he said at last.

"I imagine so," she hissed back. "Lying tends to be."

"I'm not lying, I'm—"

"—investigating?" she finished for him. "From my side, what's the difference?"

"I know how this looks," Jack said. "And all can say is that an investigation will only get to the truth, and if you really don't know what Evan has been up to, then the truth is in your favor."

"So you think that Evan is up to something and that I'm involved."

"That's the working theory. Is there any truth in it?" he asked.

"No!" She gritted her teeth and turned away from him, then spun back around. "How am I connected? Will you tell me that much?"

"It's—" He looked ready to deny knowing, then he shrugged. "It's through some real estate deals that went through joint accounts. Plus, you were the one to deliver documents."

Her stomach sank. She'd been an idiot…

"This place—" She gestured blindly around her. "My store… Is it connected, too? What happened?"

"There were some complaints about the sale—that's how it started. And it's more involved than that. Look, I'm not supposed to even tell you that much."

"So how much of what's happened to me is true? Did I even have a stalker? Or was that made up to gain my trust?"

Jack sighed. "No, you didn't."

"So you planted letters to freak me out…" Her mind went through the frightening evidence. "The pictures. Did you leave those pictures on my doorstep?" she said, gasping.

"Not personally," he replied with a shake of his head. "But yes, they were a plant."

"A plant! You make it all sound so civilized, but it isn't! You terrorized me!"

"I'm sorry, Liv. I am! But we needed to know."

She didn't care to listen to his excuses. They were the police—they'd band together regardless, and she wasn't foolish enough to place the full blame for an investigation on Jack's shoulders. But he'd been the face of it all. He'd been the one leading her down the garden path, making her believe anything he wanted…

Just like Evan. Lies and subterfuge. And she'd fallen for it all a second time.

"I couldn't figure it out—nothing made sense!" Liv pulled a hand through her hair, tugging it away from her face. "I couldn't figure out who would want to chase me away or hurt me. But no one did! No one wanted to get rid of me, did they? I was right—this all felt wrong because it was all an elaborate lie!"

And for the first time, it all added up! This looked crazy because it was supposed to look crazy. They were trying to knock her off-balance so that she'd tell them about her ex. If they wanted to know about him, all they had to do was ask her! She would have been happy to share all she knew.

"Yes, the first couple of letters were fake," Jack said with a shake of his head. "But not all of it. The woman in the rain—we didn't send her. We didn't slash your tire. And that latest letter wasn't our plant, either. Someone *is* threatening you—"

"I don't believe you," she said, her voice low but steady.

"Liv—"

"Why *should* I believe you?"

Jack sighed, then licked his lips. "I get it. You're angry. We've scared you and put you through the wringer. But I'm telling you the truth, Liv. What started out as a simple investigation has gotten a whole lot more complicated."

"You're telling me the truth—just like you did before?" she demanded. "I asked if I was in danger, and you made sure I was good and freaked out. All for what, exactly?" She shook her head, the pieces falling slowly into place. "And what did you find out about me, Jack? Anything that would stick in court?"

She heard the disdain dripping from her own voice, but she couldn't help herself. "You found nothing because there was nothing to find! I have no business with my ex-husband! I'm the only one who has been telling the truth!"

Liv looked around the apartment. Her home—her fresh start away from Evan, his lies, his new wife… This store she'd opened with such a full heart and so many hopes for her future… It was all tainted now. She'd wanted time to herself to get comfortable in Eagle's Rest again, to find her niche. All she'd wanted was some peace and quiet to recover from all that had happened, and what had she gotten? A cop who convinced her she was in danger in order to get in close enough to sift through her personal life!

And idiot that she was, she'd trusted him.

That hurt the most—that she'd opened up. She'd told him things she hadn't told other people. She'd welcomed him into her home, cooked for him, talked with him so freely that now she felt a rush of dread. What all had she said? Had she been accidentally incriminating herself? She'd had no idea she was under any kind of suspicion—not until today, at least, when Jack had started pushing her for some sort of confession.

"And what about Evan?" she asked. "What did he do, exactly?"

"We need more evidence against him," Jack said with a faint shrug. "We're pretty sure we know what he's up to, and eventually we'll nail it all down, but right now—"

Jack's expression was dismal.

"But what did he *do*?" she repeated, her voice shaking.

"Fraud." Jack met her gaze tiredly. "And I can't tell you more than that."

"Fraud…" she murmured. Lies built upon lies. How many untruths and betrayals had she navigated in the past years? She'd thought she was free of it now that she was single again. She could put her life together in the sunlight, live openly and happily. She'd thought she'd see it coming a mile away this time, because if nothing else, her painful divorce had been a wealth of experience.

"I have one question for you, Jack," Liv said quietly.

"Okay." Jack stepped closer, those dark eyes still riveted to her face.

"When you kissed me—what was that?"

He shut his eyes for a moment. "That was—" He looked toward the window, then exhaled a sigh. "Like I said at the time, that was a mistake."

She nodded slowly. Was it ever! So he'd been investigating her, and he'd crossed that line. It was more than a mistake. It was a fireable offense.

"I want you out of my home," Liv said, her voice trembling. "Right now."

"Liv, you do have someone after you—"

"Get out, Jack." Her voice firmed and she looked around the living room. His duffel bag was packed neatly in a corner as it had been since his arrival. She'd thought it was cleanliness on his part, but it wasn't. He'd been prepared for a quick exit this whole time—prepared for this moment.

Jack studied her for a beat, and she couldn't read the emotions that flickered deep behind his gaze. He nodded twice, then headed over to the corner where his bag sat. He bent and picked it up.

"Liv, you have every right to be angry with me, but please understand that this is far from over. You *are* being targeted, and I have no idea who it is."

"Just go—" Her voice cracked, and she sucked in a stabilizing breath.

Jack walked to the door and pulled it open. He cast her one more look of regret, then stepped outside and pulled the door shut behind him. Liv swept forward and flicked the dead bolt into place.

She stood there for a moment, her heart hammering in her throat. He was gone—it was over, whatever this had been. And she was alone in her new home once again.

As it should be.

But a shiver crept down her back, because while she'd kicked out the man who'd lied to her for the last two weeks, she had more to fear than Jack Talbott. There was the ex-husband who seemed to be closing in, and who just might drag her down with him if he was involved in something illegal. There was the cousin who'd maintained a relationship with her ex behind her back, a woman who'd stared at her in rainy darkness, someone who'd slashed her tire and now a new letter, so much creepier than the last…

The woman in the rain hadn't been a police plant—or so Jack claimed. And neither was the flat tire or that last letter. *Pretty, pretty Liv.* She shuddered. Had he been lying to keep her afraid and dependent on him? Or was someone really targeting her? And how could she possibly figure out what was true and what was made up for the sake of the investigation?

Liv was living in the cozy town of Eagle's Rest, with her family and longtime friends, and she'd never felt more alone in her life.

The tears started to flow.

JACK SAT IN his car. He rubbed his hands over his face and heaved a sigh. He didn't feel right leaving her unprotected, but she was certainly done with him. He couldn't blame her, either.

He'd been stupid to have updated the chief so close to her home. He should have walked farther away, been more aware of his surroundings. He'd pushed her—another mistake. But he'd wanted to make sure that if she was involved, she confessed early enough to get off with a plea bargain. It was his job to find the truth, but he wasn't interested in putting Liv Hylton behind bars. If she was connected to her ex-husband's ruse, Jack was now quite certain that she hadn't entered into it knowingly or willingly. But once a person was trapped, they could be manipulated. And if Evan was still manipulating her—

Jack leaned down so he could look up at her apartment. She stood in the window, then pulled the curtains, blocking his view. Blast it! He wasn't the threat. But try to convince her of that now…

Jack pulled out his cell phone and dialed the chief's number. The chief picked up on the first ring.

"So you've lost your cover," the chief said, forgoing a greeting.

"Yes, sir."

"All right…we'll pull you out and put another officer in as soon as she cools down."

"Sir, I know I don't have a lot of say in this, but she's scared enough as it is. And now she's scared of us. She's not going to come running back to the police at this point. She's upset, she feels betrayed and she's trying to figure out who she can trust."

"Exactly, and she no longer trusts you," the chief said.

"I know that, sir, but—" was he crazy to be asking this? "—sir, I need another chance with her."

"I'm not sure that's wise," the chief replied. "You've tried and failed to repair this. We've been listening through the bugs."

"I'm not so convinced that she's guilty, sir," Jack said.

"Based on what, exactly?" the chief asked.

"Based on my gut instinct. She's genuinely

afraid, and when she opens up, she doesn't sound guilty. Confused, yes. Besides, she's got someone out there threatening her, and you've seen that note. It makes my skin crawl. My bet is that she's innocent, but there's someone blaming her for Evan's handiwork."

"You're letting your personal feelings sway you, Talbott. What was she talking about— you kissing her? I thought we discussed boundaries."

Jack had known that would come back and bite him. He'd known it in the moment he'd pulled her into his arms, and he'd done it, anyway. It was stupid—beyond stupid. He was playing with his career here!

"It was a mistake, sir. I know it. And nothing ever went beyond a kiss. I swear."

"You realize that this taints your integrity in the case."

"I get that, but this isn't about any attraction between us. I knew her before, and I know her better now," Jack said firmly. "Someone found out about our letter planting, and they took over. I'm willing to bet it's someone close to her—someone she confides in. But the Liv Hylton I know is honest, straightforward and determined to start her life over as far from her ex-husband as possible."

"And the property sales? What about her delivering the documents?"

"She might not have known what Evan was up to. It's a possibility. She's scared, sir. We can't blame her for that!"

The chief was silent for a moment. "We'll continue monitoring anything we can get from the bugs in her apartment, and in the meantime, you can continue the investigation and see where it leads you. But stay away from her."

"Thank you, sir," Jack said, a flood of relief washing over him. "I appreciate that. She needs police protection, though, whether she realizes it or not."

"I've got an officer on the way to her apartment now. I'll post a cruiser in front of her building. She'll be safe. But, Talbott…"

"Sir?"

"Keep your personal feelings out of this. We need evidence and a conviction. I'm writing you up for inappropriate contact with a suspect and compromising a case. This is serious, Talbott, and there will be disciplinary consequences. If you even come close to crossing lines with Ms. Hylton again, you'll be suspended until further notice and I'll personally recommend your demotion and possible dismissal."

Jack's stomach sank. He hadn't expected anything less, but it still quickened his blood to hear it. He'd worked long and hard for his career, and a misstep like this could cost him everything he'd worked for.

"I understand, sir."

"Take the night off, go home. Get your priorities in order. I need you back in the morning with a clear mind. In the meantime, we'll continue working the case without you."

"Yes, sir."

Jack ended the call and glanced up at the building once more. He didn't belong in that apartment with Liv—he knew that—but somehow the last week had become more meaningful to him than it should have. He'd miss seeing her in the morning, figuring out dinner with her, hearing her talk about chess and the books she loved... She'd been the most pleasurable assignment he'd ever had, and the most dangerous for his career. And he couldn't blame her for a bit of it—this was all on him.

But she was also in danger, and he was going to have to leave her safety up to other officers. Logically, that shouldn't be a problem. He entrusted his own life to other officers every day, but something in his gut just wouldn't settle down.

The chief of police had warned him off, and if Jack knew what was good for him, he'd do as he was told and go back to his hotel room. He'd have to accept any discipline coming his way and hope to ride it all out. His opinion wasn't going to change anything in the course of an investigation. They'd follow the evidence, just like they always did.

But something had been nagging at the back of Jack's mind... If Evan Kornekewsky knew about the minable gold under this town, then he couldn't be the only one. There were more people involved here, and Jack needed to figure out who they were.

A cruiser approached from the west, and he spotted an officer he recognized. He gave her a salute and she flashed her lights at him. She'd take over in guarding Liv. It would have to be good enough, because he didn't have any other choice.

If he wanted a job come morning, he'd better clear out and do his investigating away from Liv. He had a few things he wanted to check into at city hall. And he needed to find the town's most cynical journalist. They needed evidence, and Jack was going to find it.

CHAPTER FOURTEEN

LIV WATCHED AS various cruisers took turns parking in front of her building. They seemed to trade off every three or four hours. Guarding her must be the most boring post in this sleepy town! And yet when the sun set that night and a dull, driving rain started up, Liv couldn't help but look toward the spot on the pavement where the woman had stood with that stroller…

The spot was empty. Of course. She told herself she was just spooking herself for nothing, but she was even more aware that she was alone in this apartment. And there was no longer a beefy cop to stand between her and danger.

Not up here in her apartment, at least. And the cop currently down there had the light on in the cab of his vehicle, was bobbing away to music no one else could hear, and seemed to be eating some Chinese takeout at the same time. So much for discretion. She could probably cartwheel past the cruiser and the cop wouldn't notice.

Liv watched him for another moment, then turned from the window. She should probably contact a lawyer, but right now, she didn't have any ready money.

She'd expected more from Jack Talbott. He'd suspected her all along—they all had. And she'd been blithely going along with anything Jack suggested, thinking that she was being smart—cooperating with the police who were trying to protect her.

But the cops weren't on her side. Sure, they wanted to keep her in one piece, but they also wanted to prove her guilty of some sordid connection with Evan! And she had no idea what Evan had even done besides that nebulous description of "property fraud!"

She picked up her cell phone and looked at it for a moment. Dare she call him? She could sit tight, be good and hope that the police would recognize her innocence, but she was already a suspect.

Liv dialed her ex-husband's cell phone number and let it ring. On the third ring, Serena picked up.

"Hello?" She sounded groggy.

"Hi, could I talk to Evan, please?"

"May I ask… Wait, Liv?"

"That's right. I need to talk to my ex-husband. Is he there?"

"No, he's busy." Serena suddenly sounded very much awake, and her voice was tight.

There was a murmur in the background, a muffled back-and-forth between Serena and Evan, and then Evan came on the line. "Liv, what's going on?"

Liv's mouth went dry. If he was up to something, he wouldn't tell her. And she didn't want to reveal too much information, either. What was she even thinking?

"I'm sorry to disturb you," she said. "I'm just wondering about my property here in Eagle's Rest. It seems that someone is really angry that I've moved back."

"Really?" Evan's voice softened. "Why? You're home, aren't you?"

"I've gotten some threatening letters."

"I mean, how threatening?" Evan asked with a short laugh.

"Very."

"Okay…well… Are you asking me as a police officer, or are you asking me as a friend?"

"You aren't my friend, Evan," she snapped. "I'm asking you as my ex-husband. Was there was some sort of complication in the purchase of my building?"

"None. I don't know what to say. You were there for all of that, Liv!"

He sounded so relaxed that it would feel natural enough to go along with what he was saying. The words *You're right. Sorry to bother you* were on her tongue, but she bit them back. He wasn't right—he was just smooth.

"I was there for *part* of it," Liv replied. "You did the initial haggling while I was away at my brother's wedding in England. And we got it for a steal."

"That's an ugly word, Liv." He sounded reproachful.

She smiled bitterly to herself. "Sorry. We got an amazingly low price."

"I highly doubt anybody is upset that you got a good deal five years ago," Evan said with a sigh. "Now, it's late, Liv."

"It wasn't *my* deal, Evan," she said curtly.

"You signed off on it," he snapped back. "Now, Serena has been infinitely patient here—"

"Apparently not as patient as I was," she retorted.

"Good night, Liv." And he hung up. She stared at her phone, her teeth gritted.

"Idiot!" she muttered under her breath. So

very noble of him to protect his wife's interests against *her*!

Liv resented the fact that she'd even given him a retort. It made her seem petty and jealous when she was anything but. Betrayed? Absolutely! But not jealous. Not anymore, at least. Even if Evan came begging on hands and knees, she wouldn't take him back. Serena could have him, if she could manage to hold him. He was greasier than even the new Mrs. Kornekewsky imagined. Hot Pants could perch over his cell phone every waking hour, and if Evan wanted to cheat on her, he'd do just that.

Liv went back to the window and looked down into the street. The cruiser was gone, and there wasn't another car in its place. The wind picked up again and drove a sheet of drizzle into the window. She shivered, then looked over her shoulder at her living room once more.

The low light, once so warm and inviting, seemed eerie. And the couch where Jack had been sleeping these last few nights seemed so clean and sparse. Tears rose in her eyes, and she attempted to blink them back. She'd gotten used to Jack being around…even started to count on him. She didn't want him back, either, but she did miss what she *thought* she'd had with him—an actual friendship.

"I'm the idiot," she whispered to herself.

She crossed the room briskly and flicked on the overhead light. Then she went to the side tables and flicked on those lamps, then into the kitchen and turned on the fluorescent light with its annoying hum. She flipped on every light switch in the apartment. Lamps glowed on tables, fixtures blazed overhead. It would cost a fortune in electricity, but Liv didn't care. She wasn't leaving one dusky corner tonight.

It would be strange to sleep in the brightness, but if she turned the lights off, she wouldn't sleep at all.

THE NEXT DAY, Liv opened the store as usual. It was a busy morning, and she made several large sales. A local church put in a bulk order for their ladies' book club, and two older women came in with lists of books for their grandchildren to start their Christmas shopping. Hylton Books seemed to be just what Eagle's Rest had been waiting for—most of the town, at least. There was still the question of who wanted her out of business so badly.

The rain from the night before continued. It drummed the sidewalk, puddles filling and wind gusting the steady downpour into the faces of passersby. They ducked behind umbrellas and dashed from vehicles into stores. Outside the display window, Liv could see a cruiser on the street once more. Inside was the female cop again, and when she spotted Liv looking, she nodded in acknowledgment.

Liv stepped away from the window. She had no idea whom to trust anymore. The police were suspicious of her. Her ex-husband was "handling" her like he always had. And the one man she thought she could trust had been lying to her from the get-go. She'd come home because she wanted to belong somewhere. That's what home was all about—having people you could trust to both criticize you to your face and have your back when you were vulnerable. Yet she felt more out of place, more unwelcome here, than she'd imagined possible.

The store's front door opened, and the bell dingled cheerfully. Tanya pushed inside, her head ducked down. She shook out her umbrella before looking up, and Liv felt a flood of relief to see her cousin's friendly face. Tanya shuddered dramatically. She wore a pair of tartan-patterned rubber boots and a tan-colored trench coat that was drenched, despite the umbrella.

"What weather!" Tanya laughed, unbuttoning her coat. "How are you doing?"

"I'm great." A socially acceptable lie. She wasn't in the mood to tell anyone about Jack just yet. She wasn't sure how she felt about it all—or more the point, she didn't know how she was supposed to feel about him.

"Yeah?" Tanya came farther into the store and glanced around. It was empty for the moment, but the morning's sales had Liv optimistic, at least. "Where's your bodyguard?"

Liv's smile slipped. "Um. Gone. There's a cop out front, though."

"Gone?" Tanya's eyebrows lifted. "What happened to him?"

"We had a falling-out." Liv sighed. "I don't really want to talk about it."

"What happened?" Tanya pressed. "He seemed…so nice."

"He had a job," Liv said. "We went over this. Not a real boyfriend. This isn't a breakup."

"No?" Her cousin didn't look convinced. "Then I take it he isn't coming to Rick and Amy's wedding."

The wedding! Liv shut her eyes and grimaced. She'd forgotten about it with all the drama lately. Was there any way to get out of attending?

"You forgot," Tanya said.

"I did." Liv sighed. "And I was looking forward to having a fake boyfriend to trot out with me. I guess I'll have to do the single life sooner or later. I might as well start now, right?"

"I really thought I saw a spark between the two of you," Tanya said. "Like a genuine spark. You looked… I don't know. Happy. In control."

"I don't know what to tell you." Liv didn't want to listen to this. She hadn't been in control at all—it had all been a farce at her expense. "It's over. No more playacting."

"But the way he looked at you." Tanya blew out a breath. "He didn't look at any other woman like that! And right about now, I'd give my eyeteeth to have my boyfriend look at me that way."

"He wasn't my boyfriend!" Liv said, but then reconsidered her cousin's words. "Wait… do you have someone, Tanya?"

"Me?" Tanya's face colored. "We're talking about you!"

"Not anymore!" This was more comfortable ground, and Liv felt the smile return to her face. "Who is he? Do I know him?"

"You—" Tanya pressed her lips together. "You definitely wouldn't approve."

"Since when?" Liv pressed. "I'm more open-minded than you think. Look at me— I'm a single woman again. Who is he?"

"I'm not saying," Tanya replied, and from the look in her eye, Liv knew she wouldn't get much further on that track.

"Then what's he like?" Liv asked. "You can tell me that, can't you?"

"He's sweet." Tanya shrugged weakly. "But not just sweet, you know? Like he's all man, and he makes me feel like I'm all woman. But he understands me like no one else has. I can't see him too often, but in between visits, he talks to me every day. I wake up to a good-morning text, and before I go to sleep, he tells me that he's thinking of me…"

"So it's long-distance?" Liv asked.

"Stop it!" Tanya retorted. "Quit being such a detective."

"Well, either it's long-distance or he's married!" Liv laughed. "So which one is it?"

Tanya's face flushed, and she looked away.

"He's *married*?" Liv felt all the amusement drain out of her. She'd been on the receiving end of that kind of behavior, and her cousin was right that she wouldn't approve.

"It's *long-distance*," Tanya retorted. "He lives in Denver, okay? So I don't see him too often. But that's not the point, is it? The point is that he makes me feel beautiful."

"Yeah, I know that feeling…" Liv sighed. Jack had made her feel beautiful, too, for all that it mattered. "Is this the real thing? I mean, is it love?"

Tanya nodded. "Yeah, it's love."

"Oh, Tanya…" Liv smiled wistfully. "I'm happy for you! You deserve a good guy. And one of these days, you'll have to introduce us to him."

"Yeah…" Tanya didn't look entirely convinced about that, but from where Liv was standing, she couldn't hold off forever. What was she going to do, disappear into Denver and never see her family again? But if Tanya wanted some privacy with her newfound love, who was Liv to quibble?

"So what happened with you and Jack?" Tanya asked. "Tit for tat, Liv."

"Fine," Liv conceded. "He turned out to be just as career-focused as my idiot ex-husband. It wasn't about me, it was about the job. And it turns out that he's a really, really good actor."

"You're saying all that was fake?" Tanya shook her head. "I don't believe it."

"It was. He actually suspects me in some criminal investigation!"

"You!" Tanya's eyes widened. "That's impossible!"

That's what Liv had thought, too, until very recently.

"Not entirely. There was some sort of complaint in the sale of this place. It's connected to fraud somehow."

"What?" Tanya shook her head. "No, that can't be right. Besides, she didn't sell it to Evan. She sold it to both of you."

Evan's argument coming out of Tanya's mouth. Liv's breath caught in her throat, and it was like the store slowed to a crawl around her.

"Tanya…"

"I'm just saying," Tanya said with a shake of her head. "You and Evan can back each other up. You were involved in that sale. From the start."

"Not from the start," Liv countered. "I was at my brother's wedding in England when Evan found the place and made the first offer. I came back in time to sign papers—that's it!"

Tanya shrugged. "On paper, your name is there. Your signature. I know you don't like Evan, but he needs your help. You need to back him up in this. If you support him, this goes away. It's easy."

"It goes away…" What was happening here?

"It's something to think about, Liv." Tanya met her gaze.

"When did you last talk to my ex-husband?" Liv asked.

Tanya rolled her eyes. "Who cares?"

"I do. Was it last night? When he was telling you that he was thinking of you before you went to sleep?"

Tanya stilled, and for a moment, all was silence between them. Had Liv gone too far? She'd just accused her cousin of getting involved with her married ex! This was the cousin who had been by her side through her tumultuous divorce, giving her moral support and being the voice of reason in the midst of all that chaos. What was she even doing? Was she so turned around in her own personal life that she'd hack apart the relationships that mattered most to her? Remorse rose up inside her. She was suspecting everyone of everything now, and she had gone too far.

"Tanya—" Liv took a step toward her cousin.

"He loves me!" Tanya interrupted. "I know you find that hard to believe, but he *loves* me!"

Liv stopped, her cousin's words swimming through her head but not quite landing.

"I know it didn't work between the two of you, and I'm not excusing what he did!"

Tanya went on. "But Serena doesn't understand him. He's got a soft heart, and Serena just keeps hurting him again and again, and he wants out! He's going to divorce her!"

"So you're... Wait." Liv swallowed hard. "Tanya, you're sleeping with Evan?"

"It isn't as sordid as you make it sound," Tanya retorted tightly. "I'm in love with him, and he's in love with me. The situation is just a little complicated. You can't exactly respect that sham of a marriage!"

"No, I don't," Liv breathed. "But once upon a time, I was the one who supposedly didn't understand him... And one day, that'll be you, too."

Her cousin had been sleeping with Evan. It was all too much. Tanya wasn't supposed to be that stupid! She knew what Evan was like from everything Liv had told her. Why would she do this—to Liv or to herself?

"I'll look after my own interests," Tanya said, then she licked her lips. "I need to go."

Liv had nothing to say. Tanya turned and walked briskly toward the door. Liv stood there in the center of her store, her heart sinking within her.

Tanya...her cousin, her first friend. Now this was betrayal, and she felt so tired and worn that she could sit down on the floor and cry. But she wouldn't.

Tanya looked back at Liv once more, and her expression was conflicted. Her cousin was guilty—that much was clear. And she was scared, too.

"Liv, back him up!" Tanya repeated. "You can both get out of this unscathed! Just back him up, and it goes away!"

Then she pushed out into the rain, and the door swung shut. Liv let out a slow breath. And now there was one more person who had betrayed her...one more person she couldn't trust.

And as stupid as it was, the only thing Liv could think right now was that she wished she could talk to Jack...because the Jack she'd known would understand all this. He'd give some perspective. His quiet strength would be so very comforting...

But that wasn't the real Jack, and she couldn't forget it. The real Jack thought she was tied up in Evan's ugliness. And the real Tanya was in bed with Evan...

How deep did this go?

JACK WAS GRATEFUL the chief had let him stay on the case, though he regretted having to steer clear of Liv. They needed boots on the street to suss out more evidence, though, and Jack was willing. He had a theory, but before he told anyone about it, he needed some evidence of his own. So he spent the day poring over local news stories on microfiche in the library. They hadn't digitized them yet—a job for an intern, probably. The librarian had never been asked for so much information at once, and she was having the time of her life pulling out box after box of microfiche.

Jack found what he was looking for—not evidence, exactly, but it certainly fed into his current theory.

The next morning dawned cloudy and windy, but at least the rain had stopped. Jack knocked on the door of a little house at the end of a raggedy-looking street. A dog barked inside in response to his knock, but there wasn't any other movement. He sighed. This was the last known address for Brent Villeneuve, a disgraced local reporter who had been fired two years ago when he was accused of some sexual impropriety with the mayor's daughter.

Jack stepped back and looked around. The yard was ill-kempt. The leaves hadn't been raked yet this season, and they appeared to cover an overgrown lawn. A pile of local newspapers leaned against the corner of the porch, and Jack would have wondered if the guy even lived here anymore if it weren't for the dog barking inside. He knocked again, this time harder. There was the scrape of a window opening above.

"What?" a growly voice demanded, and Jack stepped off the porch to get a better look at the speaker. A gray-haired man with deep creases in his face and a raspy, three-day stubble on his chin stood in an open window wearing a bathrobe. Despite his ragged appearance, Jack recognized the man from his column photo.

"I'm Jack Talbott from the local PD," Jack said. "I was hoping to ask you a few questions."

"About what?"

Jack shaded his eyes. "I guess we could holler at each other right here, but I figured you might want more privacy from your neighbors."

Jack glanced over his shoulder and spotted a middle-aged woman walking her dog, her steps slowing as she looked at them curiously.

"Fine." The window closed with a bang, and a minute later the front door swung inward. The dog, which had sounded bigger than it was, currently sat nestled in its master's arms. "Come inside, then."

Jack stepped into the gloom. Despite the terrible appearance of the yard, the inside of the house was immaculately kept. Brent led the way into the kitchen and nodded to the table.

"Sit down if you want," he said. "I'm making coffee." He deposited the dog on the floor in a scramble of nails against linoleum.

Jack wasn't sure if he was being offered coffee or not, but he took a seat. The dog growled at him a few times, then took up a protective stance around Brent's bare ankles.

"So what do you want?" Brent asked after he'd started the coffee maker.

"I need a few details," Jack said. "And you're the one who knows the most around here."

"Depends who you ask," Brent replied. "Local opinion isn't in my favor these days."

"Because of Mayor Nelson's daughter's accusations," Jack clarified.

"She didn't accuse anything. Her father did. But she went along with it. And I get it—the optics weren't in our favor. She was twenty-two and had her whole life ahead of her. I was fifty-eight and a stubborn old codger. But there was no sexual assault involved."

"I believe you," Jack replied.

"What?" Brent eyed him suspiciously. "You'd be the first."

"There were no criminal charges," Jack replied. "And if the mayor's daughter was assaulted, there would have been charges. Instead, there was a big public furor, you were fired from your post at the paper and then Chantilly Nelson left for law school."

"Hmm…" Brent nodded. "All right, you've earned yourself some information from me. What do you want to know about?"

"What you were investigating when the scandal erupted," Jack replied.

"Because you think the mayor used me as a diversion," Brent said with a slow nod.

"That's my theory." This had to go further than some cop in Denver picking up on a lead. But the local PD wouldn't look into the mayor without a very good reason, and Jack had been banging his head against local politics.

"No one else believed me," Brent replied. "Why should you?"

"I'm here right now, but I'm not local. I have no preconceived ideas or die-hard views one way or the other." A small lie—he was emotionally involved in this, just not in the same way the rest of the town seemed to be.

"Fine. I was looking into a local government cover-up."

"Involving property values, and the discovery of minable gold underneath this town," Jack finished for him.

"Yeah. That's right. So if you know about it, why come to me?" Brent pulled out a chair and sat down, then scooped the dog up into his lap.

"Because I need to know who knows about this minable gold," Jack said. "Exactly."

"Mayor Nelson, of course," Brent replied with a shrug.

Jack tried to cover up the swell of satisfaction at those words. That's what he'd needed to hear! Even though it had been his working theory, having Brent confirm his suspicions gave them more weight.

"And he was hell-bent on keeping me from blowing the lid off the whole thing," Brent went on. "He insisted that I needed to keep quiet about it or our town would lose out on this massive opportunity to make money."

"The town would lose out on the money." Jack frowned.

"His words, not mine," Brent replied with a shrug. "You ask me, though, I think there's a select few who are poised to make money off this."

"What makes you so sure?" Jack asked.

"First of all, three families have always held the money in this town," Brent said. "The Nelsons, the McConnellys and the Davidsons. You'll find them in all the local government—aldermen, school trustees…they get voted in because they seem to care the most. And really, who wants to be an alderman?" Brent made a face.

"Not you?"

"The pay is dismal," Brent replied. "Not the point. These three families fight among themselves for local power. Mayor Nelson is currently winning this round. Anyway, he didn't want anyone else to know about this gold until he could set up something with a local mining company. Then he could be the town's savior."

"Savior? Would a mining outfit even be popular around here?" Jack asked. "You've got a pristine area—mountains, forests, the lake…"

"Yeah, yeah, beautiful," Brent went on with a wave of his hand. "What we need are jobs. People are leaving in droves because they can't find decent work. There's the tourists who come for the wilderness and the fresh air, but they only bring so much money. But if a big mining outfit set up in town, that would bring some stable union jobs, and that's what our town needs. At least that was the way the mayor was billing it."

"So you were in favor of this," Jack said, squinting at the man.

"Not at all!" Brent barked back. "Because it's only worth something if people are willing to sell their land. And if they sell, where are they going to go? All we'll end up with is a town emptied out of the locals, and a bunch of newcomers swooping in after those jobs."

"Who owns most of the land in the downtown core?" Jack asked.

"It used to be a good mix among the Nelsons, the McConnellys and the Davidsons. But then Mayor Nelson started buying up properties here and there. Going into some real debt to do it, too. He made out like he was doing people a favor. He'd take some useless property off their hands really quietly. He acted like he was doing it out of the goodness of his heart because his family was relatively wealthy compared to everyone else. Helping out some retiree who just needed to sell. But I got wise to it."

"So the mayor was buying up land."

"And some outside buyers, too," Brent said. "Some fella with a god-awful name who married this local woman. He started picking off the properties, too."

"Kornekewsky?" Jack asked.

"Yeah, that's it. Evan Kornekewsky. He was a cop in Denver. He had some family money behind him—not a lot, but enough to get his feet wet. I didn't get that far into my investigation."

That was pointing to the evidence they needed. They could look up the property sales in the area over the last five or ten years to confirm it all, but it still indirectly connected Liv to the story. And that was the connection he was trying to test.

"The local woman—" His heart softened even at this indirect mention of Liv. "Was she involved?"

He watched Brent for any sign of deception, but Brent didn't look nervous at all.

"I don't know. But the strong-arming—that was all Kornekewsky himself. When his wife came into it, it was always at the end, delivering an envelope or something with a smile and a plate of cookies. In all my digging, she was nothing more than a delivery person. You police will investigate whoever you want, but my focus was on the husband."

No evidence that she was involved. In his heart he could feel it—she'd been telling the truth all along. She was as innocent as she looked, and Evan had been keeping her linked to his fraud for his own reasons—maybe so he could throw her under the bus later and claim she was the mastermind?

"No evidence of her pressuring people to sell?" Jack clarified.

"Not that I saw. Everything pointed to the husband," Brent said. "I was getting information on that Denver cop when Chantilly and I started up. She wasn't quite the daddy's girl that everyone thought she was. She had some real issues with her dad, and half of my appeal was that I didn't idolize him. Anyway, the mayor found out about us about the same time I started poking into those high-pressure sales. And then *pow*—it all blew up in my face."

Jack moved this new information around in his mind. "So why did Chantilly go along with it?"

"Because her father was the one paying her way through Harvard," Brent said. "You think I could afford that? I wasn't anything long-term for her. She thought I was all bitter and sexy. And maybe I was!" He chuckled. "But Chantilly's smart. She knew what she wanted, and she wanted Harvard."

"And you're not mad about that..." Jack said slowly.

"Furious. Who said I wasn't mad?" Brent shrugged. "She let her father ruin my career and my good name, and she just waltzed off. She's engaged to some twenty-five-year-old upstart. And maybe I should have seen that coming, but it's possible to dump some starry-eyed old guy without cutting his legs out from under him."

"True," Jack said. "Did she know what you knew?"

"Not all of it," Brent replied. "I wasn't a complete idiot."

Suddenly a thought occurred to him. "Chantilly—any connection to Evan Kornekewsky that you know about?"

"He was like you—all young and muscle-bound. She was attracted to him," Brent said with a shrug. "And I couldn't compete with that, could I?"

"Was she sleeping with him?" Jack asked.

"It was a short fling before she picked up with me. The Kornekewskys came back to visit family and stuff from time to time. Chantilly wasn't looking to break up a marriage. Liv Kornekewsky used to babysit Chantilly, and think what you want about her, Chantilly had her limits on who she'd till under."

So Evan had been getting it all over town… Poor Liv. He knew she hated having anyone pity her, but Jack couldn't help it. She'd deserved a whole lot better than Evan.

"So how angry are you?" Jack asked. "Are you mad enough to testify in court?"

The gurgling of the coffee machine stopped, and Brent met Jack's gaze cautiously. "Depends."

"On what?"

"I'll only do it if you don't press charges against Chantilly Nelson."

A soft spot for the woman who had allowed her father to ruin his career and reputation? Jack shook his head.

"Why?" Jack asked. "She hasn't helped you."

"I knew what I was doing." Brent winced. "Look at me. Chantilly was a beautiful woman in her early twenties. It was consensual, but she was a lot younger than me, and I feel like I owe her this much."

Jack sighed. "I'm not in a position to make those deals."

"Then I'll have to talk to someone who is," Brent replied, rising to his feet. "You want coffee?"

"No." Jack rose, too. "Thanks, though. I appreciate the chat. I'll be in touch."

"Do that." Brent reached out and they shook hands. "But I don't remember anything unless Chantilly's left alone."

Clear enough. Brent had had a weirdly inappropriate liaison with the mayor's daughter, and now he was having a weirdly inappropriate protective streak. Whatever. Jack didn't care too much about Brent's complexities, as long as he could get the man to testify.

But this didn't prove Liv's innocence, either. Not when it came to a court of law. If Jack wanted concrete proof that she wasn't involved in this scheme, he might never get it. But with every beat of his heart, he longed to find something that could cut her free of this mess. Because even if other people weren't, Jack was convinced that she was innocent.

Maybe he wasn't so different from Brent, after all. Even if Liv wasn't connected to Evan's fraud, they still had no future together. She was a suspect in what would be a very high-profile case, and she was the ex-wife of a police officer who, if Jack had his way, would be doing some serious jail time. But Internal Affairs required an officer's unquestionable integrity. Nothing could appear to sully Jack's name—and even if they couldn't find enough to press charges against Liv, doubts about her involvement would linger.

And still, Jack wanted to rescue Liv. Even if she moved on with some other guy.

CHAPTER FIFTEEN

LIV LEANED BACK in her bed, her phone tucked up against her ear. The wind howled outside her bedroom window, and she tried to ignore it, but every moan felt like it echoed inside her.

"I can't believe it," her mother said into her ear. "Tanya and *Evan*?"

"Apparently so." Liv stared up at her ceiling. "She claims to love him."

"And he's cheating on Hot Pants," her mother said wryly. "There's some justice there."

"He's cheating with my cousin!" Liv ran a hand through her hair. "How could she do this to me?"

"Evan obviously got to her." Her mother sighed. "Dear, I know you and Tanya were always close, but that girl is an idiot. She always was. She'd do anything for a boyfriend. Do you remember that high school teacher she dated?"

"She had already graduated." Liv sighed.

"Yeah, but he was fifteen years older than her, and he'd taught her from grade ten through twelve."

"I'm not saying Tanya has great taste in men," Liv countered. "I'm saying this is a personal betrayal."

"Oh, granted."

Liv shook her head. Her mother always had been the one least inclined toward drama.

"Why do you think Evan was trying to buy your lake cottage?" Liv asked.

"I have no idea." Her mother sighed. "Love nest for him and Tanya? Is that too crass to even say?"

"It might be true, though," Liv agreed. "One woman never seems to be quite enough for him, does it? Will I never be free of him?"

"You will be, dear," her mother said, "the minute you decide to be. You'll have to let him go. Emotionally wash him out so that if he walked down the street in front of your store, you'd feel nothing for him besides pity because he's the one who can't seem to get over *you*."

"Is this about me, Mom? Evan's fixation with this town, I mean."

"I'm sure his fixation with your cousin has everything to do with you," her mother replied with a bitter laugh. "As for the town…

what do I know? You said the police are convinced he's involved in some sort of fraud."

"I wish I could make sense of everything that's happened. It's the confusion that gets to me," she admitted.

"Here's what you need to know," her mother said firmly. "First of all, you're a good person, and you're worthy of better than Evan. Second, you know that you're innocent in all of this, so don't start questioning yourself. Evan is the liar and the manipulator. He's good at that—he did it all through your marriage. He made you feel crazy and question your own instincts. And third, you need a lawyer, Liv."

Liv's heart felt heavy, but she knew her mother was right. She needed someone on her side, even if she had to pay that person to be there. And she couldn't let her life get dragged down by her ex-husband. Running away from the man wasn't going to fix this. He'd chosen her cousin for a reason, and it wasn't because he'd fallen in love with her. Tanya was delightful, but Evan was no idiot, either. He'd sent her cousin with a message—back up his story.

"I know," she said. "But it costs a lot, and right now I feel like I've been hit by a truck."

"Dad and I can sell something. You're not going to be on your own."

Liv wouldn't let them do that.

"Thanks, Mom," Liv said. "But that's not necessary. I'm tired. I'm going to try to get some sleep."

"All right. Have a good night, sweetheart."

Liv smiled sadly as she hung up. Her mother was her very last bastion—the one Evan couldn't influence against her. And Tanya... stupid, stupid Tanya... What on earth was she thinking? She knew what Evan was! Or maybe she didn't care. And that hurt most of all, because Liv cared about family. She'd uprooted her city life and come back to Eagle's Rest for *family*!

Liv pried herself off her bed and grabbed her nightgown. It was time for a hot shower and a good sleep. Things would look better in the light of day. Or maybe they wouldn't, but at least there would be daylight and work to occupy her thoughts. One step at a time, one day at a time. Life would get better, and these raw emotions would be further behind her.

Liv ambled into the bathroom and deposited her phone on the counter, then leaned over and turned on the hot water. She fully intended to stay in this shower until the hot water ran out.

The steam billowed out of the bathtub as Liv dropped her robe and stepped into the drumming spray of hot water. She shut her eyes, her muscles melting under the heat. She tipped her chin up and let the water flow over her. Sometimes all she wanted was a little bit of comforting...

There was a *thump* somewhere in the apartment. Liv paused, listening. Had she heard that right? It might have come from outside—a garbage truck or something. She wasn't used to all the nighttime sounds on this street yet. She strained her ears but couldn't hear anything else.

It was nothing. She was jumpy for good reason, but she couldn't let herself slide into complete paranoia, either.

Her more immediate problem right now was her cousin, because that wasn't resolved! Tanya had walked out of the store, and neither of them had texted to say anything. Liv didn't know what Tanya could say to make any of this better. And Liv had nothing to say. She was shocked, heartbroken...and furious.

Tanya had been her best friend and steadfast ally for the last thirty-two years. And now...what? This wasn't the kind of betrayal Liv could bounce back from, and her heart felt sodden and filled with tears.

Another *thump*. This one *was* from inside the apartment, and Liv held her breath. She reached to turn off the water but pulled her hand back. No, that would only announce that she had heard. But someone was in her apartment… She sucked in a quick breath, trying to calm her clamoring heart.

Was it Jack? He hadn't returned the key yet… Had she dead-bolted the door? She stepped carefully out of the shower into the foggy bathroom and snatched up her bathrobe. It stuck to her skin as she pulled the terry cloth on, and she shivered. She grabbed her phone. Creeping to the door, she slowly turned the handle and eased it open a crack.

She couldn't see anything, but she could hear the clatter of glass breaking. She slowly shut the door again and crept to the back of the bathroom, dialing her phone with a trembling finger—

"911. What's the nature of your emergency?" a woman's voice said.

"Someone's in my apartment," Liv whispered. "I need help."

"What's your address, ma'am?"

"Seven twenty-eight Main Street, Eagle's Rest. I'm right above Hylton Books. Someone's in my home! I need help!"

She was trying to whisper, but her voice was shaking too much to do it very well. The shower was at least masking any sound she might make.

"The police are on their way, ma'am. I want you stay quiet. Where are you?"

"In the bathroom—"

"Good. Stay there and stay hidden. Don't say anything else, but remain on the line with me. I'm right here, and the police are on their way. You're going to be okay."

Liv crouched down next to the clothes hamper, her breath coming in ragged gasps. Her skin was wet and chilled next to the cold bathroom tiles, and she tugged her robe closer around her knees. It felt like ages that she crouched there—her knees starting to ache and her hands trembling with fear or cold, she wasn't sure which. The steam in the bathroom was starting to dissipate, and she was breathing hard, but she held that phone to her ear, listening to the soft breath of the 911 operator. If Liv died tonight, another sympathetic human being would hear it!

Outside the door, there was another *crash* and the *thud* of boots.

"Police!" a voice barked. Liv knew that voice, and she crumpled with relief. It was Jack. Something hit the floor with a *bang*.

"Stop—police!" A pause. "This is Officer 2962. A suspect is fleeing on foot west through the alley. Requesting backup."

"He's here," Liv breathed into the phone. "I know that cop. Thank you."

She hung up the phone and stood up just as the bathroom door opened and a gun appeared in her face. She slowly raised her hands and met Jack's drilling gaze. He was dressed in uniform this time—the crisp, dark blue fabric tugging at his muscled biceps. He held the gun in two hands, and his eyes flashed with steely intensity.

"Hi," she whispered.

"Liv... Oh, my God..." Jack lowered his weapon and crossed the tile floor in two quick steps. He pulled her against him and lowered his mouth over hers in a hard, hot kiss. She could feel the side of his gun in the small of her back, and she allowed herself the momentary luxury of sinking into those strong arms.

"Are you okay?" he asked, pulling back.

She nodded quickly. "What was that?"

"I don't know. They got out the back window—you've got a lot of broken glass, but we can take care of that. You sure you're okay?"

"I'm shaken, but I'm in one piece..." She paused, pulling her bathrobe together at her neck and eyeing him suspiciously. "How did you get here so fast?"

"I was patrolling your street when the call went out on the radio," he said. "And no, I'm not supposed to be patrolling your street, if that's your next question."

"Who was it?" she asked.

"Female. Five ten. Slim build. Armed."

"A woman?" she squinted, her mind spinning back. "I saw a woman on the street that night. You didn't believe me!"

"You're right, I didn't at first. Though you did convince me." He kept his voice low. "I'm sorry. I was blinded by our other investigation. But I'm looking into some new leads, and I'm getting somewhere—"

"All the good that does me!" she snapped. "You think I'm involved!"

The shower was still pummeling into the tub, but the steam was gone, which meant the hot water had run out. She moved toward the shower to turn off the water, but Jack caught her arm and shook his head. There was a warning in his eyes.

"Don't," he murmured.

"Why?"

"Your apartment is bugged. All but the bathroom."

Bugged? She stared at him, stricken. Why did this surprise her? She should have thought of it herself! There was a time that she'd have said she had nothing to hide. But that didn't seem to matter anymore with a police force determined to tie her to her ex-husband's crimes.

"Listen to me," he said softly, leaning closer. "The other cops will be here any second. I'm going to point out bugs, and you're going to drop them into a cup of water. Don't say anything, just do it."

"Why are you telling me?" she asked suspiciously. He'd lied to her often enough. What did he have to gain from this? She studied him uncertainly, and Jack met her gaze evenly.

"Because I know you're innocent, Liv, and I'm going to prove it."

JACK GRABBED A cup from the bathroom counter and filled it with water. Then he marched out to the living room and moved a vase to point out the tiny device. Liv snatched it up and dropped it into the water. He led her to a picture frame, pulled it back and revealed another tiny microphone taped to the wall behind it. She snatched it off the wall, taking some paint with it, and dropped it into the water. She followed him around the room in silence until all the microphones had been drowned.

"What makes you so sure I'm innocent in all of this?" Liv asked. "Do you have proof?"

"Not yet."

"But you believe me—" She turned toward him, scanning his face nervously. "You do believe me."

"Yeah, I believe you." He was tempted to leave it at that, except her taut expression hadn't relaxed. "I dug up a local journalist, and let's just say I got the confirmation I needed. But there are people who would try to make you look guilty just to have you share the blame."

"I was telling the truth… I might have been the only one!" Liv looked down at the bugs, her lips pursed. "You've all been listening to me, my conversations. When I talk to myself. When I sneeze!"

"Yes." He couldn't sugarcoat that.

"What did you hear?" Her voice trembled. In anger? He couldn't tell. "Never mind. I'm not sure I want to know. Why did you tell me?" she asked, her voice low. "You could have left them there. Is this part of some police plan to gain my trust?"

So she didn't believe him yet, either. Could he blame her?

"No, it's part of *my* plan to gain your trust."

She raised an eyebrow, her gaze icy. "What

does it matter? If you don't think I did it, then don't press charges against me."

"Because I can't keep you safe unless you trust me," he said. And maybe it was selfish of him, but when all this was past, he didn't want Liv remembering him as the lout who'd deceived her.

"Will you be in trouble?" she asked, looking down into the glass of water filled with little black mics.

Jack didn't want to think about his professional future right now. He'd done what he thought was right, and it wasn't going to be good for his career, but he could still recover if the fates were in his favor.

"Maybe. But I've got evidence that will move this case forward. I'm counting on a little forgiveness and some fast talking."

"Like you've been doing with me?" That glittering green gaze met his again.

He shot her a grudging smile. "I had that coming, but Liv—I'm the only one who's convinced that you're innocent right now. And you've got bigger problems." Jack took the cup from her hands and shoved it into the fridge. "We'll deal with those later."

"If my apartment was bugged, why didn't someone hear the break-in?"

So the shock was wearing off and she

was back to her logical, methodical self, it seemed. He'd need that brain of hers if they were going to crack this case and prove her innocence.

"That's what I want to know."

The front door opened and two more uniformed officers came inside, McDonald being one of them. They lowered their guns when they saw Jack, and they all exchanged nods. They were on the same team, after all. Even if McDonald was a joke in a uniform.

"What took so long?" Jack asked bitterly. "We're fine in here. Who's chasing down the suspect?"

"Everyone else," McDonald retorted.

Jack crossed the room and lowered his voice. "Who was listening to the surveillance?"

McDonald glowered at him. "I used the bathroom. Bad timing. What can I say?"

Jack bit back a retort. "Okay. So…"

"The chief was clear that you weren't supposed to be here," McDonald said. "We'll take it from here."

"No." Liv's voice rang out, cutting off their hissed conversation. Jack turned to see Liv standing behind him, her arms crossed. "You can arrest me if you have cause, but I'm not being babysat by any of you."

"Ma'am, your home was just burglarized," McDonald pointed out. "You need our help."

Liv looked back toward the kitchen, the floor littered with broken glass, and Jack laughed softly.

"Liv, I'm not leaving you alone here. This had nothing to do with the police. We planted a few vague notes, and the chief figured he was really upping the ante with the pictures some of the officers took of you around town over a few days. That's as nasty as we can do. This—" He gestured around them. "That's someone else. You need protection, and you've got it. So you can choose—McDonald or me."

McDonald looked surprised, then straightened his shoulders a little. Did he actually expect Liv to trust him? He repressed the urge to roll his eyes.

"Thank you, Officer McDonald, but you can go," Liv said with a sigh. "I'll take Jack. The devil you know and all that."

"It's not your choice, ma'am," McDonald replied icily.

"It damn well is!" she snapped. "If you want an officer with me, it'll be Jack. Otherwise, you can all get out!"

McDonald and the other officer took their leave. Soon enough everyone would figure out that the bugs were dead, and he'd deal with that then. In the meantime, he had a few things to hammer out with Liv.

When the door was shut and locked once more, Jack turned toward her. "Did you lock the door?"

"I must have forgotten the dead bolt."

Jack nodded slowly, looking around. "Missing anything?"

Liv looked around, then shook her head. "Not that I can tell. I don't really have anything worth stealing!"

"This was a message," he concluded, more to himself than to her. "Someone wants you terrified."

"Like you did," she said pertly, and he glanced back toward her.

"Liv, I'm sorry. That wasn't personal. I was given an assignment—that's all. We needed to get in close to you to see if you were involved. And you *aren't*."

"Except no one else believes that!" she retorted.

"Well, I do. So you made a good choice in me over McDonald. Now let's get this place cleaned up and board up that window. I'm sleeping on your couch tonight, for the record."

He was in no mood to argue about it, either. She didn't have to like him. She didn't even have to trust him 100 percent, but he'd be keeping her alive and in one piece, regardless. He looked over to where Liv stood in that lopsided bathrobe. She clutched the fabric together at her throat, and her eyes had misted with unshed tears.

"Liv—" He took a step toward her, and that green gaze flickered toward him. She was on the verge of crying, but she wasn't inviting him in.

"I'm fine," she said curtly.

She wasn't, and he knew it. But while he could stomp around here and act like the bodyguard he was, he couldn't pull her into his arms and act like the boyfriend.

"What are you, anyway?" Liv asked, eyeing him cautiously. "Are you a local cop like you said?"

"No." He cleared his throat. "I'm still based in Denver. I'm here investigating some internal issues with the police departments in Denver and the surrounding area."

"Internal Affairs?"

"Not yet. I hope to be one day, though."

"So that's what you want—to arrest fellow officers?"

"No, I want to arrest dirty officers," he snapped back. "I want to catch the guys planting evidence on fourteen-year-old kids! That's what happened to Berto, and he never pulled out of it. There are other kids, fathers, families…people being torn apart because of dirty law enforcement, and it's my life's goal to put an end to as much of it as possible. Whoever I am, it was formed by the family I love."

She nodded slowly. "So you're not after my stalker, you're after Evan."

"I'm after whoever's doing this, Liv. And yes, I suspect your ex-husband is connected. But I'm not one of those cops planting evidence. If he isn't dirty, I have no beef with him." Jack sighed. His deeper need for justice wasn't her problem. "Look, I don't know what you want to tell your family about all of this, but I'm going to be around for a bit longer."

"No need to update them on anything," she said quietly. "As far as they know, you're the adoring boyfriend, remember?"

"Okay. If that's how you want to do it."

"Do I have a choice?"

"I don't even know if I have a choice," he admitted. "The chief knows I kissed you, and he's told me to keep clear of you. I'll talk to him and see if he can understand why I rushed to the scene when I heard that 911 call. Fingers crossed."

"My cousin's wedding is this weekend," she said. "I guess that means you'd be coming to that, too."

"Let me call my boss. I'd better get that out of the way."

The phone call took about fifteen minutes. The chief wasn't pleased, but he grudgingly admitted that he understood why Jack had disobeyed his orders. And seeing as Jack was the only one Liv trusted right now, the chief agreed to let him stand in. It was a relief, because Jack could have found himself jobless or demoted. When he hung up, he came back into the room where Liv was waiting for him.

"Looks like I'm in the clear," he said. There was no way he was letting her out of his sight again until this case was wrapped up.

"Congratulations," she said drily.

"Thanks."

"What if I don't take you as my date?" she asked.

"After all that? Then I come as your bodyguard with an obvious gun." He raised one eyebrow. "Your call."

She smiled faintly. "My cousin's bride would never forgive me for drawing the attention away from her."

"So how do you want to do this?"

"You'll have to be my adoring boyfriend."

She didn't sound pleased with that arrangement. "Find an appropriate suit."

"Okay. Go get dressed. I'll start cleaning up."

Liv nodded and headed to her bedroom. The door shut softly, leaving Jack alone in the living room. He went to the kitchen and snagged a broom out of the closet. His mind was spinning. Why was Liv the target? What did she know—or what did they think she knew?

He turned his attention to sweeping up the shards of glass, his senses all on high alert. But whoever had broken in seemed to be long gone. There was a brick on the floor by the fridge—thrown there? Hard to tell. He'd missed it on his first perusal of the kitchen. A note was secured to it with a dirty plastic band. The words were written in pencil—*So pretty.*

Jack's blood chilled. Who was doing this? He could only imagine the kind of person who would lurk after a woman like this. He swallowed hard and pulled his mind back to the case at hand.

He'd gone against orders when he'd removed their surveillance, but without Liv's trust, they weren't going to get anywhere, either. All they'd heard so far were a few personal conversations with family—nothing even remotely linking her to her ex-husband.

Jack went down to his car to retrieve some plastic to cover the window for the short term. When he came back upstairs he found Liv in the living room dressed in a pair of soft pajama bottoms, slippers and a bulky sweater. Her hair was pulled back into a ponytail, and her face was clean of makeup. She looked tired and worn down.

"So are you willing to tell me what's going on now?"

Jack locked the door behind him and headed toward the kitchen with the plastic under his arm.

"There's a bit of a development," he admitted. "But first, do you have tape?"

She found the tape in a drawer and Jack stretched the plastic over the window. Liv tore off a strip of tape and they got to work blocking out the chilly night air.

"You mentioned a journalist who was disgraced a few years ago. I found him. His name is Brent Villeneuve, and he had a romantic relationship with the mayor's daughter at the same time that he was digging into this situation with the minable gold," Jack said. "Apparently Mayor Nelson knows all about it, and he was insistent that Brent keep the secret."

"Why?" Liv asked, tearing off another piece of tape with her teeth.

"The reason he gave was that he didn't want anyone to know until he'd made a deal with the mining company, bringing union jobs and economic stability to Eagle's Rest. Anyway, the mayor started throwing around allegations about sexual assault, and Brent's career was over. So it looks like the mayor was using the journalist as a distraction from what was really going on."

Liv shook her head. "And Evan? How does he fit in?"

"You pretty much know it all now, anyway. He's buying up properties for much less than their value, and we suspect he's planning on selling them to the mining company for a major profit." He caught her eye and smiled grimly. "And having told you that could do bad things to my career."

"You said you need a witness."

"We do. I also need time to find out what's really going on around here, and that will keep the chief at bay. For the moment."

"Is buying properties and reselling them illegal?" she asked with a frown. "I knew he was flipping properties. Lots of people do that."

"It is if you strong-arm the owners into selling using your police influence," he said.

She nodded slowly. "And my building—he pressured the owner into selling?"

"That was the second complaint—the old woman's son came forward last year when his mom died and he found out that she'd sold the building. He remembered that she'd been afraid of a police officer, and he'd brushed it off as dementia. When he found out that an officer had bought her building, he got suspicious. It wasn't enough to press charges, but it was enough to get Internal Affairs to take note. They've been slowly gathering evidence ever since."

Liv sucked in a deep breath. "How do I clear my name?"

"We'll find a way," Jack said. He'd have to, because he wasn't keeping her alive to hand her over for a prison sentence. And while he was dedicated to finding the truth, his emotions were leading him in deeper than was wise.

He needed to prove Liv innocent—not only for her, but for him. When he left her to her life in her beloved Eagle's Rest, he'd know he'd given her everything he could—a cleared name and a chance at a quiet life free from all these unwanted cops.

He wanted to offer more, he realized...but that couldn't work. There was no way around it.

CHAPTER SIXTEEN

RICK AND AMY'S wedding was being held in a little country church about a mile up the mountain from Eagle Lake. Liv had memories at that little church—being taken there by her grandmother every Christmas and Easter. She'd sit in the hard-backed pew and listen to the soft drone of a preacher's voice while Grandma played tic-tac-toe with her on the back of the bulletin.

Every sidewalk crack and stretch of gravel road in Eagle's Rest held memories for Liv. She'd grown up here, come of age here. Eagle's Rest had become an integral part of who she was. This was home.

And yet the small town wasn't all she'd assumed it to be, either. Tanya wasn't the loyal confidant Liv had thought. Her ex-husband wasn't only a cheating louse—and ironically, she missed the days when that was the worst thing she knew about him. Someone in this town wanted her out, but where was she supposed to go when home had become a dangerous place?

Liv stared out the window of Jack's car at the passing autumn foliage of the open country outside town. They couldn't see the mountaintops from where they were, nestled in a winding, upward-turning road. The forest had been cut back from the road, but it sprang up almost violently on either side of them—fiery leaves contrasted against evergreen neighbors.

She wore a fitted burgundy dress that fell to about midcalf with a black wrap to block out the chill in the air. The heat pumped onto her feet, and it felt good, her strappy heels doing nothing to keep her warm. Weddings weren't the time to dress sensibly.

Jack had dressed up rather impressively, too. Liv wished he hadn't pulled that off as easily as he had. He wore a black suit paired with a gray shirt and a charcoal tie. It fit him perfectly, the smooth lines of his suit falling over his muscular physique in a way that drew her eye. Did he have to be so good-looking?

"What?" Jack glanced over at her, catching her watching him.

"I talked to my cousin Tanya, and as it turns out she's been sleeping with Evan."

Jack shot her a look of surprise. "For how long?"

"I'm not sure. But she was pressuring me to back up Evan's story about the purchase of my store."

"In what way?" Jack asked.

"He wants me to say that I was part of the sale from the very beginning and that the seller dealt with both of us."

"Is it true?"

"No. He did all the work of getting the sale. I just signed on when I got back from a wedding in England."

Jack was quiet for a moment, then he nodded grimly. "He's obviously getting nervous if he's sending Tanya to talk to you."

"It would seem so," she agreed.

He looked over at her, his gaze softening. "I'm here for you, Liv. You know that, right?"

"You're here for your case," she retorted. "Let's not blur any more lines."

"Hey, you chose me!" He gave her a small smile.

"My other option was that skinny idiot!" she shot back, and Jack burst out laughing.

"I'm saying it was a good call," he said.

They fell into silence for a couple of minutes and Liv leaned her head against the window. She hated fighting with him like this.

She'd missed him, longed for his comforting presence, and now she couldn't stop arguing with him.

"Full confession?" Jack said quietly. "McDonald drives me crazy. He's a wimp. When I was in high school, I was always a big guy, but I was pretty quiet. There was a wiry guy who was like a bucket of testosterone on two legs. He was tiny but obnoxious. McDonald reminds me of him."

"So you were bullied?" she asked.

"Nah. I could have flattened him if I wanted to. He was like a mosquito. Relentless and annoying."

"I had a guy like that in high school," she admitted.

"Yeah?"

She shook her head. "Not that it matters. Enough sharing."

"Why?" Jack didn't take his eyes off the road, but she saw his expression harden.

"Because I was being stupid before, and you know it. You've been lying this whole time—"

"Not all of it," he interrupted. "Yes, I lied about why I was there as part of my cover, but the personal stuff we talked about—that was all true. You didn't want to be the only one sharing. You expected something in return. That wasn't stupid, it was having standards. Everything I told you about my family, about my life…it was true. I think we got to be friends."

"Friends!" she exploded. "This is not friendship, Jack! This is—" She cast around for the right word and came up empty.

"Then humor me," he said. "What about that guy in high school?"

"I don't feel like humoring you."

"Tit for tat, Liv. I shared. You share. That's how this works."

He was using her own words against her. But maybe it didn't matter. "Fine. He was the same as you described—steeped in testosterone—and he hit on me constantly. Except—"

His gaze flickered toward her and then went back to the winding road. "Except?"

"I think he was making fun of me." She hadn't admitted that out loud before. Matt Clinger—skinny, full of attitude and the collector of every single pickup line known to a tenth-grade boy.

"He couldn't have just been hopeful?" Jack asked.

"I was a big girl, Jack. I was well-liked—don't get me wrong—but no one asked me to prom."

Jack was quiet for a moment. "You've obviously moved beyond that."

Liv looked down at her dress. She looked good—she knew it. And she was now at a place in her life where she appreciated having a womanly body. There was a strange power in curves, and she'd discovered that in her adult years.

"For the most part, yes," she agreed. "I found clothes that fit me properly, a style that accentuates my assets. But there are still times when I feel like that high school girl all over again—when how I see myself doesn't matter a whole lot in the face of an obnoxious guy."

"Ouch. The obnoxious guy isn't me this time around, is it?"

Liv laughed softly. "I was actually thinking of Evan, but if the shoe fits…"

"You're a beautiful woman," he said quietly. "I figured you knew that. We guys can be dolts that way, but we tend to assume that you know what you do to us. I'm willing to bet that the testosterone-filled idiot from high school was hoping he'd wear you down and you'd go out with him. Not that you should have, of course."

"Maybe. It doesn't matter now."

Liv felt off-balance all over again. It was

the same feeling from adolescence, like she was on the cusp of this whole new life and didn't know how to step into it. She could pretend not to care what people thought, but she did. And one day soon, her family was going to learn that Jack Talbott was a fake, and she was tired of pretending.

"Jack, I don't want any more PDA," Liv said suddenly.

"Okay." He gave her a sidelong look. His GPS quietly announced their upcoming turn. *In fifty yards, turn right onto Range Road 356...*

"No cuddling. No hand-holding. None of it."

"How exactly am I supposed to look like your boyfriend with all these rules?" he asked, slowing to take a tight corner as they approached the turnoff to Deer Lake Church.

"Figure it out," she retorted, and it felt good to be back in control. He'd leave town when he was done with this case, and she'd be left with the fallout.

"I do have one demand of my own," Jack said, stepping on the gas again as they sped along the cracked narrow road.

"I'm not sure you get to make any," she said.

"Sure I do," he shot back. "Whatever this

is—friendship or not—I'm part of it. And I'll respect your boundaries, but I want you to play by the original rules. Tit for tat. I share, you share."

She could claim that she didn't trust him, but that wasn't entirely true. She did trust him... He'd shown her the bugs in her apartment, and he'd told her about the case. He was also the only one who thought she was innocent right now.

"Fine," she said with a sigh. "Tit for tat."

"Thank you."

They crested a steep hill, and as they looked down into the small valley, sunlight glowed over the scene. Patches of oranges and yellows blazed against the evergreens, and a brilliantly white church sat in the midst of it all. It was old-fashioned, with a steeple and a graveyard out back. Liv could see the cars turning in to find parking, and she smiled wistfully.

"Rick's fiancée asked me a good place to get married—I said Deer Lake Church."

"Is this where you got married?" Jack asked.

"No." She'd hoped to get married here, but Evan had wanted it to be somewhere closer to his own family, and the logistics just hadn't worked out. Maybe that was for the best, because this tranquil spot was untouched by her failed marriage.

They came down the road and signaled a turn into the same drive behind a carload of people Liv recognized. They'd turned some of a side field into additional parking, and it was probably best that they were in Jack's car. Her own car would have struggled. He parked in full view of the church and turned off the motor.

Jack got out of the vehicle, and Liv took a moment to adjust her wrap, gather up her purse and check her lipstick in a mirror. Then her door opened, and she looked up in surprise to see Jack standing there with a hand out.

"I don't need—" she started, but he reached in and took her hand, giving her a gentle tug.

"Come on," he said.

"I thought we said—"

"This is neither a kiss nor a cuddle. This is common manners, Liv. When I take a woman out, I open doors and I treat her the way she deserves to be treated. So get used to it. Let's go."

"This isn't a date," she said, but she couldn't help the reluctant smile that came to her lips.

"I know." He slammed the door shut as she joined him at his side, and she stared at the grassy expanse spread out ahead of them. "All the same, you can lean on me until we get to firmer ground. If you want."

Liv adjusted her wrap once more. These strappy heels required a male arm, it seemed, and she sighed, slipping her hand into the crook of his arm. He was solid, tall, and gave her a sense of sure footing. She hated this. She'd rather carry a pair of boots with her than have to rely on something so fickle as a man—at least right now.

"And, Liv?" he said as they started out toward the church.

She looked up.

"You look amazing."

JACK SCANNED THE cars as they made their way across the grass. He was watching for anyone watching her—which was silly, because as soon as they'd arrived all eyes turned in their direction. And Liv did look amazing. That burgundy dress hugged her curves in a modest yet tantalizing way. She was stunning, and he was the family's newest source of gossip, so the attention was understandable. But still—he was looking for someone with a different intent.

Whoever wanted Liv out of town might very well be part of her extended family or a family friend. Jack wasn't ruling out anyone at this point. But he was willing to bet it was connected to Evan's plans for her property. Follow the money—that was the safest bet most times.

When they got across the grass, Liv let go of his arm and took a side step away from him. He shouldn't be insulted, he knew, but those few inches stung. There had been a time when he'd hoped for an opportunity to be this close to her...and that hadn't changed. Maybe he was terrible for her. And she wasn't any good for him, either! If he took a chance on Liv Hylton, he'd never get that position with Internal Affairs, and he'd never be able to root out the dirty cops on behalf of all those kids in the projects. But he couldn't help what he was feeling. She was stuck in his head, and he couldn't seem to get her out.

Jack recognized Marie Hylton from the barbecue, and he paused at Liv's side when she stopped to hug her aunt. Marie looked severe, even dressed in her wedding best, which turned out to be a brilliant blue lace-covered dress.

"And we have Jack here," Marie said, turning to Jack with a smile. "At a wedding no less! This is a big step in a relationship."

"Uh, yeah," Jack said, nodding slowly. "I'm glad to be here."

What was he supposed to say to that?

Liv looped her hand through his arm and dragged him forward, shooting her aunt a warning look as they hurried farther toward the church. He had to admit, he didn't mind this—even being dragged—since it meant closing those few inches between them. But the minute they were clear of Marie, Liv stepped away from him once more.

"I don't bite," he said softly, leaning toward her so that his words would stay between them.

Liv shot him a wry smile. "I might."

He laughed at that. "We'd have made good friends, Liv."

She relaxed a little, then eyed him uncertainly. "But we aren't."

And whatever they were, she was right. It had shot right past friendship, and there was no pedaling it back, either. They were stuck in that zone where hearts got involved whether they wanted it that way or not. Not everything came down to logical choice.

"For what it's worth, I wish we were," he murmured back.

They arrived at the church doors at that moment, and Liv stopped to say hello to a few friends. Jack studied each person—two men and three women—and then scanned the milling crowd once more. He knew what he was looking for—suspicious attention directed at Liv, someone keeping her in their sights. So far, nothing.

Which was good—wasn't it? His number one priority was to keep her safe, but he couldn't very well do that if he didn't know who was after her. The worst-case scenario wasn't an outright attack, because he was very well trained in hand-to-hand combat. Whoever attacked her would have to get through him first, and he could guarantee that he'd win. No, the worst-case scenario was that this person would slide back into the woodwork and wait until Liv wasn't quite so well protected.

And then Jack spotted him—coming from the field where he'd parked, apparently, and striding across the grass like he owned the place. He was alone, no wife to be seen, and there was probably a reason for that. Didn't he have a new mistress now? But even Tanya was notably absent.

Evan Kornekewsky was a tall man, lanky but well-proportioned. He was wearing a pair of dress pants with a button-down shirt and a vest, no jacket. He didn't look bothered by the chilly wind that ruffled his shirt and hair, and he stopped to talk to an older man with a wide, casual smile.

He looked like he was coming home.

Jack's heartbeat sped up, but he took a deep, calming breath. What he needed was presence of mind. Evan was in town—more than that, Evan was staking out his turf with Liv's family. And Jack could see why—if Evan was buying up land, he'd need people who trusted him enough to recommend him to others who might own that coveted real estate. But where did Tanya come in? Unless she was just some sordid little side deal.

Liv seemed to sense a change in him, because as she said goodbye to the last friend, she glanced up at him, then turned, following his gaze.

"Oh, great..." she breathed.

"Yeah."

Evan paused to talk to someone else—a man his age who laughed and gave him a rough hug. Evan wasn't exactly hated in these parts, it seemed. He'd managed to cheat on Liv, dump her for another woman and still keep up relationships with her friends and family. It was creepy, and a little frightening. Jack would be truly amazed if Evan hadn't spotted them yet, but the man was deftly ignoring them.

Liv straightened her shoulders, and it was then that they both saw Tanya. She had just arrived, wearing a knit dress and knee-high brown boots. There was a hitch in her step as she saw Evan, and her face flooded with color. She hadn't been expecting him, it seemed.

"You didn't know he'd be here," Jack said quietly.

"I knew it was a possibility. I was hoping he'd stay away," she replied. "Tanya will be thrilled."

Liv's voice was dry, and Jack watched as Tanya moved closer to Evan and glanced around uncomfortably before putting out a hand. Evan shook her hand obligingly, but her hand lingered in his several beats longer than necessary, and he leaned in closer to say something to Tanya that made her smile.

"I'm not watching this." Liv spun on her heel and marched into the church. Jack paused, watching the couple behind him for a beat or two until Evan looked up and met Jack's gaze evenly. He smiled slightly—a thin, victorious-looking smile—and Jack's skin crawled.

Jack headed into the church after Liv and

found her standing by the doors, her arms crossed over her stomach protectively.

"Liv?"

She was looking into the church, and he followed her gaze. It was lovely—the pews all decorated with fresh pink roses on the ends, and several candelabras lit at the front of the church. The lighting was low and a harpist played a soft tune—was that the *Titanic* theme song?—as people wandered in and took their seats.

"Liv—"

She looked up, and he saw tears sparkling in her crystal clear eyes. He longed to bend down, gather her up in his arms…or maybe he wanted to march back out there and slam a fist into Evan's smug face. Either-or. In a perfect world, he'd get a chance at both.

"It's not *him*," she said through gritted teeth.

"No, it's the fact that your cousin would do this to you," he replied.

Liv nodded, her chin quivering. "That sums it up."

"So what do you want?" he asked, his voice low. He fixed her with a steely look.

"What?" She looked from him, back to the church door and the flood of autumn sunshine outside. "What do you mean?"

"What's the best outcome here?" he said. "Considering all our facts, what do you want from this?"

"I want—" She seemed to straighten herself as she blinked back the tears. "I want to get through this with a little dignity. If possible."

"Very possible," he said. "How are you going to do it?"

She shrugged miserably. "How do you feel about a little more PDA in this sham of a relationship?"

Jack grinned, and he was so tempted to stoop down right then and catch those beautiful lips with his, but he held himself back.

"Just so we're clear here," he said, bending to keep his voice close to her ear. "You're asking me to treat you like I treat a woman I'm interested in…very, very interested in."

Some pink tinged her cheeks, and he knew his words had hit home.

"Yes."

"All right," he agreed with a roguish grin. "Only if you're sure."

The doorway darkened, and Jack turned to see Evan walk into the church. Tanya looked awkward next to him, and she kept a couple of feet between them and wouldn't look at him directly. She wasn't ready to announce that she was a known cheater's mistress to her family, apparently.

Jack slid an arm around Liv's waist and leaned in to murmur in her ear.

"I'm going to enjoy this. You mind?"

She glanced up at him. He tugged her a little closer, relishing this chance to have her back in his arms.

"Jack—" Then she smiled up into his eyes. "You're a good actor, you know that?"

"Who's acting?" He bent down and pecked her lips.

He knew this would mess with his emotions. He wasn't the kind of guy who could get this close to a woman and not have his heart entangled, but he'd just have to deal with that later when he could be alone and lick his wounds.

When he looked up again, Evan brushed past them, shooting a dark look in Jack's direction. Was that jealousy Jack saw? For Liv's sake, he hoped it was. Let her have this—let her rub a real man in that scoundrel's face. Because Liv deserved a guy like Jack—someone strong enough to protect her, man enough to stand by her and passionate enough to bring pink to those cheeks just by murmuring a few words in her ear.

"Let's go sit down," Liv said.

Suddenly, Jack knew exactly what he was missing in his life—and it was *her*. Liv Hylton, the woman who had intrigued him for years. Except he couldn't have Liv and chase justice the way he wanted to. He could be her hero, or he could get in the thick of it and root out the cancer in the department in the most effective way he knew how. It was Liv, or it was Berto's cause. One or the other.

CHAPTER SEVENTEEN

THE WEDDING WAS TOUCHING—though Liv couldn't fully enjoy the occasion. Rick and Amy said their vows, and Liv sat two rows behind Evan, staring at the back of his head the entire time. Tanya sat a row ahead of Evan, perhaps afraid to make her mistress status too obvious. Anger simmered as Liv looked at her cousin.

Relationships changed, but Liv had counted on that one to be enduring. How wrong could one woman be?

Jack played the role of doting boyfriend to a T, and Liv appreciated that he was helping her to avoid the pity she resented so much. He kept his arm behind her, comforting and warm. And while she knew she was fool-hardy to enjoy it, she did. She'd miss Jack when he was out of her life again. This might have been playacting from the start, but it had begun to feel ever so real.

The reception was held two miles down the road from the church. The hall overlooked the lake, which glistened with the golden reflection of autumn trees. Inside the hall, all was decorated with twinkling lights. Liv heaved a sigh.

"How long do you want to stay?" Jack asked quietly as they found their table—they were seated a stone's throw from the head table, where the bride and groom were just taking their places.

Liv looked over at Jack helplessly. "They'd see us leave. Rick would never forgive me."

And that was part of the problem with a hometown—along with the support and the comfort came the duty. This was Rick and Amy's day. She needed to be here for them.

Dinner was served—chicken—and the music started up for dancing. Rick and Amy had their first dance as husband and wife, and Liv watched mistily as her cousin looked down into his new bride's upturned face.

"They're happy," she said, and Jack slid an arm around her and tugged her gently against his solid shoulder. Liv tipped her head over and heaved a sigh.

"That's what happiness looks like, huh?" Jack murmured.

"Yeah…"

Rick dipped Amy, and then the music changed to something more upbeat and people started to stand up to join them on the dance floor. Here was hoping that this new couple was happier than she and Evan had been. And Liv also hoped that she'd have that kind of happiness again—except this time, the kind that lasted.

Jack moved the tips of his fingers up and down her arm, and she closed her eyes, enjoying the sensation.

"Jack, you're supposed to convince onlookers, not me," she murmured.

"I'm not that good of a liar, Liv." His obsidian gaze met hers, and something sizzled between them. Neither was she a good liar, for that matter. The room seemed to quiet around them, blurring into the background as the dancers swept around the floor laughing. She was going to miss him when all of this was over, because despite the lies, despite the spying and trickery, she'd foolishly fallen for this cop.

"Am I interrupting?" a deep voice asked, and Liv whipped around to see Evan standing in front of them, a half-cocked smile on his face. "Hi, Liv."

"Evan." She swallowed. "You know Jack Talbott."

Jack's posture hadn't changed a bit, but she could feel the tension of his muscles. He was taut, alert, ready to spring into action—and yet his fingers kept moving in slow circles over that one spot on her arm.

"Jack…yeah…" Evan's tone chilled. "What brings you to Eagle's Rest?"

"I'm on duty—looking out for Liv," Jack said easily.

"Then she's in good hands, because there's two of us," Evan said with a slow smile.

"And what brings you here?" Jack asked.

"A wedding—" Evan spread his arms. "When you marry a woman, you marry a family, right?"

"What about when you divorce a woman?" Liv asked curtly.

"Liv, it's never so easy, is it?" Evan's attention was back on Liv again. "Dance with me."

"I'd rather not," Liv retorted.

"Liv…" Evan's tone got that slightly paternal sound to it. "I just want to…talk. Please."

He held out his hand, and Liv considered for a moment, then sighed. Evan wanted to talk—maybe he'd let spill something she could use in her own defense.

"Fine." Liv rose and reluctantly took his hand. "A short dance."

She felt cold where Jack's body had been warming her, and she glanced back at Jack, but Evan was pulling her into the midst of the dancers. Then he slid a hand into the small of her back and positioned her so that she couldn't see Jack without craning her neck. She turned once more, and she caught a glimpse of Jack staring at them, those glittering dark eyes fixed on them like a drill. And she felt better. She wasn't alone in this, and if Evan thought he could separate her from her bodyguard with a simple dance, he was very wrong.

"What do you want, Evan?" Liv asked, moving into step with her ex-husband. This was a two-step, and Liv's body fell into the rhythm without any thought from her.

Evan tugged her a little closer—too close for her comfort—and moved her in slow, languid circles over the dance floor.

"Just checking in," Evan said with a shrug. "When you called the other night, I started to worry."

"Where's Serena?" she asked pointedly.

"Home. She's tired—needed some me-time."

He was off the leash for a couple of days, it seemed, and there was something familiar in the way he was looking down at her.

"I've missed you," he said, then pivoted them again, her breath jumping as he did so. He knew how to dance, how to make her heart leap with the joy of simple movement.

"Apparently, you've been missing Tanya, too," Liv replied with an icy smile.

Evan lost the rhythm for a second, then he caught up. "Liv, you know me. I'm no angel. And now Serena has to put up with me. What can I say?"

That was probably the best response he could have given, because Liv had zero sympathy for Officer Hot Pants.

"But I owe you something—" Evan went on.

"The books," Liv replied.

"The books?" Evan looked mildly confused. "Oh, yes. But I was talking about something…deeper. I owe you some help. Some protection. You matter to me still, Liv."

"And you want me to back up your story about buying my property," Liv replied.

"That would be helpful," Evan said, pulling her in a little closer as the music slowed once more. She doubted he simply wanted her on the record as his business partner—he had something lined up to blame the whole thing on her. That was more Evan's style—his priority was always number one.

He sighed. "Liv, I heard from Tanya that you're being threatened by someone…"

They were nearing their table again where Jack sat. She turned to look at him and found his gaze still locked on her. She was safe as long as Jack had her back, and her courage returned.

"That's why Jack is here," she said. "I'm not your problem, Evan."

"Sure you are." Evan's voice lowered seductively. "You'll always have a piece of me, Liv—"

"Oh, cut that out," she retorted. "I'm fine."

"You're not," he countered. "I know you."

"And what do you propose?" she asked, shaking her head. "Unless you know who's doing this—"

"Of course I don't know," Evan replied. "But I could help you out here. From what I hear, someone wants you out of town. And Liv, Eagle's Rest was a step backward for you. I'm sure you feel it by now. You aren't the same woman who left."

"What's that to you?" Liv snapped, but Evan spun her again, and she found herself almost floating through the air as Evan kept her moving with the music. When he pulled her back in against his lanky body, he shot her a playful smile.

"I can make the problem go away. I'll buy you out."

"Buy me out?" Liv pulled her hand out of

his and stopped dancing. A couple nearly ran into them, and then another.

"Liv, we're causing a traffic jam here," Evan said with a short laugh, reaching for her hand again.

"No!" Liv took a step back and spotted a path of escape that would get her to the side of the dance floor. She took it, and when she was safely out of everyone's way, she found Evan pinned to her side again.

"I can't imagine the stress you must be under," Evan went on. "Threats from God knows who, all the pressures of starting up a new business... I also heard about the hike in property taxes. I mean, that's not going to be easy on you. You came back to Eagle's Rest in order to breathe for a bit, and I get that. I wasn't much of a husband, and you needed some time to yourself. But I feel bad. I knew this wouldn't be what you thought when I signed that property over to you—"

"Evan, shut up!" Liv shook her head, anger boiling up inside her. "My life—my stress—is none of your business! You caused most of it!"

"I'm just offering some help here," Evan said. "I'm in a position where I could offer you a fair amount for that property. Not what we paid, mind you. A little less. But it would be fair."

"From what I hear, it's worth a whole lot more than that," Liv said with a short laugh. "If I'm going to sell, it's going to be directly to a mining company."

Evan's face blanched, and the cajoling stance evaporated. He had nothing to say, and for the first time, she saw him falter. He still thought that little detail was a secret.

"You still want to help me out?" she asked innocently.

"Liv—" Evan reached for her again, and this time he clamped down on her arm with an iron grip. She tried to jerk free, with no effect.

"Someone wants to hurt you," Evan said, his voice low and flat. "And I'm willing to help you. Think about that. What's money worth if you're dead?"

Liv's heart hammered in her throat, and she stared at him in shock. Was that a threat? She wasn't even sure! But Evan wanted her property—that much was obvious. She swallowed hard, and a dancing couple bumped up against them on their way past, knocking Liv off-balance. But then a warm hand slid along her waist, and she heard Jack's voice just behind her. "Evan, let her go."

Evan dropped her arm, and the smile was back. "Thanks for the dance, Liv. Just like old times."

JACK'S ENTIRE BODY was tensed in response to that look of horror on Liv's ashen face. He'd been watching them dance, watching the way Evan moved her around the room so effortlessly. At first he'd wondered if what he was feeling was jealousy, but then he saw Liv pull away from Evan, her whole body recoiling from his touch. That was when Jack had stood up and started moving around the dance floor toward them. Liv could talk to anyone she wanted…she could dance with anyone she wanted. But when a man laid a hand on her in an effort to control her, scare her, hurt her—that was no longer okay.

And now, with his hand on her waist, Jack could feel her straighten, get her balance back.

"Are you okay?" he asked Liv.

She rubbed her wrist but nodded. "I'm fine."

"She's fine," Evan said with a shake of his head. "We were having a conversation that didn't include you."

"Well, now that conversation does include

me," Jack snapped. "Keep your hands to yourself."

"Jealous?" Evan asked with a short laugh. "You always did have a thing for my wife, didn't you? Did you think I didn't notice? You were pathetic! Sitting on the sidelines staring at a woman who didn't even know you existed."

Jack glared at the other man. "She isn't your wife, Evan."

Evan didn't answer that, but a muscle along his jaw began to twitch. Jack had hit a nerve there. Evan liked to own turf, and he liked to keep women jumping. Liv wasn't jumping anymore—and that made Evan a whole lot more dangerous.

"You haven't changed," Evan went on with a sneer. "You're still the loser who came from the wrong side of the tracks looking in at how the big boys play."

Jack's anger rose, but he wouldn't take the bait. Evan wanted a fight, and Jack wasn't interested in that. He needed evidence, and when he came for Evan, it would be with the authority of the law behind him, not his fists. But it was tempting—really tempting.

"Have a good evening, Evan," Jack said, keeping his voice low, and nudging Liv close to him. Liv moved in tandem with him, and they headed away from the dance floor, leaving Evan behind them. He claimed to be part of this family still, and he had a mistress staring at him from across the room, misery all over her face. Evan should have his hands full without them in the mix.

"I need to get out of here," Liv breathed, and Jack caught her hand with his, giving it a warm squeeze.

"Me, too. Let's get some fresh air."

Jack tugged her along, and they edged past some chatting guests. Someone called a hello to Liv, and she raised a hand in blind greeting but plunged on. He was no longer tugging her with him; she was pushing ahead toward the door.

And then they were outside, the crisp October air enveloping them in a welcome embrace. Jack heaved a sigh and looked over at Liv.

"What was that about?" he asked.

"Evan wants to buy me out." She met his gaze, then shook her head. "And he's low-balling me."

"Yeah, I saw that coming." Jack rubbed his hands over his face. "What did you tell him?"

"I said no. He didn't much like it. That's when you showed up."

"Gotcha." Jack slipped his arms around

Liv's shoulders and pulled her against him.
"You okay?"

She relaxed into his arms and nodded
against his shoulder, and he smoothed her
hair away from her face. It felt good to just
hold her, a strange relief to be alone with her
again.

"Jack…"

"Hmm?"

Liv pulled back, looking up at him. "When
Evan said that you'd had a thing for me—"

She paused, licked her lips.

"I mentioned it before. I was attracted to
you. Obviously I didn't hide it as well as I
thought."

"Evan can be a jerk," she said.

"But he was right about one thing—I'm
crazy about you now. Before, it was a crush,
and now—" He swallowed. "Liv, I've fallen
in love with you."

Liv froze, her gaze searching his. "You…"

"What can I say? You're amazing—smart,
sweet, gorgeous, funny. The last couple of
weeks… I was supposed to keep my distance.
That didn't work."

"Jack…" She shook her head slowly.

"Hey—" Jack touched her cheek with the
back of his finger. "It's not your problem. I
wasn't supposed to fall for you, and I'm not

throwing myself at your feet, either. I'm just acknowledging it."

Liv blinked, and her lips parted as if to say something, but no words came out. So Jack did what felt most natural and dipped his head down, catching those lips with his. She sucked in a quick breath through her nose, then her eyes fluttered shut and she leaned into his kiss. He loved the feel of her in his arms—the softness of her body, the warmth of her skin. She pulled back, and she put her fingers to her lips.

"I wasn't supposed to do this, either," she whispered.

"Kiss me?" he asked.

"Love you back," she admitted miserably.

Jack bent to kiss her again, and she leaned back. "No, Jack. It doesn't matter, does it? You love me, and I love you, and—" Tears misted her eyes. "I can't do this, Jack! I've been married to a cop, so I know the life. There are priorities, and I'd never make the top three!"

"Not true," he growled. Even as another man's wife, she could have made him jump for her. "I'm not Evan. I'm nothing like him."

"And what about your precious Internal Affairs?" she asked with a shake of her head. "I'm the ex-wife of a dirty cop. How long will it take you to catch him? Who knows, right? And even once I clear my name, that's a legality. It would cling to you. You know what it's like—if you want to work in Internal Affairs, you've got to be beyond reproach, and I'm a stain."

"You're not a stain!" He wouldn't let her describe herself that way. She might be misunderstood, but she was far from a stain. She was right, though. Not everyone looked into those green eyes and saw what he did. There would be questions, rumors…and his career track into Internal Affairs would be over. Justice for guys like Berto…well, he wouldn't be the one dishing it out.

"I have to make a difference, Liv," he said quietly, his heart breaking inside him. "You understand that, right?"

Liv nodded, tears welling in her eyes. "I know. I told you before—I know cops, and you're a cop to the bone."

"So what do you want?" Jack asked miserably.

"I want to get over you—" Her voice trembled. "I want to stop feeling…all of this! I want to find some boring, everyday guy who won't break my heart, and I want a regular civilian life. That's what I *want*."

"And I want you," he whispered.

"Not enough." She licked her lips, her chin trembling. "You don't want me enough, Jack."

"I can't change who I am," he said huskily. "I can't change what drove me to become a cop in the first place."

"Any more than I can change who I am." She wiped a tear from her cheek. "This wasn't supposed to happen, Jack. It was supposed to be fake…"

But it was far from fake. What Jack felt sank down into the very deepest parts of him. He loved her, and she loved him back—which was a miracle unto itself! But it wasn't enough. That flimsy, impossible coincidence that she should love him, too, as rare and beautiful as it might be, couldn't make up for who he was.

"I'm sorry," he murmured.

"You need to go." Liv took a step away from him.

"I need to protect you," he countered.

"I have my family, Jack!" She shook her head. "Call someone else. You need to go."

She sucked in a wavering breath, and he could tell that she was holding back tears. Then she turned and headed back for the hall. She stopped in the doorway, cast him one indecipherable look, and disappeared inside.

It took all of his strength to keep from following her, because she was right. She was with her family, and she belonged here. He was the outsider. He pulled out his phone and dialed the station.

He'd call for a replacement, and when the officer arrived, he'd go back to the hotel. Whatever he'd come here to do, it wasn't to fall for the suspect. She was right—being a cop went right down to the bone. And someone had to get some justice for kids like him, like Berto, who grew up in the projects. He'd known this for some time—it was her or Internal Affairs. This wasn't just a job, it was a chance to make a difference, to help fix a broken system.

He couldn't make his heart, his own desires, the priority. No matter how much it hurt to walk away.

CHAPTER EIGHTEEN

THE NEXT MORNING, Liv stood in the mystery section of her store, scanning the titles. She was irritable and heartbroken. Everything inside her was in a jumble, and she hated feeling so out of control. Outside, the sun was shining, and dried leaves blew and scraped down the sidewalk. It was the kind of day that went with the smell of new books.

But Liv's heart ached, and even a fresh box of books delivered from a favorite publishing house did nothing to ease that pain.

Last night, Liv had stayed at the wedding, watching the other couples dance. She'd declined any more offers to dance with friends and cousins. She was tired, and her heart was so heavy in her chest that she felt like she could drown. And when she got home that night, she'd lain in her bed and sobbed her heart out. She'd cried until she was dry, and still her heart ached.

She loved him. That was the problem. Liv had fallen in love with Jack. And she knew better than to take a chance like that! She'd done this before…she'd thrown her heart into a marriage hoping that if she just loved her husband hard enough, everything would be okay. It hadn't worked.

For the moment, Hylton Books was empty, and Liv looked around herself, taking in the shelves of books, the straight spines, the red armchair off to the side, her trusty little stepladder for reaching top shelves.

This was hers—she'd built this herself. And yes, Evan might have arranged the purchase, but the land was not the store. Hylton Books was more than real estate—it was sweat, tears and a whole fresh start for a woman whose heart had taken enough.

This was the life she'd dreamed of for years, and when she'd realized her marriage was over, this was the dream that had kept one foot going in front of the other. And yet anything connected to Evan seemed to get tainted, and her store was no exception.

Someone wanted her out of town—well, they could forget it! She was giving up a man she loved, but she wasn't giving up this dream. This store was all she had left, and Liv wasn't going anywhere. And if Evan had done something illegal, she wasn't going down with him, either. She'd been a good wife, a good citizen, and damn it, she wasn't going to cave in and back that man up in his lies. Nor was she going to give up on the life she'd just begun to build.

So what could she do? Her mind ticked through the facts, lining them up like pieces on a board. There were options, some easier than others…

Liv picked up her cell phone and looked down at it. Evan had never lost gracefully to Liv, even in chess. But that was the problem. If you didn't win, you lost. And she was tired of stepping back for that man, being less for him, *losing* for him.

Liv had her name on her business, and she needed to clear that name. Two could play this game. She dialed Evan's cell phone number and let it ring.

"Liv?" Evan sounded tired.

"Hi, Evan." She tried to sound pleasant. "So I've been thinking. Do you want to know what about?"

"Uh—" There was a rustling sound. "This isn't really a good time, Liv."

"Tell Tanya to hold on," Liv replied with an eye roll, imagining exactly what was occupying her ex-husband's time. "This is worth it."

"Fine…" Evan sounded annoyed now. She must have nailed that one. "What?"

"I want in."

There was a pause, more rustling. He was probably moving away from the bed now. He lowered his voice. "What? What are you talking about?"

"Don't play dumb, Evan. Here's the thing. You're offering to buy me out because this land is about to be worth a fortune. And I want in. You used my name to buy this property to begin with, so I figure you owe me. If you want me to play along and back up the story about this place, then I want a cut."

"What kind of a cut?"

"That depends on how many people have a slice of the pie, doesn't it?" she said. "But at the very least, I'm keeping this property, and I'll sell it to the mining company myself. But if you want to buy my parents' property by the lake, or if you want a chance at Marie and Gerard's summer house, you're going to need me to nudge them into it."

"Are you trying to set me up?" Evan asked. "Is Talbott with you?"

"And if he were, would I say?" She laughed lightly. "Evan, I'm serious. I want in. And if you don't let me in, I'll start making things up. Talbott is eating out of my hand right now. I'm sure I could feed him enough stories to keep Internal Affairs after you for a decade."

"Blackmail?" he asked incredulously.

"Business." Her tone hardened. "I'm a single woman now, and I have a bottom line to worry about. Come by the store tonight. I want to talk. There will be no cops, I promise. Well, besides you. If you want my cooperation, there's a price."

There was silence on the other end.

"Nine tonight," she said. And when there still hadn't been an answer, Liv hung up without a farewell. Evan was used to having the upper hand, and he wouldn't risk her ruining everything he'd worked so hard to put together.

She had been a good wife, a good citizen, but she was an excellent chess player, and she was tired of waiting on men. Jack would work his fingers to the bone to prove her innocence, but it was very likely that there was no concrete proof to be found. Evan was good at this, too, and he wouldn't have left that kind of thing to chance. Besides, given half a chance, he'd pin the whole thing on her… and likely had most of that lined up already.

If she was going to clear her name, then she'd have to do it herself. Here was hoping she didn't get herself killed in the process. *Pretty, pretty Liv.* Forget that. She might be attractive, but she was also smart—and innocent!

WORK WAS THE great comforter when emotions got too strong. Jack had always been that way—a workaholic, some said. Yeah, well, it was a whole lot better than facing his feelings for Liv. He'd fallen in love with her all over again. He'd thought he could stay aloof, keep his emotions in check, but she was the one woman who could topple his defenses without even trying.

Hell, she didn't even want him.

Jack hadn't slept that night—not much, at least. And the next morning, he decided to do what he did best and start chasing down some clues. Nate Lipton had had a few run-ins with Evan Kornekewsky, hadn't he? Maybe that was another place to dig.

After a day of fruitless investigating, and after the sun sank behind the mountains, Jack found the old man's address—a little apartment building at the edge of downtown Eagle's Rest. But when he buzzed, no one answered.

"Who are you looking for?" An older woman came out the front door with a little dog.

"Nate Lipton. Do you know him?"

"Oh, Nate. You won't find him home at this time of night," she said with a wave of her hand. "He'll be at dinner—that café on the corner."

A little late to eat, but to each his own.

"Thanks." Jack looked the way she'd pointed, at a striped awning poking out onto the street, aglow in the yellow light of a streetlamp. He shrugged his coat higher up on his neck and headed in that direction.

The café itself was small and quaint. At this time of year, there weren't many tourists, and Jack spotted Nate at a table near the window. He was with another man and what looked like a teenager, but Jack couldn't see either face until he pushed inside and angled past the tables. Then he saw him—Brent Villeneuve was the adult. The teenager wasn't anyone Jack knew. Next to three empty plates there was a little travel chessboard. That was a friendship he hadn't guessed!

"Good evening," Jack said, and both men looked up.

"Hello, Officer," Brent said. "What can I do for you?"

"Actually, I was looking for Nate," Jack replied, pulling up a chair and straddling it. "Who's winning?"

"Hard to tell," Nate replied.

"He's winning." Brent chuckled. "It's just a matter of how long he toys with me."

"Ah." Jack glanced toward the kid. "Friend of yours?"

"We're teaching him the game," Nate replied. "Gotta pass these skills on to the next generation somehow. So what do you want, Officer?"

"I'm looking into a police officer," Jack said. "Evan Kornekewsky."

"That idiot," Nate said, not taking his eyes from the board. "What'd he do now?"

"I'm trying to find out."

"Get evidence, you mean," Nate replied with a bitter laugh. "We all know what he's done."

"I hear he pressured you into selling," Jack said.

"I reported that," Nate replied, and he move his castle forward five spaces, then looked up. "He didn't have as much to hold against me as he did my neighbor, Ruth Kripke."

"What did he have against Ruth?" Jack asked.

"Her son was dabbling in drugs, and Ruth was a single mom. She'd scraped to buy that house. Officer Kornekewsky had arrested her son on some misdemeanor in the city, and he said he'd drop the charges against her boy if she sold to Mayor Nelson. So she did. You'll never get her to say anything, though. She's too afraid of her son seeing the inside of a jail."

Of course. The mayor was as dirty as the cops he used for muscle. If Jack had to guess, those golf games between Evan and the mayor were less about the sport and more about their plans to swindle the community. Brent made a move, and Jack silently watched the men play for a couple of moves. It would be a slow process of putting together the bits and pieces of evidence. On their own, it was all pretty circumstantial, but maybe this Ruth Kripke would be willing to testify. Maybe. Hopefully… He made a note in his pad.

An image of Liv rose in his mind, and his heart clenched. He was doing this for the sake of justice—for all the kids who had been pushed around by dirty cops, for all the moms who'd been willing to do anything to save their boys from jail. And he was doing it for Liv, for her chance at a new life away from Evan. Cops like Kornekewsky had ruined the lives of too many people, and even if it took him years, he'd never stop trailing after these monsters.

And yet there was a very tantalizing life here in Eagle's Rest—one that wasn't available to him, regardless. Liv knew what she wanted, and it wasn't the likes of him. Even if she had fallen in love with him. Not much of a victory when the woman could love him and still know she was better off without him.

"Don't make that move," Nate said, his voice monotone.

Brent took the move back. "Why?"

"I'll win in three moves," Nate replied. "No, not that one, either."

Brent took another move back. Jack chuckled softly.

"I know that feeling. I played Liv Hylton, and she kept making me take moves back, too."

Even romantically, it was the same. Don't make that move… Hearts didn't matter as much as Jack used to think.

"Brent's too defensive," Nate said, glancing over at the teenager. "He's always trying to close the holes, stop my attacks. But you can't win on defense. You can only prolong the game a little bit. The only way to win is to make a positive move—do something. Attack."

Brent shot Jack a wry smile. "He's always right."

But constant offense didn't win, either. Sometimes a man had to defend what was most important to him at home instead of endlessly attacking…like he was trying to do for Berto—for the kids who kept getting tilled under by a handful of selfish authority figures.

But a long time ago—before Berto was arrested for drugs he'd never seen before in his life—Jack had wanted to be more than this. He'd dreamed of a house and a car in a real driveway, a pretty wife and a few kids. He'd wanted a "good job" and family vacations— all the stuff he'd never had growing up. He'd wanted to move his mom and dad into his home, safely away from the drugs and violence of that old neighborhood. Once upon a time, he'd wanted to be a good guy living a good life. He'd wanted to be able to walk down a street and see respect in people's eyes. He'd just wanted a shot at the same stuff everyone else wanted. He'd called it "rich." Heck, it was just plain old middle class.

Once upon a time, Jack had dreamed of being happy.

And that had suddenly become obscured in his desire for justice. Would Jack be happy once he'd chased down every single dirty cop in Denver personally? Would he find that elusive light he'd been looking for? Or would he look back on his time here in Eagle's Rest and kick himself for walking away from the one woman to capture his heart?

"Not that move, either. You put yourself in check," Nate said.

"Fine…" Brent sighed.

"There's more than defense, Brent," Nate admonished again. "There's a move—I see it! You just have to take it!"

The teenager leaned closer, and Jack looked down at the board, the pieces all arranged in their battle formation. Jack suddenly saw it— Brent's way to win. It was a direct attack, and he'd lose his queen in the process…

"There." Jack pointed it out. "That's your move."

Brent shook his head and moved the piece. In a matter of three moves, the game was over and Nate grinned at his buddy.

"Good game, Brent."

"I've never beat you before." Brent chuckled, and they shook hands over the board.

"Well, to be fair, you still haven't," Nate retorted. "It was this fella."

But more had fallen together in that moment than just a chess strategy. He'd been so focused on defense, he'd forgotten who he wanted to be. A defender of the defenseless? Of course, but also a husband, a father and a good cop who did more than just chase down his dirty colleagues. He wanted to be the first on the scene—and do the job right. He wanted to mend fences, and not only stop bad cops from taking advantage, but set a few kids on firmer ground. He wanted to be the cop he'd needed in his community as a kid.

"Did you see that, Mike? That's how it's done. Don't give up just because it looks like you're losing." Nate swiped the board clean and started arranging the pieces again. "Your turn, kid. You're going to play Brent, and I want to see what you can do without me giving you tips this time…"

Nate was doing what Jack had needed when he was young. He was passing along some skills, giving a kid a leg up. He was being a mentor. That kind of relationship could open up options a teen had never dreamed of before.

Jack couldn't stay in defensive mode. He had to take a step up and look at the whole game. Was it possible to be more than a guy chasing down his personal demons?

Jack glanced at his watch. It was almost nine—Liv wouldn't be in bed yet.

"I'll leave you to your rematch," Jack said. "Thanks for your time."

Jack got to his feet and turned the chair back to its proper position. He needed to talk to her. It might not make any difference in the grander scheme, but he had to try!

CHAPTER NINETEEN

LIV WASN'T SURE what to expect when the clock crept closer to nine that night. She'd thrown down the gauntlet, and she was beginning to worry that she'd dangerously misjudged her ex-husband. Evan had clearly been involved in some very shady things, and she was counting on some sort of fondness for her to keep him from bulldozing her along with everyone else who got in his way. She'd meant something to him at some point—but would that be enough to protect her?

She stood in front of the counter of Hylton Books, waiting. Would Evan even come, or had he seen through her bravado and found her laughable? Or worse—would he send someone else to take care of the issue for him?

Her skin crawled at that thought, and she wondered if she'd been wrong to try to deal with this alone. Maybe she should have called Jack and told him what she was up to, if only for a little personal protection.

But Jack would only try to stop her, and if Evan saw even a trace of police presence, her chance to catch him in his own words would fall flat. Evan *was* a cop. He knew what to look for.

The store was chilly—she'd turned down the heat for the night—and she rubbed her hands together for warmth.

This is foolish, she thought miserably. *This is downright dumb! I've just threatened a very dangerous man—*

But then the front door rattled, and she didn't have time to reconsider her plan. She sucked in a shaky breath, wiped her hands down the front of her jeans and headed over to unlock it.

Evan stood outside, a stack of old books in his hands, but he wasn't alone. Behind him was a cop she recognized. He was tall but skinny, and his face was lined and gray in the wan light of a streetlamp.

"Officer McDonald?" she said hesitantly.

"You wanted to talk business," Evan said with a cool smile. "McDonald is part of that."

"Oh…" she breathed.

A couple of options flashed through her mind. Was Evan setting her up to take the fall for his crimes? Or was it the obvious thing— McDonald was a dirty cop, too? Her mind spun, and she stepped back to let the men inside. Officer McDonald stepped too close for comfort, but Liv wouldn't give way. She held her ground, letting the man brush up against her as he slid past. He looked different out of uniform—weaker, maybe. But if she had any chance of pulling this off, she had to appear a whole lot more cocksure than she felt, because she was suddenly much less confident in her ability to navigate this conversation. She knew Evan's buttons, but he'd brought along some protection against that.

"Thanks for coming," she said, locking the door behind them. She led the way into the store, closer to the counter.

McDonald put the books down on the counter, and Liv looked over at Evan curiously. He was making good on the promise to give her those books, it seemed. But she still didn't trust him.

"Are you sure you don't just want to let me buy you out?" Evan asked, his tone gentle. "This can't be easy for you, Liv. I know you. I've brought the books—I know you're the only one to really appreciate them. And I want you to remember that I care. You're a good woman, and I think you're in over your head."

"I'm perfectly fine," Liv replied with a

shrug. "But thanks for delivering those. I appreciate it."

"Life isn't easy, Liv," Evan said. "I do understand your desire to run a bookstore, but there are other ways to stay connected to your passions. Maybe a collection of rare first editions." He tapped the pile of books temptingly. "I could even help you out with a few more as I come across them."

Yeah, as he robbed old people of their property.

"I could do both," she countered.

"The property taxes alone will be a burden," Evan pointed out. "I'm only here out of courtesy. If I sat back and waited a few months, you'd be out of business on your own. You can't afford to make those tax payments."

"What makes you so sure?" she snapped.

"Come on, Liv..." Evan reached out to touch her arm, and she took a step back.

"I'm not your wife anymore, Evan," she said. "You can save the sweet talk for Serena. Or Tanya, for that matter."

Evan's expression iced over. "I'm trying to be nice, Liv."

"Then stop being nice and talk business!" she said. "I want in. You're about to make money hand over fist, and I don't think it's fair that I should miss out on that after ten years of marriage. You owe me something, Evan."

Evan sighed. "You want in."

"I do. You used me, but now I know about it, and I want a cut."

"What do we get in return?" Evan asked.

"My compliance?" She raised her eyebrows. "A sense of having done the right thing?"

She let a smile quirk up one corner of her lips. She was teasing him now.

"This is bigger than you or me," Evan said, clearly exasperated. "I can't just cut you in. There are bigger people who run this. And they don't like being threatened."

"So why did you come?" Liv asked.

"Because I wanted to protect you. You're playing a game you don't understand. Our marriage might not have lasted, but I do care... I think I'm proving that here."

"How much bigger?" Liv asked, frowning. "Like the kind of people who send women to break into my apartment?"

Something flickered in his eyes when she said that. She'd hit on something.

"She was yours, wasn't she?" Liv pressed. "Because there was a woman outside my apartment in the rain before that. With a baby stroller of all things…" She let out a bitter laugh. "Weird. I could have sworn she looked like Serena, but—"

"Leave her out of it," McDonald said, his voice low.

Her heart hammered in her throat. The woman outside her home, the woman breaking in… It wasn't a thug—it was a cop!

Evan snorted. "I didn't send her anywhere. She does what she wants. She's no delivery girl."

Like Liv had been. She heard the insult between the lines.

"This is personal for her, then," Liv guessed. "What…don't tell me she suspects you're cheating already, and she thinks it's me!"

The look on Evan's face confirmed that, and she bit back the nasty comment that popped to her mind. She was trying to get Evan to open up, not clam up.

"Oh, Lord…" Liv murmured. "Look, Evan, if you need me to tell her that we're over, I'm happy to do that. Whatever you have going on with my cousin has nothing to do with me. I mean, if we're going to be in business together, I'm glad to smooth that over for you."

"It's fine," Evan muttered. "It's just…" He paused. "She lost a baby, okay? So cut her some slack. I think you could understand what she's going through."

That explained the stroller...sort of. If Serena was really struggling with the loss, and Evan had been the idiot he'd been with Liv in a similar situation... That poor woman was being dragged along in Evan's wake, trying to keep him faithful. It was like trying to keep a dog away from a bloody steak.

"No, no, understood." Liv softened her tone. Evan always had thought the world revolved around him, so maybe he'd believe that she was falling into line, too. "I'm not completely heartless. So...about business, then. Who else am I working with here? You said there are bigger people. Who are we talking about? The mayor? Because I used to babysit his kids, and he likes me."

Evan's mouth twitched in annoyance. She needed him to say it out loud, though, or it wasn't much good.

"Let's bring him into this talk, then," Liv went on. "I'm willing to chat with him. I can play ball, Evan."

"Mayor Nelson doesn't want the payout to get any bigger than it already is," Evan snapped. "So you're going to be a problem. Don't you see that?"

"There have been some disturbing events

lately," McDonald added, his tone equally oily. "Tires get slashed…don't they, Pretty Liv?"

The words sounded a little too comfortable on the man's lips, and Liv stared at him in disgust. He leered down at her, and she noticed Evan's jaw tightening.

"So that was you, was it?" she said with a short laugh. "I have to say, you'd have been smarter to keep your mouth shut. The tire was annoying, but I'd chocked that up to kids. Now the letter was very creepy, I'll give you that, but now that I know who was behind it—"

"You should leave town while you can," Evan snarled. "I appreciate that you want to work with me, but I'm giving you an out. Out of respect for our marriage."

Liv eyed him for a moment, weighing her words. It was time to stop begging.

"See, this is the thing. You're both much creepier on paper. But looking you in the face—" she shrugged "—you're a lot less scary, I have to say."

"Liv!" Evan's voice turned a few degrees colder. "I've tried to be nice about this, but I'll be straight. You aren't getting a cut in this deal. You do have a chance to leave town alive, though. And I'm strongly urging you to take me up on the offer."

Her heart hammered in her throat, and she sucked in a deep breath. She couldn't let him see that she was scared. She needed more.

"So who exactly is going to kill me?" she demanded. "McDonald here?" She considered him skeptically. "No, not McDonald. He likes me too much. He's got a bit of a crush. He couldn't help himself—he had to tell me he was the one behind the Pretty Liv thing. And his very manly tire-flattening skills. He wants to impress me."

McDonald's expression became an ugly grimace, and she had a sudden sense that she'd been very wrong about him. He would hurt her quite easily. But she couldn't stop now— she was tap-dancing as fast as she could here.

"Or you?" Liv turned to Evan. "Would you kill me if the mayor asked you to?"

She was expecting Evan to patronize her again, soften his tone and give her a few more warnings. Instead, Evan's hand shot out and clamped onto her throat. He hauled her in close enough that she could smell the coffee on his breath, his eyes narrowed in fury.

Liv scrambled to stay on her feet, trying to dig her fingers under the grip on her throat, but the harder she tried, the harder he squeezed. She'd misjudged all of this, and Evan had been right about her being in over her head. She had a sudden yearning for Jack. His strength, his muscle-bound protection... his heart, his dark, soft eyes... She should have called Jack...

"Yeah, Liv," Evan growled. "It would be me who hurt you. And you might think you can control me, but you can't. You never could. You're aren't a part of this deal, baby. You never were. You were oblivious to all of it, and now you want to try to get in on it? Not a chance!"

Liv couldn't breathe, and she felt her muscles going slack, black spots appearing in front of her eyes, when suddenly a bang jolted the attention of both men away from her and toward the door. Evan dropped her, and Liv sagged against the counter, sucking in a ragged, painful breath.

Her balance slowly returned and she looked up in time to see Jack Talbott in the doorway—the door hanging in a broken sort of way. Crap. She'd have to fix that. He must have kicked it in. He stood there with a gun trained between Evan and McDonald.

"What's going on?" Jack growled.

"It isn't what it looks like," Evan said with a sigh. "This is...domestic."

"And that's better?" Jack snapped.

"This is *not* domestic," Liv said with a sigh. She reached under the counter and pulled out her cell phone. "I recorded everything."

"You little—" Evan started, but Jack made a sound in the back of his throat that stopped the man short.

"Don't move, Kornekewsky," Jack said, and he glanced toward Liv. "What did you record?"

"Everything," she said. "They admitted to it all—and I'm pretty sure this clears my name."

"You should have told me!" Jack growled, then he flicked the gun toward the floor. "You two—on the ground."

Evan and McDonald slowly bent down, then did as they were told. Jack pulled out a set of cuffs and tossed them to Liv. She caught them, and Jack pushed a button on his radio.

"This is Officer Talbott, requesting backup at 728 Main Street. Two suspects have been apprehended." Then he released the button and dialed down the chatter on the radio. "You know how to use these?" Jack pulled out a second set of cuffs.

Liv couldn't help the grin that came to her

lips. "What self-respecting cop's wife hasn't figured it out?"

She knelt in the center of Evan's back, grabbed an arm and slapped on the cuff. She rotated off him and cuffed the other hand securely. That felt better—at least Evan wouldn't have a chance to lay a finger on her again.

Then she looked up at Jack, who had just finished cuffing McDonald, and she shot him a weary smile.

"Thank you."

"Yeah," he said, leaning over and pecking her lips lightly. "Anytime, Liv."

THE NEXT TWO hours were busy. Evan and McDonald were both arrested and charges were laid. The mayor was picked up at his home, and they discovered Serena there, too. That was where she'd been hiding out since breaking into Liv's apartment. Liv's recording turned out to be even better than she'd hoped, and after she'd given her statement, signed all sorts of forms, and told and retold her story, she was finally released to return home.

"I'll give you a ride," Jack said, draping her jacket over her shoulders.

"Thank you." Her voice trembled. She was so tired, and with a simple act of kindness coming from this man she couldn't help loving despite herself, her emotions were starting to resurface. She put on her jacket properly and then followed Jack outside into the starlit darkness. She needed to go home, to crawl into the warmth of her bed and cry this out. Because if she let herself do what she wanted, she'd be slipping into Jack's warm arms and staying there forever.

But that wasn't an option.

Jack led the way to his car, but before they got there, he tugged her to a stop, then bent down and covered her lips with a tender kiss. She leaned into him, sinking into the feeling of safety he provided. He pulled back, looking into her eyes.

"God, I love you," he breathed.

"Jack, we can't make this harder—" she started, her breath in her throat.

"What if it didn't have to be?" he asked, frowning slightly. "I know you don't want a cop, Liv... I know you've had that life and hated it, but I'm not Evan. And I could very easily make you my top priority. I admit it— I'm a cop to the bone. That can't be helped. I am who I am! But I'd also be yours to the core...if that counted for anything."

Liv stared at him, emotion misting her eyes. "Because I've just cleared my name?"

She shook her head. "So I'm safe now because you could go on and build your career in Internal Affairs?"

"No—" Jack frowned, then shook his head. "Liv, no! This isn't about that. I talked with Nate Lipton about chess moves, and it got me to thinking. I can't keep living defensively. I wanted to chase down the dirty cops because of my rough experiences growing up, but before I got bitter and jaded, I had a different set of dreams, and those included a house and a car...a wife. Maybe kids, if she were so inclined..." He brushed a tendril of hair away from her face. "I'm tired of living in reaction to hard times. Maybe I'd rather be the good guy in a kid's life—the cop who made a difference just by being there and being honest."

Liv swallowed hard. "Scandal will cling to me, Jack. You can't be naive about that."

"Naive?" He chuckled softly. "Liv, I'd forget Internal Affairs and take up a position here in Eagle's Rest if you'd have me."

"You'd—" She stopped short. "Really?"

"I'm in love with you, and if I don't do everything I can to win you over, I'll regret it for the rest of my life. I want a life with you. I want to wake up to you, go to bed with you—" He smiled. "I want it all, Liv. With you." He shut his eyes for a moment, then shook his head. "But you don't want a cop..."

"I didn't," she whispered. "I don't! But I realized that Evan wasn't just hiding his life from me, he was hiding a whole criminal element. What it comes down to is this—I don't want to be discounted. I don't want to be forgotten. I don't want to be betrayed, cheated on, cast aside." She fought back the tears that filled her eyes. "I don't want to be left out of your life. I don't want you to tell another cop how you feel when you should be telling *me*! I don't want to be pushed aside because I'm too *civilian*—"

Jack silenced her with another kiss, and when he finally pulled back he looked into her eyes with more tenderness than she'd ever seen in life.

"You'll be my first stop, Liv, my confidant, my everything. Too civilian? Liv, you took down Evan Kornekewsky by yourself!"

"With a little help once he was strangling me," she said with a small smile.

"I was coming by your place tonight because I'd realized I could still be the cop I wanted to be—I could have the dream I'd had as a boy. And when I realized that, the one person I wanted to tell was you. Even when I knew you didn't want me." Jack pressed his lips against her forehead. "I love you, Liv. I'd marry you in a heartbeat, and I'd spend the rest of my life eternally grateful that you shared your days with me."

Liv swallowed, her mind spinning. She knew what she wanted—she wanted him. She wanted love and kisses, laughter and plans together. She wanted the kind of life they'd been playacting these last two weeks.

She sucked in a wavering breath. "It's all a little fast…"

"I just want a life with you," he said quietly. "And I want it to start as soon as possible, but I'm not going to pressure you, either. How about this…tomorrow night, I want to take you out for dinner. And the night after that, I want to take you out for dinner again. And the night after that, and the night after that… And I'll keep taking you out for dinner until you decide you'd like to take me up on my offer of forever. And when that happens, you let me know."

"Okay," she whispered. "What time will you pick me up?"

He grinned. "Seven."

They resumed their walk toward the car, and when they got there, he opened the door for her. Her heart was full as she looked out at the starry night, the full moon, and then back at the man standing next to her.

"If we're going to make this official, we could go scandalize your aunt and tell her the whole story," he said. "What do you say? Maybe her good manners will take over, and she'll offer us more of that potato salad."

"Yes," Liv said with a soft laugh. "But you know, I can make that potato salad myself."

"No need to sweeten the deal, Liv." He dipped his head down and kissed her tenderly. "I'm already yours. But be warned—every time you break out that potato salad, I'm going to propose."

Liv laughed and shook her head. "I love you, Jack."

Standing in the open door of the car with Jack's strong arms wrapped around her, Liv felt all her misgivings drift away. She was safe with this man, both in his arms and in his heart. Standing in her hometown with all her hopes for the future swirling through her mind, she could see her biggest hope in the gentle eyes of this big cop.

She was home in Eagle's Rest, and her happily-ever-after had only just begun.

EPILOGUE

EAGLE'S REST, AS it turned out, did have minable gold, but the environmental groups rallied together to keep it unmined for the sake of the eagles who roosted there. It was all tied up in the courts, but the courts eventually ruled in favor of turning that land into a protective sanctuary, leaving the town intact and the property taxes reasonable. Jack couldn't be more pleased. Not everything came down to making money.

Tourists who were eager to catch a glimpse of eagles in the wild came pouring into town, and Liv's bookstore sold more books on eagles than any other subject matter. She had an entire section dedicated to them. Jack was proud of her. She'd made a thriving business out of Hylton Books, and he was glad that she'd be keeping her last name after she married him. She'd worked too hard to get it back.

Jack went to see his cousin in prison and they had some good long talks about what was possible in the future if Berto got clean and turned his life around.

"I'm not like you," Berto said. "But I want to be."

And that was the first step. Berto deserved a chance to set his life right, and Jack was determined to give his cousin all the help he could. He'd be behind bars for a few more months, but then Jack had arranged a job for him working with wounded eagles that were being rehabilitated for the wild. Rehabilitation took time—for humans, too.

As for Tanya, she wasn't a long-term fling for Evan—especially after his lengthy court case began. Liv didn't trust her in the same way again, but it was the beginning of a new cousin relationship—built on forgiveness and an understanding of what they both had to lose.

And then one Saturday morning in the winter, Jack put on a black tux and he stood at the front of Deer Lake Church, his heart in his throat. He'd waited for this day most patiently. Liv had needed time, and he understood that. But he'd been true to his word, and when Liv made him that amazing potato salad last spring, he'd pulled out the ring he'd been carrying around and asked her to marry him. It had taken all of a heartbeat for her to say yes.

Now, as he stood in front of the church filled with friends and family on both sides, he shot his mom and dad a misty grin.

This was it—the life he'd dreamed of as a kid. Maybe he didn't drive quite so nice a car as he'd wanted back then…but the intelligent, thoughtful, amazing wife? Yeah, he'd beaten the mark on that one. And Liv was more gorgeous than he'd ever even dreamed of in his youth.

The organ music swelled, and the doors opened to reveal Liv in a white wedding gown. It was fitted over her hips and then fell to the floor in a foam of lace. He'd never seen a more beautiful vision in his life. He couldn't see much of her face behind the voluminous veil, but he noticed the engagement ring sparkling on her finger, and he saw the way she clutched her dad's arm.

He loved her…that was all that mattered. And he'd spend the rest of his life convincing her that he was the best choice she could ever make.

She moved up the aisle, and when she got to the front of the church, her father passed her hand into Jack's, and he felt the reassuring squeeze of her fingers. He lifted her veil—

as they'd practiced—and looked down into those glittering green eyes. Then they turned toward the minister.

"Marriage is a sacrament..." the minister began, and Jack stole a look at his bride.

How he loved her.

This was what happiness looked like. If anyone cared to take note.

Jack Talbott was home.

* * * * *

Get 4 FREE REWARDS!

We'll send you 2 FREE Books plus 2 FREE Mystery Gifts.

Love Inspired® Suspense books feature Christian characters facing challenges to their faith... and lives.

FREE Value Over **$20**

YES! Please send me 2 FREE Love Inspired® Suspense novels and my 2 FREE mystery gifts (gifts are worth about $10 retail). After receiving them, if I don't wish to receive any more books, I can return the shipping statement marked "cancel." If I don't cancel, I will receive 4 brand-new novels every month and be billed just $5.24 each for the regular-print edition or $5.74 each for the larger-print edition in the U.S., or $5.74 each for the regular-print edition or $6.24 each for the larger-print edition in Canada. That's a savings of at least 13% off the cover price. It's quite a bargain! Shipping and handling is just 50¢ per book in the U.S. and 75¢ per book in Canada*. I understand that accepting the 2 free books and gifts places me under no obligation to buy anything. I can always return a shipment and cancel at any time. The free books and gifts are mine to keep no matter what I decide.

Choose one: ☐ **Love Inspired® Suspense**
Regular-Print
(153/353 IDN GMY5)

☐ **Love Inspired® Suspense**
Larger-Print
(107/307 IDN GMY5)

Name (please print)

Address   Apt. #

City   State/Province   Zip/Postal Code

> **Mail to the Reader Service:**
> **IN U.S.A.:** P.O. Box 1341, Buffalo, NY 14240-8531
> **IN CANADA:** P.O. Box 603, Fort Erie, Ontario L2A 5X3

Want to try two free books from another series? Call 1-800-873-8635 or visit www.ReaderService.com.

*Terms and prices subject to change without notice. Prices do not include applicable taxes. Sales tax applicable in N.Y. Canadian residents will be charged applicable taxes. Offer not valid in Quebec. This offer is limited to one order per household. Books received may not be as shown. Not valid for current subscribers to Love Inspired Suspense books. All orders subject to approval. Credit or debit balances in a customer's account(s) may be offset by any other outstanding balance owed by or to the customer. Please allow 4 to 6 weeks for delivery. Offer available while quantities last.

Your Privacy—The Reader Service is committed to protecting your privacy. Our Privacy Policy is available online at www.ReaderService.com or upon request from the Reader Service. We make a portion of our mailing list available to reputable third parties that offer products we believe may interest you. If you prefer that we not exchange your name with third parties, or if you wish to clarify or modify your communication preferences, please visit us at www.ReaderService.com/consumerschoice or write to us at Reader Service Preference Service, P.O. Box 9062, Buffalo, NY 14240-9062. Include your complete name and address.

LIS18

HOME on the RANCH

YES! Please send me the **Home on the Ranch Collection** in Larger Print. This collection begins with 3 FREE books and 2 FREE gifts in the first shipment. Along with my 3 free books, I'll also get the next 4 books from the Home on the Ranch Collection, in LARGER PRINT, which I may either return and owe nothing, or keep for the low price of $5.24 U.S./ $5.89 CDN each plus $2.99 for shipping and handling per shipment*. If I decide to continue, about once a month for 8 months I will get 6 or 7 more books, but will only need to pay for 4. That means 2 or 3 books in every shipment will be FREE! If I decide to keep the entire collection, I'll have paid for only 32 books because 19 books are FREE! I understand that accepting the 3 free books and gifts places me under no obligation to buy anything. I can always return a shipment and cancel at any time. My free books and gifts are mine to keep no matter what I decide.

268 HCN 3760 468 HCN 3760

Name	(PLEASE PRINT)	
Address		Apt. #
City	State/Prov.	Zip/Postal Code

Signature (if under 18, a parent or guardian must sign)

Mail to the **Reader Service:**

IN U.S.A.: P.O. Box 1341, Buffalo, New York 14240-8531
IN CANADA: P.O. Box 603, Fort Erie, Ontario L2A 5X3

Get 4 FREE REWARDS!

We'll send you 2 FREE Books <u>plus</u> 2 FREE Mystery Gifts.

FREE
Value Over
$20

Both the **Romance** and **Suspense** collections feature compelling novels
written by many of today's best-selling authors.

YES! Please send me 2 FREE novels from the Essential Romance or
Essential Suspense Collection and my 2 FREE gifts (gifts are worth about
$10 retail). After receiving them, if I don't wish to receive any more books,
I can return the shipping statement marked "cancel." If I don't cancel, I will
receive 4 brand-new novels every month and be billed just $6.74 each in the
U.S. or $7.24 each in Canada. That's a savings of at least 16% off the cover
price. It's quite a bargain! Shipping and handling is just 50¢ per book in the
U.S. and 75¢ per book in Canada*. I understand that accepting the 2 free
books and gifts places me under no obligation to buy anything. I can always
return a shipment and cancel at any time. The free books and gifts are mine
to keep no matter what I decide.

Choose one: ☐ **Essential Romance**   ☐ **Essential Suspense**
              (194/394 MDN GMY7)   (191/391 MDN GMY7)

Name (please print)

Address   Apt. #

City   State/Province   Zip/Postal Code

> **Mail to the Reader Service:**
> **IN U.S.A.:** P.O. Box 1341, Buffalo, NY 14240-8531
> **IN CANADA:** P.O. Box 603, Fort Erie, Ontario L2A 5X3

Want to try two free books from another series! Call 1-800-873-8635 or visit www.ReaderService.com.

STRS18

Get 4 FREE REWARDS!

We'll send you 2 FREE Books <u>plus</u> 2 FREE Mystery Gifts.

Harlequin® Special Edition books feature heroines finding the balance between their work life and personal life on the way to finding true love.

FREE
Value Over
$20